PRAISE FOR AMY CLIPSTON

"Hometown charm and swoon-worthy second chances make this a must read."

—KRISTEN MCKANAGH, author of *Snowball's Christmas*

"Amy Clipston writes a sweet and tender romance filled with a beautiful look at how love brings healing to broken hearts. This small-town romance, with an adorable little girl and cat to boot, is a great addition to your TBR list."

—PEPPER BASHAM, author of *Authentically, Izzy*, on *The View from Coral Cove*

"Grieving and brokenhearted, novelist Maya Reynolds moves to Coral Cove, the place where she felt happiest as a child. An old family secret upends Maya's plan for a fresh start, as does her longing to love and be loved. *The View from Coral Cove* is Amy Clipston at her best—a tender story of hope, healing, and a love that's meant to be."

—SUZANNE WOODS FISHER, bestselling author of *On a Summer Tide*

"*The Heart of Splendid Lake* offers a welcome escape in the form of a sympathetic heroine and her struggling lakeside resort. Clipston proficiently explores love and loss, family and friendship in a touching, small-town romance that I devoured in a single day!"

—DENISE HUNTER, bestselling author of the Bluebell Inn series

"A touching story of grief, love, and life carrying on, *The Heart of Splendid Lake* engaged my heart from the very first page. Sometimes the feelings we run from lead us to the hope we can't escape, and that's a beautiful thing to see through the eyes of these winning characters. Amy Clipston deftly guides readers on an emotionally satisfying journey that will appeal to fans of Denise Hunter and Becky Wade."

—BETHANY TURNER, award-winning author of *Plot Twist*

Something Old, Something New

OTHER BOOKS BY AMY CLIPSTON

STORIES

A Plain and Simple Christmas

Naomi's Gift included in *An Amish Christmas Gift*

A Spoonful of Love included in *An Amish Kitchen*

Love Birds included in *An Amish Market*

Love and Buggy Rides included in *An Amish Harvest*

Summer Storms included in *An Amish Summer*

The Christmas Cat included in *An Amish Christmas Love*

Home Sweet Home included in *An Amish Winter*

A Son for Always included in *An Amish Spring*

A Legacy of Love included in *An Amish Heirloom*

No Place Like Home included in *An Amish Homecoming*

Their True Home included in *An Amish Reunion*

Cookies and Cheer included in *An Amish Christmas Bakery*

Baskets of Sunshine included in *An Amish Picnic*

Evergreen Love included in *An Amish Christmas Wedding*

Bundles of Blessings included in *Amish Midwives*

Building a Dream included in *An Amish Barn Raising*

A Class for Laurel included in *An Amish Schoolroom*

Patchwork Promises included in *An Amish Quilting Bee*

A Perfectly Splendid Christmas included in *On the Way to Christmas*

NONFICTION

The Gift of Love

Something Old, Something New

AMY CLIPSTON

THOMAS NELSON
Since 1798

Published in Nashville, Tennessee, by Thomas Nelson. Thomas Nelson is a registered trademark of HarperCollins Christian Publishing, Inc.

Thomas Nelson titles may be purchased in bulk for educational, business, fundraising, or sales promotional use. For information, please email SpecialMarkets@ThomasNelson.com.

Publisher's Note: This novel is a work of fiction. Names, characters, places, and incidents are either products of the author's imagination or used fictitiously. All characters are fictional, and any similarity to people living or dead is purely coincidental.

Library of Congress Cataloging-in-Publication Data

Names: Clipston, Amy, author.
Title: Something old, something new / Amy Clipston.
Description: Nashville, Tennessee : Thomas Nelson, [2022] | Summary: "Bestselling author Amy Clipston returns with a small-town romance full of charm, treasure, and happily ever after"-- Provided by publisher.
Identifiers: LCCN 2022024978 (print) | LCCN 2022024979 (ebook) | ISBN 9780785252962 (paperback) | ISBN 9780785252979 (epub) | ISBN 9780785252986
Subjects: LCGFT: Love stories. | Novels.
Classification: LCC PS3603.L58 S66 2022 (print) | LCC PS3603.L58 (ebook) | DDC 813/.6--dc23/eng/20220623
LC record available at https://lccn.loc.gov/2022024978
LC ebook record available at https://lccn.loc.gov/2022024979

Printed in the United States of America

23 24 25 26 27   LSC   10 9 8 7 6 5 4 3 2 1

For my wonderful editor, Laura Wheeler, with love

one

Christine flipped the front-door sign to Open as she hummed along with Cyndi Lauper singing "Girls Just Want to Have Fun." Her favorite '80s satellite radio station poured through her store's wall-mounted speakers, and after taking a moment to appreciate both her air-conditioning and the early morning sun streaming through the large windows, she turned to scan the business she'd established nearly four years ago.

With its booths displaying everything from the old—like vintage purses and clothes and antique toys and furniture—to the new—like her best friend's handmade soaps, candles, and greeting cards—Treasure Hunting Antique Mall was a dream come true.

Leaving behind the law office she'd worked in had been a leap of faith. But thanks to the antiques she and her grandmother had collected over the years, the money she'd saved on her own, and the inheritance her grandmother left her, she'd finally opened the store Nana had always talked about owning someday. And right here on Main Street, in their hometown of Flowering Grove, North Carolina.

If only Nana could see it. She'd love it!

When a loud meow echoed throughout the large, single room, she spun to see her two resident tabby cats staring up at her. Wanda, the smaller gray tabby, blinked up at Christine, while Pietro, her orange-tabby brother, meowed again. He was at least twice his sister's size.

"Well, now. I suppose you two are waiting for your breakfast, huh?"

Pietro bellowed another response as Wanda rubbed against Christine's shins.

"Okay, then. Follow me." She strolled down the aisle between a row of booths until she reached the breakroom across from her office at the back of the store. The cats began a chorus of loud meows as she filled their bowls with their favorite food and then provided fresh water.

"Now, Pietro, don't push your sister out of the way and finish her meal. You need to start watching your weight or the vet will put you on a diet at your next checkup."

Both cats ignored her, scarfing down their breakfast as if they hadn't eaten in a week.

"You two are way too spoiled," she muttered.

The bell above the front door rang, and Christine made a beeline to the front counter.

Mrs. Ward, a frequent customer, sashayed in. "Good morning, Christine. Oh my! It's another hot morning out there. But then again, the Fourth is next week."

Christine leaned against the counter. "June sure is flying by. What brings you in today?"

"I'm looking for a bookcase." With her perfectly coifed graying-blond bob, just the right amount of makeup to accentuate her brown eyes, and designer jeans and bag, Mrs. Ward seemed to be enjoying her early retirement from the corporate world in style.

"Are you looking for any particular finish, Mrs. Ward?"

The older woman shook a finger at her. "How old are you and your twin sister now? Twenty-eight, right?"

"Yes, ma'am."

"That means you should call me Harriet like any other adult."

Christine smiled. "Well, I'll try," she said, but she would never get used to calling her Harriet. Her parents had raised her better than that.

"How is Britney doing?"

"She's great. Thanks."

"How old are her twins now?"

Christine couldn't hold back a grin as she pictured the faces of her precious nieces—her "M&Ms," Maddy and Mila. "They're four, and they're fantastic. Growing like weeds and learning to read. I'm hoping to see them this weekend."

"It's just so astounding that Britney is a fraternal twin and has a set of fraternal twins of her own." She clucked her tongue. "Now, wouldn't it be something if you had twins too?" She pinned Christine with a look. "Do you have a special fella in your life yet?"

Christine merely cleared her throat, unwilling to discuss her non-existent love life.

Mrs. Ward turned toward the furniture pieces up front, most of which Christine had found, refinished in her workshop at home, and then brought in to sell. "I have boxes of my favorite novels in the attic, and I want to put them on display."

"Oh, how nice." Christine followed her.

Mrs. Ward frowned. "I'm sure you heard about my Cameron's messy divorce. His wife decided she didn't love him anymore. Anyway, he stayed with us until he got back on his feet." Her expression brightened. "And now he's finally moved out, which means I have an office again."

"That's wonderful." Christine made a sweeping gesture toward the bookshelves, finished with varying stains. "I have a few here and more in the booths. What size do you need?"

Mrs. Ward touched a finger to her lips and then pointed to a five-shelf, solid-oak bookcase Christine had refinished and brought to the store last week. "That's it."

"Do you, uh, want to measure it?"

"Nope."

Christine inwardly grimaced as she recalled the pieces of furniture Mrs. Ward had purchased without measuring—a china cabinet, a dining room set and buffet, a triple dresser, and an entertainment center. Each time, Christine's mother, who had occasion to visit the Ward home from time to time, informed Christine the piece was scaled a bit too large or small for the room it was in. Too bad Mrs. Ward's design sensibilities didn't necessarily translate to interior design.

"Are you *sure* you don't want to measure it, Mrs.—uh, Harriet?" *Not that you would have properly assessed your space before coming.*

Mrs. Ward waved off the question and then pulled a matching wallet out of her gray purse. "How much is it?"

Christine told her, then grabbed the tag off the bookcase and slipped behind the counter. She rang up the sale and had Mrs. Ward run her credit card through the machine before handing her a receipt.

"I have a truck parked right out front," Mrs. Ward said.

"Oh. Let me grab my hand dolly, then."

"Perfect."

Christine maneuvered the heavy bookcase out the front door to the sidewalk, where Mrs. Ward stood waiting at the tailgate of a Ford pickup truck. Christine wished her brother-in-law was somewhere close by. Not only was Hunter a wonderful husband and father, but he often made time to help her haul heavier pieces of furniture to and from the store.

Christine squared her shoulders. She was strong and courageous. She could lift this bookcase by herself.

Couldn't she?

Mrs. Ward dropped the tailgate and then grabbed an armload of blankets. "I had to convince Marty to let me bring his truck today. But I knew you'd have what I wanted, and like I said, I'm ready to reclaim my office." She spread the blankets out on the tailgate and truck bed.

"Any chance Marty is nearby to help me lift this?"

"No, he went fishing with his brothers. But I can help."

Christine sucked in a deep breath. Where was a superhero— maybe Thor—when she needed him?

"All right," she said, doubtful but willing to try. "You take one side, and I'll take the other." Once their hands had grasped the bookcase, she called, "Ready? One, two, three!"

They heaved and moaned as they lifted the bookcase approximately an inch off the ground. It was even heavier than Christine had recalled. Then as they shoved it toward the truck bed, it started to slip, and she yelped.

"Whoa there!" a masculine voice said before the bookcase seemed to magically float up into the air and then gently land on the truck's bed.

Christine blinked, wondering who her hero was and where he d come from. Had Thor appeared? She turned, and her jaw dropped when she realized who was standing beside her.

"Brent Nicholson," she managed to say. "Hi."

"Hey." He jumped up on the tailgate, rubbed his left knee, and then pushed the bookcase farther in. "I thought you were going to drop this," he said as he started arranging the blankets.

"We almost did." Christine stared up at him. With those broad shoulders, that dark curly hair, and those honey-brown eyes, he looked almost the same as he had ten years ago. He just seemed taller than he had in high school. And more mature, perhaps due to the dark scruff that covered his angular jaw.

"Why, Brent," Mrs. Ward sang as he hopped down, "aren't you a sight for sore eyes. I didn't know you were back in town."

After shutting the tailgate—and rubbing his left knee again—Brent pushed his hand through his riot of thick waves and curls. They always had looked a bit unkempt. "I've only been here two days, ma'am."

"It's been a long time. I don't think I've seen you in probably a decade." Mrs. Ward turned her curious stare to Christine. "Have you?"

Christine shook her head. "No, ma'am, not since before college." Her mind's eye filled with the vision of her sister hanging all over Brent as they wore their light-blue caps and gowns while posing for photos at their high school graduation. He'd stopped by the house a few times that summer before the three of them left for college—she and Britney for UNC at Charlotte and Brent for UNC at Chapel Hill—but that image was freshest in her mind.

"So where have you been hiding yourself?" Mrs. Ward asked.

Brent cleared his throat. "In Virginia." He took a step toward the sidewalk.

"Doing what?"

"Different things." He turned his gaze to Christine, and she wished she'd styled her hair that morning instead of settling for a messy bun. Though Brent wouldn't have noticed. After all, he'd never noticed anything about her in high school. She was always invisible next to Britney.

When he looked away, she cast her eyes to his left hand. No ring.

"How long will you be in town?" Mrs. Ward said, prodding as she so often did. "Are you here for good?"

"No. Just for a while. I'm helping my great-aunt with some repairs to her house." He jammed his thumb toward the row of stores lining Main Street. "I don't mean to be rude, but I need to buy some supplies and get back."

Mrs. Ward waved him off. "Of course. You run along now. And tell your aunt Midge I said hello."

"Yes, ma'am," he said before turning to Christine.

"Thanks for your help, Brent," she told him.

He nodded. "You're welcome." Then he hustled down the sidewalk.

"He's easy on the eyes, isn't he, Christine?" Mrs. Ward gushed once Brent was halfway down the street.

"He always was."

More visions crashed into Christine's memory—Brent and Britney walking arm in arm down the hallways of Flowering Grove High, laughing with their popular friends in the cafeteria, standing on the auditorium stage to accept their crowns as homecoming king and queen. But that was a long time ago, and Brent had broken Britney's heart, leaving her twin devastated. She was much better off with Hunter, who knew how to treat her properly.

Still, Christine stared after her sister's first love, wondering why the former high school quarterback, the captain of the football team, and the most popular young man in their graduating class had returned to their small town after all this time. He'd said it was to help his aunt with home repairs, but was that the only reason? He'd also said he'd been doing *different things* in Virginia. What did that mean?

"Well, thank you for the bookcase," Mrs. Ward said. "I plan to put it to good use."

Christine smiled. "You're welcome. Be sure to let Mr. Ward help you unload it." *And I hope it actually fits in your office!*

"Oh, I'll ask him and his fishing buddy brothers to take care of it for me." She pointed to the store. "Looks like you have some customers. You'd better get back inside."

A group of women around Mrs. Ward's age were filing into the store. It looked like another busy day at Treasure Hunting Antique Mall.

◆ ◆ ◆

Brent sighed as he stalked toward the hardware store, nodding hellos to familiar faces that didn't mask their surprise at seeing him back in his hometown. So much for keeping a low profile and sneaking in and out of Swanson's Hardware without being recognized by the locals.

Grimacing, he could only imagine what Harriet Ward would say to her friends if she learned what a mess his life was on top of failing to be the college football hero the whole town had expected him to be. She'd probably portray him as the prodigal son who'd come hobbling back to his family.

He'd hoped to sneak past the woman without even making eye contact, but when he saw the bookcase shift, he had to intervene before it fell to the ground, taking her with it. He wasn't one to ignore someone who needed assistance.

While he'd recognized Mrs. Ward as soon as he looked over at the pickup truck, not until he'd hefted the thing—at his knee's expense—had he realized the tall blonde also struggling to lift the bookcase was Christine Sawyer.

Brent swallowed a groan. He'd hoped to avoid running into the Sawyer twins during his stay, but there he was, already face-to-face with his ex-girlfriend's sister. Perhaps it was best to get it over with, though. His mother had told him both Christine and Britney still lived in Flowering Grove, making it inevitable that he'd see at least one of them since he was in town for more than just a quick Thanksgiving or Christmas visit with his family.

He rubbed his hand over the stubble on his jaw as he recalled his relationship with Britney. He'd once believed he would spend his life with her, but that fantasy had evaporated years ago, right along with the bright future his football scholarship promised—all thanks to a career-ending injury.

But that was ancient history, and now he was here to help his aunt Midge before returning to whatever life he could scrounge together back in Virginia. Then except for those short, one- or two-day holiday visits with his family, he could once again leave Flowering Grove and all the painful memories it held for him in his rearview mirror.

Brent quickened his pace and swept past Miller's Dry Cleaners and the Fairy Tale Bridal Shop, which he noticed only because Britney used to love gazing at the dresses in the window. Then coming to the hardware store, he pushed the door open, grateful to find only a few customers milling about.

He grabbed a flatbed and zipped around the large store, grabbing the items on his list—four bundles of shingles, two boxes of nails, a hammer, tar paper, and a few sheets of plywood.

When he approached the front counter, the store was still quiet, and he found Mr. Swanson himself flipping through a catalog. Brent guessed the man was at least seventy-five by now, but with the same receding gray hair, matching bushy eyebrows, wrinkly face, and warm, welcoming smile, he still looked exactly as Brent recalled. He'd been a bachelor for as long as Brent could remember, and he assumed he still was.

The older man smiled, peering at Brent over his reading glasses.

"Well, I'll be. If it isn't the winningest quarterback in Flowering Grove High's history!"

"Hi, Mr. Swanson." Brent pinned a smile on his face, but heat crawled up his neck as he set the hammer and boxes of nails on the counter.

Mr. Swanson peered over the counter at the supplies he'd wheeled over. "Looks like you're repairing a roof. Are you working over at your folks' place?"

"No, sir. I'm helping my great-aunt get her house ready to sell."

"Is that right?" His brow wrinkled with concern. "Where's Midge planning to move?"

"She wants to join her friends at the retirement community over in Oakboro." Brent pulled his wallet from the back pocket of his shorts. "She's buying a condo there."

Mr. Swanson shook his head. "How about that?" He began entering purchase prices on his cash register. "So what have you been up to the last few years, son?"

Brent pulled out the stack of bills Aunt Midge had given him for the supplies. "Working in Virginia."

"What do you do there?"

Brent hesitated, then said, "I'm between jobs right now."

It would be too embarrassing to tell Mr. Swanson the whole truth of the last six months, including that he'd had his own business but then lost it, forcing him to move out of his rental home and rent a room from his friend Devonte. Especially when he himself was still trying to come to grips with the shambles his life had become.

When Mr. Swanson gave him the total for the sale, Brent reached for his wallet again and pulled out some of his own cash. Aunt Midge had told him she had enough money for the repairs—and insisted on paying him to make them—but how could he be sure she was telling the truth? Or that she truly understood that the condo and the retirement community's fees wouldn't come cheap?

Mr. Swanson handed him his change and dropped the receipt in the bag with the nails. "What were you doing before you were between jobs, son?"

"Mostly home remodeling." Brent slipped the change into his wallet and then pushed it into his back pocket.

Mr. Swanson beamed. "Then you're the man to help your aunt."

"Yes, sir." Brent swallowed a relieved sigh, glad the older man seemed satisfied with his vague responses—and hadn't mentioned his failed football career.

"You tell Midge I said hello."

"I will, and I'm sure I'll be back soon for more supplies."

Brent was grateful to dash out of the store and to his truck unnoticed. Now to return to Aunt Midge's house and get to work. The sooner he finished with the repairs, the sooner he could get out of Flowering Grove.

two

Brent steered his gray Chevrolet Silverado pickup down Main Street, passing the town hall, fire station, and library, then turned left onto Maple Avenue to head out of Flowering Grove's downtown area. He flipped the air-conditioning to high and then drummed his fingers on the steering wheel as one of his favorite hard-rock tunes blared through the truck's speakers.

His shoulders tensed when the high school football stadium came into view and memories of his high school days overtook his mind. Leading his teammates to victory after victory and then the state championship. Witnessing pride on Dad's face, which he hadn't seen since his injury stole the future his father had planned for him.

The future he'd planned for himself at the time.

Brent frowned down at the multiple scars stretching across his left knee. Thanks to blowing it, he had nothing left to make his father proud—and Dad reveled in reminding him of that.

Slowing his truck, he slapped on his right blinker and eased into the driveway leading to Aunt Midge's one-story brick ranch. Another swell of nostalgia overtook him. Many of his best childhood memories had taken place in this house, and the majority of them were of his great-uncle Sal. Brent cherished the time they'd spent together building things with wood, watching nature movies, and packing up his uncle's old pickup truck to head to his favorite fishing pond.

Uncle Sal had passed away fifteen years ago, but Aunt Midge was fiercely independent and had refused his mother's numerous offers for her to move in with her and Dad. They thought she could sell her home and then help them add a bedroom and bath to their own small house. But instead, she'd stayed where she was and only recently decided to sell it to join her friends at the retirement community in nearby Oakboro. That was when she'd called Brent and asked if he could get free to come fix up the house—almost as though she knew he was . . . lost. But he hadn't told anyone in his family about losing his business. When Aunt Midge called for his help, he'd just told her yes, he could make the time.

Brent slipped the truck into Park just as the screen door at the front of the house swung open. Aunt Midge toddled out, making her way down the front steps and then down the path that led to the driveway. Wearing her signature bright-turquoise cat-shaped glasses, a bright-pink T-shirt and matching pink shorts, and bright-purple slippers, she schlepped toward him, her right arm waving in the air.

"Did I give you enough cash?" she called as she approached him.

He jumped down onto the pavement. "You gave me plenty, Aunt Midge." He didn't have the heart to ask her for more money in case she didn't really have enough funds for all these repairs and buying a condo. Besides, assisting her was his pleasure, and quite frankly, her call for help had been a balm to his bruised soul. And it wasn't as though he was totally broke—not yet. He was even paying Devonte rent while he was here, even though his friend said he didn't have to.

"Now, Brent, you wouldn't lie to your great-aunt, would you?" She squinted up at him, lifting her chin.

He swallowed. He was at least a foot taller than Aunt Midge, but she could intimidate him with a look. "No, ma'am."

"Let me see the receipt." She held out a wrinkled hand.

He busied himself with collecting the bag of nails and the hammer from the back seat of his four-door cab. "He didn't give me a receipt."

"I happen to know that Jerry Swanson always gives his customers a receipt. You might as well tell me how much I owe you so I can pay you back." She sidled up to him, reached into the bag of nails, and plucked out the receipt before he could stop her. She might be close to eighty, but she was still quick when she wanted to be.

"Aunt Midge—"

"So I *do* owe you money." She frowned up at him. "Why didn't you tell me?"

He pursed his lips. "I just want to help you. After all, I haven't been around much since I left home."

"You *are* helping me. But you must have given up a job or two to do it, and I don't want you to lose money. Your great-uncle worked hard all his life, saved and invested well, and provided for me when he passed away. So I'm doing just fine. Money isn't a problem."

He closed the truck door, wondering why she'd never had all this work done before if money wasn't a problem. Uncle Sal never would have let the house fall into such disrepair. But at least she'd installed new windows a few years ago.

"I need to start on your roof. How about we argue about this later?"

She huffed out a breath.

"Mr. Swanson told me to tell you hello."

Aunt Midge rolled her eyes. "I bet he did. That old fuddy-duddy has been trying to get me to go out with him ever since your uncle Sal passed away."

Brent blinked, trying to imagine her dating. No, that just seemed . . . *wrong*!

"I'm not interested in seeing anyone." Her expression brightened. "Now, you, on the other hand, should be. After all, you're nearing thirty!" She rubbed her hand over his bicep. "Your mother told me you and Tara broke up. What on earth happened? I thought you two were so happy."

So did I.

He shrugged as if Tara hadn't broken both his heart and trust. "It just didn't work out."

"But she's not all that's bothering you, is it? I can tell."

"I'm changing into cargo shorts before I climb up on the roof. I'll need the pockets up there." He walked to the detached garage.

"Brent," Aunt Midge began, marching after him with her slippers slapping the pavement, "I'll let you get away with changing the subject this time, but you *are* going to tell me what's going on with you."

He heaved a sigh as he punched in the code on the garage keypad, then waited as the door hummed and lifted before placing the bag of nails and hammer on his uncle's workbench in the back.

"I'm making your favorite meal tonight," Aunt Midge said from right behind him.

He turned and smiled. "The *best* meal."

She gave his cheek a pat. "Only the best for my favorite nephew."

"I'm your *only* nephew," he deadpanned.

"That's right, and you'll stay that way until you get married and give me more nieces or nephews. You know, my sister over in South Carolina, Beverly, already has three great-grandchildren. Three! And I have zero little ones to brag about." She held up her hand, making a round shape with her fingers, then strolled out of the garage.

Leaving his aunt plucking weeds from a flower bed, Brent headed into the house through the back door and made his way through the kitchen, dining room, and family room into the hallway that led to the guest bathroom, two guest rooms, and master bedroom. After assessing all the work to be done, he knew the house better than ever.

Halting in front of the sea of photos lining the hall walls, he took in Kylie's high school senior portrait. With his younger sister's light-brown hair, hazel eyes, and bright smile, she resembled their mother.

Brent smiled at a few more photos of his beautiful sister but then groaned when he found the senior year prom portrait of him and Britney. He'd asked Aunt Midge to take it down when he visited last Christmas, but she insisted she loved that photo too much to do it. *"You looked so handsome,"* she said.

Brent took in his huge smile, looking as if he was living in the moment without a care in the world. And except for his father's constant pushing, he had been.

Britney, of course, looked like a supermodel, just as she always had. Her simple, powder-blue dress and subtle makeup accentuated her bright, baby-blue eyes. With her high cheekbones, petite frame, and bright smile, she'd lit up every room she entered. He'd had a crush on her in middle school and finally found the nerve to ask her out to a movie their freshman year of high school. They'd been inseparable from then on.

Brent snorted. Life had seemed so easy back then. He'd had a full scholarship to UNC Chapel Hill plus his beautiful girlfriend, Britney Sawyer, the woman of his dreams. He was certain they'd build a future together after they'd graduated college and he'd found a high-paying corporate job of some kind.

Until he lost his scholarship and then Britney, his whole world crumbling. But that was old news. Britney Sawyer was in his past, his feelings for her long gone, and so was football.

He entered the guest room he'd chosen to sleep in and dug his cargo shorts out of his duffel bag. After changing, he headed back outside to grab the tallest ladder in the garage, eager to turn his thoughts elsewhere. But as he stared up at the house's roof in desperate need of attention, he realized just how different his life was now from what he'd expected it to be when he was that high school senior.

Well, he might not know what he'd do after finishing his work here, but at least he could look forward to his favorite meal tonight— Aunt Midge's fried chicken.

◆ ◆ ◆

Christine smiled as a young woman carried a set of vintage pink Pyrex mixing bowls to the counter. "You must have found those in the Simply Southern booth," she said as she managed a smile and pulled the tag off the bowls. Business had been good, but she was kind of tired and just glad it was Saturday so she'd have the next two days off.

"I did." The woman pushed a lock of her straight, nearly black hair over her shoulder. "I've been looking for more pieces to match the ones my grandmother gave me."

"I knew these wouldn't last long. They're beautiful." As Christine rang up the purchase, her cell phone chimed with a text message under the counter. But she ignored it.

She shared the total, and the woman slipped her credit card into the machine. Then Christine printed out her receipt and set the bowls in a box.

"I noticed one of the booths is empty now," the woman said as she slipped her card back into her wallet.

"Yes, that's right. Melissa's Creations. Her husband was transferred to Ohio."

"Oh, well, that's good for her family, I suppose, but I'll miss browsing her cute displays." She dropped her wallet into her large tote, then placed it on top of the bowls before lifting the box with both hands.

"If you run into anyone who might be interested in the booth space, please let me know," Christine said as she held the front door open for her.

"I will. Have a great day."

Back at the counter, Christine retrieved her phone and found a text from Britney.

Game night at my house. 7 p.m. Don't be late.

Christine chuckled as she shook her head. Her sister always knew how to get straight to the point.

Yes, ma'am. What can I bring?
Just my daughters' favorite twin aunt.

She smiled down at the framed photo of her sweet nieces she kept on the counter. Especially with their bright-blue eyes, they resembled Britney and Christine's look at their age. But like their mother's and aunt's, their faces were different. Maddy's was longer while Mila's was rounder. And Maddy's hair was a dirty blond, like Christine's, and Mila's was a sunshine blond, like Britney's.

She was never too tired to spend time with her nieces. They were the light of her life, and she would never dare appear at their house without a surprise for them. She'd stop by the local bakery before grabbing a quick dinner at home. Their favorite iced cookies were always a hit.

A meow sounded before Wanda hopped up on the counter and rubbed her head against Christine's arm. "I suppose your sudden need for love means you're hungry again, huh, Wanda?"

Pietro appeared at Christine's feet and rubbed his head on her shin.

"That's a yes from both of you, then." Christine checked the time on her phone and found it was almost five. Then she started toward the back of the store. "Come on, you two. I'll fill your bowls and give you plenty of fresh water before I start closing up."

After taking care of the cats, Christine helped her remaining customers, then shut down for the day before heading to her waiting pickup truck. As she slipped inside, she realized she loved the gold Toyota Tacoma just as much as the day she'd bought it before opening her store.

◆ ◆ ◆

Christine parked in the driveway of her sister's two-story brick colonial right behind her mother's silver Ford Escape. Hunter's white Chevrolet pickup truck sat next to her mother's SUV with the words *Davenport & Sons Grading* emblazoned on the side. Her father loved cars and trucks, and Christine always paid attention to makes and models. It was one of the ways she and her father had always bonded.

She retrieved the box of pink iced cookies—they didn't have the twins' favorite purple icing today—and her purse, then climbed out of her truck. On her way to the front door, she took in her sister's perfectly manicured, lush green lawn and happy flowers. Britney had it all—a doting husband, adorable children, and a beautiful home.

Christine was happy for her twin. She only wanted the best for her, and she was happy she'd met Hunter, who'd attended Oakboro public schools, and then settled down with him before her twenty-second birthday. Yet a tiny part of her still resented how Britney always seemed to get what she wanted without even trying.

She sighed. What was she thinking? She had her store, her house, and her family, and she was happy with her life—even though at times loneliness crept in. Deep down, she had to admit she longed for a husband with whom she could share her life, but she was grateful for everything she had, especially her family and adorable nieces.

Peering through the screen door, Christine rang the doorbell and immediately heard footsteps scrambling toward her. In a flash Mila and Maddy stood before her side by side, grinning ear-to-ear and wearing matching purple shorts and purple T-shirts featuring Rapunzel.

"Auntie!" Mila announced as she flung the door open, allowing Christine to step inside.

Maddy stood on tiptoes. "What did you bring us?"

Mila folded her hands, but Maddy reached for the box in Christine's hand. "Is there a surprise in there?"

Britney came around the corner and frowned. "Madison! Mila! Where are your manners?" She rested her hands on her small hips. Even with her blond hair in a ponytail and her face free of makeup, Britney was a stunning beauty.

"It's fine, Brit." Christine smiled down at her nieces. "I'm their favorite aunt, so it's my job to spoil them, right, girls?"

The twins jumped up and down as she opened the cookie box and tipped it so they could see inside. "I brought your favorites. How do these look?"

"Yummy!" Mila declared. "Even though they're pink."

Maddy reached again. "Can—I mean, *may* we have one now?"

Britney took the box from Christine. "Yes, but"—she held up

her right pointer finger—"only one. Take them into the family room and use one of the little plates already in there. Then choose the game you want to play, and we'll join you soon." She handed Mila the box.

"Yes, Mommy," both girls sang before scooting away.

Britney shook her head. "They're a handful."

"Now we know how our mother felt, right?" Christine quipped.

They laughed as they walked into the kitchen, where Mom stood at the counter pouring potato chips into a bowl.

"Chrissy!" she announced. "You made it."

Christine had always believed her twin favored their mother. Not only did both women stand at barely five foot one, six inches shorter than Christine, but they shared the same thick, light-blond hair. And while Mom's bobbed style had started showing flecks of gray, her beautiful face was still youthful with only a few wrinkles around her eyes.

Christine dropped her backpack purse on a chair as a murmur of conversation filtered in through the screen door leading to the deck. She looked out the window to see Hunter and Dad chatting. Jake, the family's patient golden retriever, sat nearby, happily wagging his tail.

"Put me to work," she said as she stepped to the sink to wash her hands.

"How about you pull out the crackers from that cabinet up there?" Britney nodded in that direction, then opened the refrigerator and took out a block of cheese. "You can slice this too."

Christine opened the cabinet and found a box of Ritz crackers, then located a cutting board and knife and started slicing.

"How was it at the store this week, Chrissy?" Mom asked.

"It's been busy, but I have an empty booth now."

Britney spun to face her. "Who moved out?"

"Melissa Gorman. Her husband got a big promotion, and they're moving to Ohio."

Britney opened a bag of pretzels. "No way! I loved her handmade jewelry. It was so colorful."

"It *was* nice. So you have an empty booth." Mom took a container of dip from the refrigerator.

Christine nodded as she arranged cheese slices on the crackers. "I'm designing new posters and flyers with information about it, and I'll advertise the opportunity on my website and Facebook page too."

Mom patted her arm. "I'm sure you'll find a new vendor soon, then. In the meantime," she began with a coy smile, "have any tall, dark, and handsome men stopped by and swept you off your feet?"

Christine's thoughts immediately snapped to Brent, and she couldn't stop a snort. "Uh, not really."

While Brent Nicholson absolutely fit the tall, dark, and handsome description, he would never sweep her off her feet. He'd dated Britney, the beautiful and popular twin, cheerleading captain, and homecoming queen who could have been a supermodel if only she were taller. But that was beside the point. Even if he did notice her, Brent had broken her sister's heart, and Christine would never date him, let alone consider trusting him. That would be a violation of the unwritten sister code.

"What did that snort mean?" her twin asked.

Christine waved her off. "Nothing."

"Whoa there." Britney latched onto her arm and turned Christine to face her. "Tell me."

"Like I said, nothing."

Britney folded her arms over her green T-shirt. "Spill it, sis."

Christine sighed and peeked at her mother, who was watching her with curiosity sparkling in her blue eyes. "Fine, but you won't like it."

"What do you mean?" Britney's electric smile fell away.

Christine ran her fingers over the edge of the counter. "I ran into Brent on Thursday."

"Brent Nicholson?" Mom asked.

"The one and only."

"Brent is back?" Britney's eyes widened as she covered her mouth with one hand.

three

"Yes, Brent's back." Christine explained how he'd helped her and Harriet Ward load the bookcase into the truck. "Then Mrs. Ward tried to pull information out of him. You know how she always wants to know everyone's business. But he just said he'd been living in Virginia and was here for only a little while to make repairs on his aunt Midge's house. He was on his way to buy supplies."

Britney studied Christine. "Helping his aunt?"

"Why wouldn't he come back to help Midge if she needs it?" Mom shrugged as she filled glasses with iced tea.

Britney shrugged. "He always said he wanted to leave Flowering Grove behind for good after college. But he was also close to his aunt Midge, so . . ."

The screen door squeaked open, and Hunter walked in with Dad and Jake in tow. "Who said he'd never come back here, babe?"

Britney's bright smile was back in a flash, and she stretched up on her tiptoes to kiss her husband's cheek. "No one important."

The twins appeared in the doorway, their lips caked with pink icing. Christine had a feeling the box of cookies was at least half empty.

"Are you ready to play now?" Maddy whined.

"Yes, we are!" Dad announced, rubbing his hands together. A smile filled his handsome face. Most people who noticed the wrinkles around Bob Sawyer's hazel eyes and his mouth and the gray threading through his light-brown hair would correctly guess he was in his mid-fifties. But Dad always insisted he was young at heart.

Christine helped carry the snacks to the family-room coffee table, then took her usual spot between the twins on the sofa. Soon the whole family was seated, a Charades for Kids box lying on the table beside the bowl of chips.

"Before I forget, what are we doing on Tuesday for the Fourth?" Hunter asked as he lifted his glass of iced tea.

Christine had always thought Britney and Hunter resembled the Barbie and Ken dolls her nieces loved so much. The two of them were both blond and blue-eyed, fit, athletic, and attractive, and their daughters had inherited their good looks.

Dad shrugged. "We'll have a cookout and then go see the fireworks together like we do every year. Right, Karla?"

"That's the usual plan." Mom looked at Christine. "Are you closing the store?"

She nodded. "I always close it on holidays since nothing else is open on Main Street."

"Perfect," Dad said. "It's settled, then. A cookout and fireworks." He beamed at his granddaughters, and Maddy clapped her hands with obvious excitement.

"Can we please play now, Poppy?" Mila asked.

Dad grinned. "Only if you're on my team."

Christine laughed. If she never had children of her own, at least she would cherish these two for the rest of her life. They were a blessing.

◆ ◆ ◆

After a rousing game of charades, Christine and Britney stowed the leftover snacks in the kitchen. Then Britney grabbed Christine's arm and pulled her back into the family room. "Tell me everything about when you saw Brent."

"There's nothing more to tell."

Her sister's eyes narrowed. "Chrissy, you're holding out on me. Hunter and Dad are on the deck talking sports, and Mom is upstairs reading the twins a bedtime story. So tell me everything now, while we have a moment alone. Is he married?"

"I hate to admit it, but I did look at his left hand. No ring. Listen, we talked for only a few minutes, and he just said he was on the way to the hardware store to get supplies for his great-aunt's house. That, and he's been living in Virginia."

Britney tapped one finger against her lips. "Huh. Did he look good?"

"Very."

Britney sank onto the sofa. "It's ancient history, but I was crazy about him. We dated for almost six years, and even though we hit a rough patch when he was injured and going through all those surgeries, I believed we'd get married someday. But then he up and cheated on me." She leaned back, a sour look on her face. "I thought I'd never have to see the man again." She groaned. "I can't imagine how awkward it would be to run into him now. And truthfully? I still get angry when I think about what he did to me."

Christine sat beside her. "Brit, you have no reason to feel awkward around him. *He* hurt *you*. He's the one who should feel awkward if you see each other. And it's time to let the anger go, don't you think?"

Britney ran her perfectly polished fingernails through the tassels on a throw pillow. "I suppose. I'm just so grateful I found a good man."

"Right," Christine scoffed. "As if you ever had to worry about finding a man. Even in middle school, Daddy had to keep a baseball bat by the front door to fend off the droves of boys who wanted to ask you out."

"Whatever!" Britney laughed as she tossed the pillow at Christine. "But I doubt any of them would have been as good to me and the girls as Hunter is." She gave her a pointed look. "We have to find *you* a husband, Chrissy!"

Christine groaned as she threw the pillow back, then stood. "Now you sound like Mom."

"But she's right."

Christine rolled her eyes as she headed to the deck to join Dad and Hunter. If a husband was in her future, she'd just as soon find him on her own.

◆ ◆ ◆

"We need to leave for the fireworks now," Aunt Midge announced as she stood at the bottom of the ladder and looked up.

Brent stopped hammering a shingle and sat back on his heels. When pain shot through his left knee, he lowered himself and sat, facing her. "I already told you. I have too much to do around here." He gestured toward the rest of the roof.

"But you'll run out of daylight." She pointed toward the lowering sun.

"There's still plenty I can do when it's dark. For one thing, I need to look at that leaky faucet in your master bathroom."

When Aunt Midge narrowed her eyes, he knew he was in trouble.

"Brent Theodore Nicholson, either you take me to the fireworks or you're fired!"

He laughed and picked up his bottle of water. How he adored his aunt, especially her feisty nature and sense of humor.

"I've never missed the Flowering Grove Fourth of July fireworks, and I don't plan to start now." She shook a crooked finger at him. "Both your parents had to work, so like I told you well in advance, I expect you to take me." Then she muttered, "I can't believe Donna agreed to take inventory at that store on a holiday, but she wanted the extra pay."

Despite feeling bad that his mother felt she had to sacrifice seeing the town's fireworks, Brent grinned, resting his bottle of water on his bent knee. "I would imagine Mr. Swanson would be more than happy to take you."

"I'm going to pretend I didn't hear you say that. Now get down here. We need to get there before all the best spots at Vet's Field are taken. Besides, my friends will be waiting for me. They're getting a ride over from Oakboro."

"Yes, ma'am."

He gathered the box of nails and his hammer. Risking running into his former classmates at one of Flowering Grove's biggest events of the year was the last thing he wanted to do, but he couldn't let Aunt Midge down. "I just need to get changed."

"You'll look handsome either way. In fact, I imagine you'll find plenty of pretty young women thrilled to watch the fireworks with you."

He shook his head. "I'm not looking."

"That's when you find someone—when you're not looking and least expect it. Now, take me to the fireworks!"

◆ ◆ ◆

Brent stood in line at the Dreamy Ice Cream truck, waiting for his turn and nodding hellos to a few more familiar faces. He was grateful that, so far, no one had forced him to participate in an awkward conversation.

The air smelled of freshly mowed grass, pizza, and funnel cakes as he took in the crowd sitting on lawn chairs and blankets, all waiting for the fireworks display. Aunt Midge was sitting with several of her friends who'd come from the retirement community to enjoy the show. After he'd settled her in one of the two lawn chairs they'd brought from the house, she'd asked him to buy her a mint chocolate chip cone.

Especially after the other women refused his offer to get ice cream for them, too, he suspected her request was meant to force him into mingling with people. But he didn't argue. He'd do anything for her. After all, she was the one person he could count on to defend him when his father started in on what a disappointment Brent's life had turned out to be. Owning a business hadn't been enough to change Dad's mind, and now Brent didn't even have that.

When the couple in front of him left with their frozen treats, Brent stepped up to the window.

"May I help you?" a teenager inside the truck asked, her smile revealing braces as she pushed her bright-red braid off her shoulder.

"One single-dip mint chocolate chip waffle cone and one double-dip chocolate peanut butter waffle cone, please."

"Coming right up," she said before barking his order to a boy who had the same red hair. Must be a family business. When she gave Brent the total, he paid her and then slipped his change into the tip jar. Then she handed him his cones, and he thanked her before turning toward the sea of people.

He'd just taken a step when a little girl rushed toward him, giggling as her blond braids bounced off her shoulders.

"Maddy! Maddy, no!" a voice scolded just as the little girl crashed into him, knocking both ice cream cones out of his hands.

Brent stared down at his gray T-shirt, now sporting a large brown stain. Then he looked up and found himself face-to-face with Christine Sawyer again.

He ran his tongue over his teeth and breathed in through his nose. Of all the people here, why couldn't he have avoided running into her?

"I'm-I'm so sorry." Christine's face flushed as she released the hand of a second little girl, who also had blond braids and wore a red, white, and blue shorts outfit that matched the first little girl's. They resembled each other physically, too, yet they looked about the same age. He surmised Christine had her own set of fraternal twins.

Christine reached behind her and grabbed a handful of napkins from the funnel cake truck. She leaned toward him, but then just cleared her throat and held out the napkins for him to take. "Here you go."

"Thanks." He rubbed a napkin over the stain but only managed to make it bigger. *Perfect.*

Christine frowned at the first twin. "What do you say, Madison?"

The little girl looked up at him, her expression hesitant and her blue eyes wide. "I'm sorry, mister."

"It's okay." Brent felt kind of sorry for the child. He remembered what it was like to be a kid.

Christine bent at the waist to be at eye level. "I warned you too many people are around, so why did you run off? I asked you to hold my hand."

"Like I did!" the second twin chimed in, looking pleased with herself.

Madison looked down at her red sandals. "I know."

"I'm so sorry, Brent." Christine reached into her pocket as she stood straight and then held out a few bills. "Here. Get two more cones on me."

He shook his head. "That's not necessary."

"I insist."

"It's fine." He stepped away from her. "Enjoy the fireworks." Before she could respond, he returned to the ice cream truck line.

While he waited, Brent turned toward the line of porta potties and spotted Christine ferrying the two little girls into one. He briefly wondered how long she'd been married and how old her twins were, but he didn't really care. He didn't want to think about either of the Sawyer twins.

After making his purchase, Brent started back to Aunt Midge. But then he heard a male voice call his name, and he held his breath, hoping whoever it was would give up.

"Brent!" the man hollered again. "Brent Nicholson!"

Pasting a smile on his face, Brent turned to see his old friend Steve Barnes jogging over. He breathed a sigh of relief. He and Steve had struck up an easy friendship in Spanish class their freshman year, and Brent was happy to see him—especially since he wasn't a member of the football team. Chances were he wouldn't grill him about losing his college career.

"I thought that was you," Steve said, pushing his dark hair off his forehead. "When did you get back?"

"Last week. I'm here helping my aunt Midge with repairs so she can put her house up for sale. What have you been up to?"

Steve rubbed the dark-brown stubble on his jaw. "Well, for one thing, I followed one of my older brothers into his plumbing business."

"That's great."

"And you remember Pam Gannon, right?"

"Of course I do."

"We've been married for two years now."

"No kidding."

"How about you? Married?"

"Still single." Brent lifted his cone and licked the melting ice cream trailing down one of its waffled sides.

"Why don't you come sit with us?" Steve pointed toward the knot of people.

Brent followed his gaze and spotted Pam sitting with a group— *including* Britney. Her parents were there, too, as well as a good-looking blond man, her husband for all he knew. Or maybe he was Christine's. "It's probably not a good idea for me to sit over there."

"Because of Britney?" Steve shrugged. "But that was a long time ago, and—"

"I should get this other cone to my aunt before it completely melts."

"So go deliver it and then come."

Brent backed away from him a step. "No thanks, but maybe we can get together sometime before I leave."

"You need to come over for a barbecue." Steve pulled his cell phone from his pocket. "What's your number?"

Brent rattled it off, and moments later his phone dinged.

"Now I have your number and you have mine." Steve tapped Brent's shoulder. "I'll be in touch."

"I look forward to it."

Brent weaved through the crowd until he came to his aunt and her friends.

Aunt Midge took her cone, licked the drips, and then nodded toward his shirt. "What happened to you?"

"I had a run-in with a little blonde, which destroyed my initial purchases," Brent said as he lowered himself down onto the lawn chair.

Aunt Midge pushed her turquoise glasses up on her nose with her free hand. "Did you get her phone number?"

Brent snickered. "I think I'd have to wait at least fifteen years for her to be legal." He took a bite of his ice cream and savored the delicious flavor.

Aunt Midge snapped her fingers and looked at her friends. "Listen, do any of you have single granddaughters around Brent's age? We need to get him fixed up with a nice young woman."

While the group discussed the possibilities, Brent's gaze moved toward the porta potties just as Christine steered the twins toward her family. He took another bite and wondered how often twins had twins of their own.

"Did you hear that, Brent?" Aunt Midge asked, interrupting his thoughts. "Blanche's granddaughter is single. She's thirty-five, though. How do you feel about dating an older woman?"

He turned his attention toward her eager smile. "There's no need to play matchmaker, Aunt Midge. I won't be here long enough."

"Pish-posh," she said, waving off his remark. "I have a feeling you will."

Brent sighed and looked up at the sky as complete darkness crept over his hometown. Aunt Midge had her plans, and he had his. He'd be back in Virginia before she knew it.

◆ ◆ ◆

Christine led the twins to where everyone sat waiting for their return.

"Mommy!" Maddy announced, leaping into Britney's arms. "I spilled ice cream on a very tall man!"

Christine sank into her lawn chair, and Mila climbed onto her lap.

Britney turned to Christine as Maddy snuggled against her shoulder. "What happened?"

"Your daughter ran right into Brent Nicholson, and he dropped both his ice cream cones. One scoop landed on his shirt. And it was chocolate."

Britney smirked. "Serves him right."

"That's easy for you to say. You weren't the one awkwardly trying to apologize and wrangle children at the same time. I don't think I've ever been so embarrassed in my life."

A man selling glow sticks walked up, and the twins jumped to their feet, immediately begging their parents to buy some. Britney and Hunter both stood and turned their attention to the vendor.

Pam leaned toward Christine and lowered her voice. "Did I hear you say Maddy ran into Brent Nicholson—literally?"

"You sure did." Christine pulled two Diet Cokes from her small cooler and handed one to Pam. "And today is the second time I've seen him." She summarized her first encounter with Brent, leaving out how handsome he'd looked since Steve was listening.

Steve brushed his wife's shoulder-length dark hair off her shoulder and then looped his arm around her. Christine noted how much younger Pam looked than twenty-eight. Even now she was sometimes asked which high school she attended.

"I just spoke to him too," Steve said, "and he told me the reason he's making those repairs is so his aunt can sell her house. I said we'll have to have him over. Maybe for a barbecue. I have his number."

"Sure, but you'll be the one grilling," Pam quipped, her dark eyes twinkling.

"It's a deal," he said, his own dark eyes sparkling as he kissed the top of her head.

Christine looked down at her soda can. She was happy for Pam and Steve, who seemed to have a wonderful marriage. But sometimes she felt like an intruder when she spent time with them.

"Auntie!" Mila hollered as she jumped into Christine's lap again. "Look what I got!" She pointed to the green glow stick in her hand and then the glowing red necklace hanging around her neck.

Christine smiled. "How neat!"

Maddy joined them. "Look at mine, Auntie!"

"Wow. They're beautiful."

"When will the fireworks start?" Mila asked.

"Soon, baby. Really soon."

Christine's gaze moved over the crowd, and her eyes found Brent's looking at her from across the field. He nodded, and as she nodded back, for some reason she felt certain she'd run into him again—and soon.

four

"Good night," Christine told her cats after feeding them. "I'll see you when I come by tomorrow afternoon. Be good."

She yawned as she locked the store's back door after another long and busy Saturday, then dragged herself to her waiting truck. She'd arrived extra early that morning to update the books and print out checks for her vendors. Then she was on her feet helping customers until it was time to flip the front-door sign to Closed. Eating a quick sandwich at the counter between customers at noon had been fine, but now she was ready for a real meal at home.

She wanted to make a stop first, though. She was so pleased when she saw how many items Pam had sold in her Handmade Haven booth that she wanted to drop off her check. She motored away from downtown and turned onto Maple Avenue before turning down Linwood.

When she came to Pam and Steve's yellow, two-story house, she steered into the driveway and parked beside a gray Chevrolet pickup truck with Virginia tags. Could that be Brent's truck? At the fireworks the other night, Steve said he wanted to invite him over.

For a moment she considered backing out of the driveway and

heading home. But then she decided to stay even if Brent was here. She'd just leave the check with Pam and go. So she climbed out of her truck and hurried up the front path to the porch. The enticing aroma of grilled burgers wafted over her as she knocked on the door. Maybe this was the barbecue Steve suggested.

After only a few moments, the door opened and Pam grinned at her. "Chris! Hi!"

"Hey." She pulled the check from her pocket. "I just wanted to bring this to you."

Pam took the check and grinned. "Wow. Looks like I sold a lot."

"Mostly your tote bags, greeting cards, and soaps, but the doll clothes were a hit too."

"Thank you for dropping this off." Pam beckoned for her to come into the house. "Stay for dinner. Steve's grilling up some burgers."

Christine held up her palms. "Oh no. You have company, and I don't want to intrude."

"Oh please!" Pam scoffed. "It's just Brent."

Christine held back a frown. The idea of spending a whole evening with him sounded painful after their last encounter—as awkward as the first. "Oh, I don't—"

"Who's at the door?" Steve called from somewhere inside the house.

Pam turned. "It's Christine! I've told her to join us for dinner."

"Oh hey, Chris! We have plenty."

Pam took her arm and yanked her into the house. "Stop acting like a stranger and come in, for heaven's sake."

Reluctantly, Christine allowed Pam to steer her into the kitchen, where she deposited her purse on the table and then stepped to the sink to wash her hands. "I feel guilty for eating your food when I didn't bring anything."

"Oh, knock it off, Christine. You're family."

Steve poked his head in as he pushed open the sliding glass door. "Let's eat out here on the deck. It's a beautiful evening."

"Okay."

Steve left, and Pam pushed a bowl of macaroni salad and one with baked beans toward Christine before draping a folded tablecloth over her arm. "Here. Take these out."

Brent slipped inside, his hair the same mess of dark curls that, coupled with yet more stubble on his angular jaw, gave him the rugged look she'd noticed outside her store. Wearing shorts and a plain black shirt that hugged his wide chest and muscular biceps, he nodded at Christine before turning to Pam. "Steve says the burgers are about ready. How can I help?"

Pam handed him a stack of paper plates, then placed regular utensils on top of them along with a stack of plastic cups. "You two start setting the table. I'll gather the condiments."

"After you," Brent said to Christine.

She walked onto the deck with Brent close behind, then placed the tablecloth and bowls on the table.

"So, Brent," she began, hoping to break the ice as they followed Pam's instructions, "we need to stop running into each other like this." She faced him and snapped her fingers. "And I still owe you at least five dollars for those ice cream cones."

He shook his head and grinned, his handsome face lighting up as he arranged utensils by a plate.

She grimaced as she lifted the stack of cups. "Did you get the stain out?"

"I'll have you know that my aunt Midge can get out any stain— even chocolate peanut butter ice cream."

She leaned forward with one hand on the back of a chair. "I

suspected you were here when I saw a Virginia license plate outside. You told Mrs. Ward and me that's where you're living now."

"It is." He set the last place and then looked up at her. "How old are your twins?"

So you don't want to talk about yourself. Okay, then.

"They're four, but they're not mine. They're Britney's."

"Oh." He paused. "They could pass for yours."

She smiled. "I hear that a lot. They're my little M&Ms."

He lifted an eyebrow.

"Mila and Maddy."

"Oh." He nodded as understanding filled his face. "Cute."

"Who's ready for a burger?" Steve sang as he climbed the deck stairs holding a platter. The delicious aroma permeated the deck as the cicadas sang day into night.

The glass door slid open, and Pam stuck out her head. "Chris? Steve? If you're done setting the table, could you please come help me?"

While Christine carried out a tray of condiments, Pam brought a pitcher of iced tea and a bag of chips, and Steve brought buns and dip. Soon they were all gathered around the table, building their burgers.

"So, Brent," Steve began while placing an impressive load of dill pickles on his burger, "how's your aunt's house coming along?"

"Pretty well. I'm about finished replacing shingles on the roof, but there's still a lot to do. I'm just getting started."

Christine's eyes flickered to Brent's left hand again, and she was still surprised to find it naked of any jewelry. How could he not be married? Of course, that didn't mean he was truly single. He could still have a girlfriend in Virginia.

"I have to paint over some water damage on the kitchen ceiling," Brent was saying, "and the screens on her porch look like they're about to fall out. I also have to remove all her wall hangings to spackle holes and repaint every room, not to mention dealing with leaky faucets and the commode that never stops running." He added mustard and relish to his burger and then put the top of his bun on it.

Pam touched Steve's arm. "Don't forget Steve's a plumber."

"I won't," Brent said.

"Where's your aunt Midge moving to?" Christine asked.

"A retirement community over in Oakboro. That's where all her good friends live now. She's been talking about going there for a few years, and a couple of weeks ago she called out of the blue and asked if I could come help get her house ready to sell." Brent shook his head. "It's pretty obvious she hasn't had any work done since my uncle Sal died back when I was a young teenager."

He frowned before popping a chip into his mouth, then swallowed before adding, "Aunt Midge never got rid of anything. She told me her mother taught her you never know when you might want something or even need it. But still, you won't believe all the stuff in her basement and attic. Anyway, she says she doesn't want any of it now."

"I guess your mom will go through it?" Pam asked.

"No. She's already told Aunt Midge she doesn't want anything. She doesn't have room in the house she and Dad still live in anyway. It's not even as big as my aunt's, and I'd say they could use a clearing out of their own."

"How are your folks?" Christine asked. When Brent gave her a strange expression, warmth crept up her neck and she looked down at her plate. Why did she keep managing to embarrass herself in front of this man?

"They're fine. Mom still works evenings at a clothing store in the mall, and Dad is a night security guard."

Christine met his gaze and was grateful to find him smiling at her. "Your mom drops by my store sometimes." *And never says a word about you.*

"You have a store?"

Pam leaned forward. "Christine owns the Treasure Hunting Antique Mall on Main Street."

"Oh." Brent divided a look between Christine and Pam before his eyes focused on Christine. "So when you were helping Mrs. Ward with that bookcase, she'd bought it from your store?"

"Yes, that's right."

"Cool."

They stared at each other, and yet another awkward moment passed between them.

Christine cleared her throat and looked at Steve. "These burgers are delicious."

"Thank you," he said as he lifted his glass of iced tea.

Pam dropped a small pile of chips onto her plate. "Brent, do you think your sister would want to go through your great-aunt's stuff?"

"I doubt it. She lives in a tiny apartment with a roommate."

"What's Kylie doing these days?" Christine asked.

"She's working on her master's degree to become a pediatric nurse practitioner. She's in a program at the University of Virginia and also working in Charlottesville, Virginia, at a children's urgent care facility."

"That's amazing. She was always so sweet around school." Christine forked some macaroni salad. "She might want you to keep some of your aunt's things until she does have room for them. You should ask her before you get rid of anything."

"Well, it's obvious to me what you need to do," Steve said.

Brent's brow wrinkled. "What?"

"Take anything Kylie doesn't want to Christine's store and sell it." Steve gave him a palms-up.

"You think so?"

"What sort of items are we discussing here?" Christine asked.

Brent shrugged. "Great-aunt stuff?"

Christine looked at Pam, and when they both burst out laughing, Brent crossed his arms, leaned back, and said, "Well, ladies, what would you call it?"

"Do you mean old kitchenware, housewares, linens—those kinds of items?" Christine asked him.

Brent shrugged again. "Probably. It's all in cardboard boxes. Do people really buy old things like that?"

Christine and Pam shared another look of disbelief.

"I guess you've never been to an antique mall?" Pam asked.

Brent shook his head. "No. And I'm betting a lot of men haven't." He picked up his burger and looked at Christine. "So how does it work?"

"My store is divided into booths, and each vendor has his or her items for sale on display—artwork, collectibles, vintage clothes and dishes, old jewelry, antique toys and furniture, and even new, homemade items with a lot of charm. I charge the vendors rent for the booths, and I also get a percentage of their sales." Christine looked at Pam. "Tell him about your booth."

"It's called Homemade Haven, and I crochet all sorts of things—hats, scarves, tote bags, doll clothes, blankets, pet toys . . . I also create greeting cards and make gift tags, candles, and soaps. It all sells from my booth."

"Really?" Now Brent looked intrigued. "That's interesting."

Pam shrugged. "Making things is a stress reliever for me after a crazy day at the bank."

"So if your aunt wants to sell some things still in good condition, I have a booth available right now," Christine said.

Brent smiled. "I'll tell her. Thanks."

◆ ◆ ◆

Christine contemplated Brent while washing dishes with Pam, who stood beside her drying and stowing away the utensils that were already clean. The house didn't have a dishwasher, but Pam said they didn't mind.

During dinner, the conversation had flowed as they all reminisced about high school, laughing over senior pranks and the fun times they'd had before graduation. She'd never imagined she'd share such an enjoyable meal in the company of her sister's ex-boyfriend.

"Penny for your thoughts," Pam said.

Christine glanced toward the deck.

"The guys can't hear us as long as we don't talk too loudly," Pam said as if reading her mind, "so just spill it."

Christine finished rinsing a dish and set it on the drying rack. "What's Brent's story?"

"His story?" Pam's nose scrunched. "What do you mean?"

Christine turned and rested her hip against the sink. "What has he been up to for the past decade? Don't you find it strange that he can just drop everything to come help a family member for an extended period of time? Is he independently wealthy or something?"

Pam set a dried bowl in a cabinet. "I don't think so. All I know is he told Steve he's fixing up his aunt's house and then going back to Virginia, hopefully before Thanksgiving. If he told my husband what his work is there, Steve didn't tell me."

Christine began washing the baked beans bowl while pondering how friendly Brent had been. In fact, he reminded her of the boy she'd known in high school—always sweet and respectful of her sister and cordial to her. Though they'd never spoken much. Whenever he was at their house, he focused on Britney, just like everyone else in their popular group did.

"I saw your email about the available booth," Pam said, her words breaking through Christine's thoughts. "I don't know any potential vendors, but I posted your flyer in the breakroom at the bank. Even if Brent and his aunt take the space, it won't be for very long. But if they have a lot of great stuff to sell, that will be good for your store while you wait for a more long-term vendor to show up."

Christine smiled. "You're right."

When the dishes were all put away, Christine grabbed her purse. "I need to go, Pam. I've had a long day." She hugged her. "Thank you for a delicious meal."

"You're welcome, but you need to thank the grill master." Pam took Christine's arm and gently towed her out to the deck, where Steve and Brent still sat at the table.

"I'm heading home. Again, the burgers were amazing, Steve," Christine said before meeting Brent's gaze. "It was nice seeing you again."

Brent pushed back his chair and stood. "I should head home too. I'll walk out with you." Reaching over the table, he shook Steve's hand. "Thanks again for inviting me over. This was fun."

"Let's do it again soon," Steve told him. "For sure before you leave town."

Brent thanked Pam as they all walked through the house to the front door, where he held it open for Christine as she said good night to their hosts. Then she stifled a yawn with her hand as they walked toward their waiting trucks. "Excuse me. It's been a long day."

Brent sauntered over to her Tacoma and gave a low whistle. "Nice truck."

"Thanks. I bought it gently used from a local dealership when I opened my store."

He pivoted to face her. "I never imagined you driving a pickup."

"And what did you expect me to drive?"

"I don't know." He looked sheepish as he gave her two palms-up. "A Prius?"

With a frown, Christine folded her arms over her chest and squinted her eyes, her backpack purse dangling from one wrist. "Because I'm the nerdy twin, right?"

"The nerdy twin?" He blinked.

"Oh, come on, Brent. Britney was the beautiful twin—the cool, popular, gorgeous, perfect twin—and I was the wallflower, the artsy weirdo."

He studied her, and an unreadable expression overtook his face. "I never thought that at all." He pointed at his Chevrolet. "And what did you expect me to drive?"

Her lips twisted as she pondered the question. "Honestly?"

"Of course."

"Okay." She took a deep breath. "Before tonight, I would have expected you to drive a new SUV—maybe a BMW, an Infiniti, or an Escalade. Something flashy and super expensive."

He snorted. "Not even close."

Questions about his life swirled through her mind, but the answers were none of her business. And he'd made it clear he really

didn't want to talk about himself, right? "Well, have a good night."
Her keys jingled as she pulled them from the pocket of her purse.

"Wait," he said. "How's your family? Your parents? They were
always good to me."

"They're fine." *And Britney's fine, too, if that's what you're really
asking.*

"Good." He smiled. "So I'll talk to Aunt Midge about the mountain of stuff in her basement and attic and then be in touch."

"Sounds good." She climbed into her truck, and before she backed
out of the driveway, she looked over and found Brent watching her. Or
was he envisioning her sister? Her *married* sister.

◆ ◆ ◆

"How was the barbecue?" Aunt Midge asked when Brent came in.

He set his keys on the pony wall that divided the family and dining spaces, then sat on the sofa across from her recliner. "It was good.
Did you eat?"

"Of course I did!" Aunt Midge chuckled and pushed her ever-
present turquoise glasses up on her nose. "I'm so glad you finally got
out of this house and spent time with folks your age. You need to do
that more often."

Brent rested his right ankle on his left thigh as he considered
the evening, careful of his knee. He'd been so surprised when Steve
told him Christine would join them for dinner. She was sweet and
friendly, and he'd been almost shocked when she asked about his
parents and sister. She was also funny and outgoing, and he enjoyed
talking to her.

He couldn't help but notice that she wasn't wearing a wedding
ring. That surprised him. After all, she was nearing thirty too. And

she was so attractive with her bright-blue eyes, long neck, gorgeous smile, and tall, trim stature. Especially tonight with her blond hair pulled back in a thick braid.

Had he forgotten how pretty she was? Or had he been too focused on Britney to notice? Not that he was interested. He wasn't ready to trust any woman again—not after Tara.

"What's on your mind, Brent?" Aunt Midge asked.

He pushed his hand through his hair. Seriously, he needed to make time for a haircut. "Christine Sawyer was there."

"Oh, that Christine is a sweetie. She's a pretty young woman too. I'm surprised she's still single. She's so nice and hardworking—and a great catch for sure! I love that store she opened. It's so interesting to go in there and browse."

And that brought up the question he'd planned to ask her.

"Speaking of her store, Steve gave me an idea for what to do with all the things you don't want from the basement and attic. How about asking Kylie if she wants anything, and then taking what good stuff she doesn't want to Christine's store to sell? The rest you can donate or just trash."

Aunt Midge smiled. "That's a great idea. I'll start sorting tomorrow."

He stood and stretched before pulling his phone out of his pocket and checking the time. "I need to hit the shower and then get to bed."

"Don't forget we have family dinner at your parents' house tomorrow evening," she said as she stood to join him. "Sunday is their one day off, and you didn't go with me last week."

He groaned at the idea of spending time with his father.

"Now, now, Brent. They're your folks. You'll miss them someday. I sure wish I could talk to mine."

He inspected his fingernails as he felt a twinge of guilt. "I love my parents. I just get tired of Dad's constant digs about how I messed up my life by dropping out of school. Although I still don't know how he expected me to pay for tuition after I was injured and lost my scholarship. I just don't need him to remind me of my failures, or his disappointment that I went into construction and home remodeling. He might be right about that, though. I'm happy to help with your house, but the passion I had for this as my life's work has faded." *Like my business.*

Aunt Midge reached up and patted his cheek. "Brent Theodore Nicholson, you are *not* a failure. And if home remodeling isn't your passion, then you just haven't found yours yet. But when you do, you'll become a wonderful success because your heart will be happy and you'll enjoy every day of work."

"I hope so, Aunt Midge." He was so grateful for his sweet aunt's unwavering faith in him and emotional support. He could always count on her when his father—and even his mother—let him down. And if he did find another path in life, she would stand behind him. He just had no idea what that would be.

"You will. Now get some sleep."

five

As Brent bit into one of his mother's meatballs, his eyes drifted to peer at the walls of his parents' small dining room. With the same dingy brown paneling that had been all the rage of the seventies and early eighties, the room looked just as it had when he was growing up. He was astounded his parents had never changed those ugly walls. But then, they'd never had extra money. They'd poured everything they had into their children, and he was grateful for that.

The red oak hardwood flooring was just as worn as all the outdated furniture in his parents' fourteen-hundred-square-foot, three-bedroom, one-bath ranch home, and the faded and chipped round oak table with four matching chairs in the middle of this room were good examples.

Only the family photos hanging on the walls had changed over the years. Updated photos of Brent and Kylie had replaced older ones as the years went by. Kylie smiled down at him from her high school senior portrait, and she looked beautiful as always with her hair cascading past her shoulders.

Brent's gaze locked on his senior football portrait, taking in his confident smile as he proudly posed in his uniform. Back then his sights were set on UNC at Chapel Hill because of the scholarship

49

he'd won, and his parents had been proud of him. In fact, everyone in his life had been proud of him, and Brent had even been proud of himself. But other than the pride he'd felt as a business owner and from the remodeling work he'd done, that was a feeling he hadn't experienced in nearly eight years.

He swirled spaghetti with his fork, then instead of focusing on his regret, he turned his thoughts toward the idea of ripping out his parents' outdated paneling and installing new drywall painted a modern color to brighten up the place.

"So, Brent." Dad's voice brought him back to the present. "Aunt Midge told your mother you're doing a bang-up job on her roof."

Brent swallowed the spaghetti and wiped his mouth on a paper napkin as he looked across the table at his father. When he was younger, family friends had often told him he resembled his dad. They had the same dark eyes, dark curly hair, strong jawline, and smile. But as Brent took in the wrinkles around his father's mouth, the dark circles rimming his tired eyes, his receding hairline, and his round face and the spare tire around his middle, he wondered if he was peering into a mirror showing him how he would look when he reached his midfifties.

As he lifted his glass of Coke, Brent silently vowed to get back to working out even if his knee did hurt.

Aunt Midge reached over and patted his shoulder. "Barry, your son is a skilled workman. The roof looks brand-new now. Next he's going to improve my screened-in back porch."

Brent smiled at his aunt, still the buffer between him and his father.

"Oh, I can't wait to see everything." Mom's hair appeared to shimmer with more gray than the last time he'd seen her, but her eyes and smile still appeared youthful.

Aunt Midge nodded. "You'll be impressed, Donna."

"Thanks, Aunt Midge," Brent said as he sprinkled more parmesan cheese on his spaghetti and meatballs. "Dinner is delicious, Mom."

She beamed. "You know I had to make your favorite pasta."

Dad cleared his throat, and the muscles in Brent's shoulders tensed. All the times his father had lectured and scolded him for not playing football well enough, for not getting top grades, for not finding a way to stay in school after his injury . . . They all began with him clearing his throat.

"I've been wondering something, Brent." Dad's brows drew together. "How is it that you had the time to come home to help your aunt?"

Brent set his fork beside his plate. "I made the time, Dad."

"Does that mean you're out of work?"

Brent's heart pounded against his rib cage. He didn't want to admit he'd lost his business. Not yet. "It's complicated . . ."

"Complicated? What's that supposed to mean? Sounds like you're hiding something. Like when you left school without telling us and then ruined your entire future. You could have—"

"It's been *eight years*. Are you ever going to let this go?" Brent's body vibrated with anger and frustration.

"No, I'm not." Dad shook his head. "I still want you to do better in life than I have."

"Now, Barry," Aunt Midge said, rubbing Brent's arm. "Your son is doing just fine. And I'm grateful he's made time for me."

Brent turned toward his mother and found her studying her half-eaten meal. He blew out a deep, shuddering sigh. While he'd always longed for her to defend him, he also understood why she remained silent. She was the peacemaker and did everything she could to avoid conflict. Still, having her in his corner would make these exasperating family gatherings a little easier.

"Brent's also going to help me clear out everything in the basement and attic," Aunt Midge said. "Are you sure you don't want any of it, Donna?"

Mom shook her head. "No, thank you. We don't have the space. Besides, I only wanted your formal china, and you gave it to me years ago."

"I just wanted to make sure. After we ask Kylie if she wants anything, Brent is going to take the good stuff I find to the Treasure Hunting Antique Mall to sell."

Mom clasped her hands together. "Oh, I love going there! It's so much fun to walk around and look at the different booths. Christine Sawyer has done such a wonderful job with that place."

"It's a fantastic store," Aunt Midge said. "I always find something interesting when I go there. Treasure Hunting is a perfect name."

Brent took another sip of his Coke. The women's excitement about the store piqued his interest even more, and he looked forward to seeing it for himself.

"Contacting Kylie is a great idea," Mom said. "I doubt she'll want anything, but it's good to check."

Dad met Brent's gaze again. "Your sister is doing great, you know."

"I do know, and I'm proud of her." Brent managed a smile despite his father's frown.

"She worked hard for her scholarships, and she'll graduate with her master's degree soon," Dad continued.

Brent gripped his glass. "And I'll go to her graduation and cheer for her right along with you."

"Don't think I've given up on seeing you graduate with a degree," Dad added, looking more determined than ever. "That's my goal for both my children, and I won't abandon that idea even though you have."

Brent kneaded his left shoulder as he bit back a bitter retort. He'd never had the top grades Kylie earned for an academic scholarship, so did his father think he had the money to pay for tuition out of pocket? Even if he wanted to return to school at this late date, his business hadn't been *that* successful—not that Dad had ever cared anything about it.

"What do you have planned for my porch besides replacing the screens, Brent?" Aunt Midge asked. "It's needed work for years now."

As he turned his focus back to the renovations, Brent hoped dessert would be quick so he could get out of this house.

◆ ◆ ◆

Brent gripped the steering wheel of Aunt Midge's red Toyota Camry with such force that he feared he might break it. Anger, frustration, and sadness surged through him as his father's litany of disappointment echoed through his mind over and over.

"You do realize that your dad doesn't mean to lecture you," Aunt Midge said, sitting in the passenger seat with her purse perched on her lap. Only when he glanced her way did he notice it matched her turquoise glasses.

Brent snorted. "And yet he does."

"The truth is, his problem isn't you. It's a reflection of his own insecurities and shortcomings. You see, he never finished high school, and with only a GED and no money for college, the jobs he'd dreamed of were always out of his reach. When you came along, he gave up and settled for being a security guard. But he wanted—still wants—more for you and your sister."

She sighed, and when he looked over, she was running her fingers over her purse strap. "Your uncle and I used to get so upset hearing your father tell you your grades weren't good enough or that you could have somehow prevented every error on the football field."

Brent kept his eyes on the road, his posture ramrod straight, his muscles taut.

"Even from the very beginning—when you were born—he started forcing you to live *his* dreams. He pressured you into peewee football."

"I liked football," Brent said, his voice low.

"I know, sweetie, but he was overbearing, saying you needed to play harder, run faster, practice more." Brent imagined Aunt Midge pursing her lips. "I tried to convince your mom to make him back off, but she very politely told me to mind my own business. So your uncle and I did what we could, making sure you had plenty of opportunity to spend time at our house."

Brent blinked. "I-I never knew that."

"Now you do." She patted his arm. "You're a good young man with a beautiful heart. Your parents are proud of you, even though they may not say it as often as they should. And your uncle and I are proud of you. Don't forget that, okay?"

He nodded as a lump swelled in his throat, cutting off any response.

"I'll start sorting through the boxes in the basement first thing," she said.

Brent cleared his throat. "Items to donate can go into those large trash bags you already have, I think. But I'll pick up some big plastic containers for whatever you want me to take to Christine's store."

"That's a great idea. Then after I have some idea what's down there, we'll call your sister."

◆ ◆ ◆

Brent jogged down the basement steps. "Aunt Midge? You down here?"

"Over here!" She waved from one corner, where she stood surrounded by boxes and four of the large plastic containers he'd bought for her.

A musty smell nearly overwhelmed him as he joined her, noticing a thick layer of dust covering every one of the boxes strewn about. "How are you doing?"

"Fine." Aunt Midge pushed her hand through her short gray hair and then pointed to the containers. He could see they were filled with dishes, tablecloths, and other kitchen items. "It's taken me a week and a half, but I have at least this much ready for Christine's store."

"Great. I need to run to Swanson's to get paint and new wood flooring and outlet covers for the porch, so I can drop these off and any items you want to donate too."

The idea of seeing Christine again filled him with surprising anticipation. But surely he was just ready for a break after working late last night installing new storm doors on the front and back of the house as well as a new service door on the garage.

He slipped the top on the first container and snapped it in place.

"Wait." Aunt Midge touched his arm. "Let's call your sister first and make sure she doesn't want any of this."

He pulled his phone from the back pocket of his jeans and shot off a text. *Hey, twerp. Are you free to talk for a minute?*

His phone immediately rang with a video call. When he answered, Kylie gave him a pointed look.

"What exactly do you mean by *twerp*, big brother?"

Brent laughed and angled his phone toward his aunt.

"Aunt Midge!" Kylie exclaimed. "It's so good to see you!"

Their aunt beamed. "How's my beautiful great-niece?"

"I'm tired, but I'm happy to talk to you both. What are you up to?" Her nose scrunched and she squinted. "And where are you?"

Aunt Midge waved her arm. "We're in my basement. Brent is helping me get my house ready to sell."

"Oh right. Mom mentioned that when I spoke to her last week. How's it going?"

"Wonderfully. Your brother is so skilled. You should see the work he's already done. The house will look brand-new when he's finished."

Brent frowned. "I seriously doubt that."

"Anyway," Aunt Midge said, ignoring his assessment, "I'm going through the millions of boxes down here, and I want to know if you want any of the things I've found before Brent takes most of them to sell at a local antique mall."

Kylie tilted her head. "What sorts of things?"

Brent held the phone while Aunt Midge went through the containers one by one, explaining nearly every piece and its significance.

"There's more like this buried in here somewhere," Aunt Midge said. "I have dolls, knickknacks, tea sets, dish sets, and all kinds of collectibles."

"Aunt Midge, they're gorgeous, but I don't have room for them."

"I'm sure I could convince your mother to keep whatever you'd like somewhere." When Kylie bit her lower lip, Aunt Midge smiled. "Sweetie, it's okay to say no. You won't hurt my feelings."

"Honestly, I have that quilt you made for me and some of your precious necklaces and bracelets. Those are what I'll cherish forever. The other items won't mean as much to me."

"I understand."

Kylie looked down and then winced. "Oh no. I have to get ready for my shift at the children's urgent care. But I'll talk to you both soon, okay?"

"Drive safely, twerp," Brent said, teasing her again.

"I'd better see you at Thanksgiving, Kylie!" Aunt Midge said.

"You will. Love you both."

Brent disconnected the call and slipped the phone into his back pocket, then rubbed his hands together. "Well, I'll get all this loaded up, then stop by both the donation center and Christine's store before I go see Mr. Swanson. I'll tell him you said hello."

"Don't do me any favors," Aunt Midge grumbled as she started up the stairs.

Brent laughed, enjoying his aunt's dry sense of humor.

He was about to put the lid on another container when he noticed a large, partially opened box behind it. He lifted what, through the paper wrapped around it, felt like a heavy square frame. An identical package sat in the box too.

He gently unwrapped the first one, and his eyes widened as he took in a beautiful watercolor scene with mountains and a lake in autumn. Then he unwrapped the second frame, unsurprised to find a similar painting by the same artist—only the scenery in this one looked like spring. He recalled these companion pieces hanging in the family room upstairs when he was a kid, but they'd disappeared years ago.

"Brent!" Aunt Midge hollered from upstairs. "Did you get lost down there?"

"I'm coming." He carefully rewrapped the paintings and slipped them back into their box. He'd look at them again when he had more time. Right now he had to make his deliveries and get those supplies.

six

"Oh, these are amazing," Christine told the middle-aged man as she slipped his antique Chrysler wheel covers into a box.

He pulled his wallet out of his pocket. "I agree. I've been collecting Chrysler memorabilia since I was a kid."

She gave him the total, and he slipped his credit card into the reader. While she waited for the computer to respond, the bell above the door rang. She turned her attention there just as Brent held it open, allowing two young women to walk out. They each gazed at him with admiration apparent on their faces, and Christine couldn't blame them. She drank in the sight of him as he sauntered inside, admiring how his well-worn jeans emphasized his trim waist and his tucked-in tan shirt was the perfect complement to his golden eyes.

Christine gave herself a mental headshake. Brent Nicholson would never notice her as anything more than a friend, if that, and he was the last man she'd want to date after he'd hurt Britney anyway. Still, she could have done more with her hair than pulled it into a ponytail. And if only she'd worn a little bit of makeup . . .

"Miss?"

"Huh?" Christine turned back to the man standing at the counter. "Yes?"

Amy Clipston

"May I please have my receipt?"

"Oh, I'm so sorry. Have a great day."

While she helped the remaining two customers in line, she was aware Brent was wandering about the store, no doubt peering into booths and examining the merchandise. Then after finishing with the last person, she spotted him back at the front of the store, running his fingers over a maple kitchen table she'd refinished along with its three chairs on one side, one chair on each end, and bench on the opposite side.

Christine ran her hands down her yellow blouse and cut-off jeans, then straightened her ponytail before sidling up to him. "Are you in the market for a new set?"

"No, but this is nice." He ran his finger over the bench. "Beautiful."

"I appreciate your saying that. I refinished it."

He turned toward her, his dark eyebrows lifting. "Really? You do nice work."

"Thank you." She gestured widely. "I've restored most of these pieces, but some of the ones I found just needed a good polishing."

He rubbed his clean-shaven jaw as his eyes surveyed the furniture. "Wow." Then he turned toward her. "Honestly, it doesn't surprise me that you're so skilled at this."

She studied his expression, looking for signs of teasing but finding none. "What do you mean?"

"The art department had a showcase when we were seniors, and you'd painted this gorgeous picture of a beach at sunset. You have talent, and it's obviously translated into how beautifully you restore furniture."

Stunned, she blinked. "You remember that painting?"

"Yes, I do. Britney told me you took a photo when you were at the Outer Banks on vacation and then painted the scene making the colors even more brilliant—which they were. The colors were amazing."

"I-I appreciate your saying that too," she stammered.

"Whatever happened to that painting?"

"It's hanging in my parents' family room."

"I bet they enjoy it." He touched the table again.

"Thank you," Christine managed to say, not sure what to make of his compliments. "So how may I help you?"

When he faced her again, he sniffed and rubbed his eyes.

"You okay?"

"Yeah." He cleared his throat. "I'm on my way to the hardware store and have a load of my aunt's things—if you're still interested in seeing them. You'll be able to tell if anyone would want to buy them."

"Let's see what you have."

Brent held the door open for her, and then she followed him to where he'd backed his truck into an angled spot near the front of the store. He lifted out one of four tote containers from the truck bed, set it on the sidewalk, and took off the lid.

Christine pulled out a vintage dinner plate, white with light-blue flowers on it. "This is gorgeous." She kept digging. "Is this a whole set?"

"Possibly?"

"I see more pieces and matching salt and pepper shakers. She even has the gravy boat and butter dish." She looked up at Brent. "This is amazing."

"Is it?" His adorable smile made her laugh.

"Yes, it is. And I'm guessing the other containers hold treasures as well. Let's take them inside. Would you like to see the available booth, then?"

He nodded toward the door. "Sure. Hold the door open for me, and I'll carry these in."

"I can carry one." She rolled her eyes. "I'm not a fragile flower."

They each took a tote, and Brent hastened ahead of her to prop open the door with his back. Then he followed her to the empty booth, where they set them on the floor.

"I'll get the last two," he said.

She frowned. "I can help, Brent."

"Fine." He hesitated and then sneezed into the crook of his arm before rubbing his eyes again.

"Are you okay?"

Now his eyes were puffy. She nearly stepped closer to look into them but stopped herself.

"Yeah. I must be allergic to something in your store, but I'll be fine."

They retrieved the last two totes and returned to the booth.

"Give me a minute," she told him. "I'll get a vendor agreement for you to review." She hurried to her office and found the paperwork and a pen, then returned.

She stopped short when she found Brent sneezing while trying to shoo away Wanda at the same time. The cat was sitting at his feet, blinking up at him.

"Can you get it away from me?" he said, actually pleading. "Please?"

"You're allergic to cats?"

"I think so!" he said before sneezing several times in a row. "I've never really been around any."

"I'm so sorry. Come here, Wanda!" She picked up the cat and then placed the paperwork and pen on a shelf beside Brent. "Here's the agreement. I'll be right back." She hurried down the aisle with Wanda meowing and twisting in her arms.

After depositing the cat in her office and closing the door, she fetched a box of tissues, a bottle of water, and some allergy medicine from the breakroom before rushing back to Brent and holding out the supplies. "Here."

"Thank you." He took two of the allergy pills and downed a long drink of water, then wiped his eyes and nose with a tissue before stuffing it into his pocket.

She left to help a customer who'd slipped in while they'd been bringing in the totes, and when she returned Brent picked up the vendor agreement and handed it to her. "This looks fine. I filled it out and signed it. Aunt Midge says she wants me to manage all this for her."

"Great. I have more shelving units you can use in the back room, and once we set them in place, you can arrange everything and set your prices."

Brent gave her a blank look. "Arrange it? And how much should we, uh, charge?"

She inwardly sighed. But it wasn't like Brent was an average vendor. She'd have to help him. After all, he was only doing this for his elderly aunt.

"And how about a name for the booth?" she added.

"A name?" He cupped his hand to the back of his neck.

"Look around. All the booths have names. Susie's Zoo, Glitz and Glamor, Our House, Simply Southern, Christmas Town, At the Beach . . ."

He took his wallet from his back pocket. "I'll pay you three months' rent plus some extra up front if you'll set up the booth, name it, price everything . . . and I'll tell Aunt Midge we need to increase your cut."

She shook her head. "I can't let you do that last one. It's not in the agreement."

"Okay, but will you do the rest? You'll really be helping me." He held out the money.

"Deal." She took the cash and slipped it into her pocket. Extra income never hurt.

Brent's eyes focused on something behind her, and a look of dread came over his face.

Christine turned just as Wanda sauntered over and meowed up at him. "Oh no. I'm sorry. Sometimes my office door doesn't latch. Wanda! Get over here!"

Wanda rubbed up against Brent's shins, and he closed his eyes. "I think she's trying to kill me," he groaned.

She chuckled as she lifted the cat. "No, she's not. She likes you."

Pietro jumped out from behind a nearby display and bellowed a meow that seemed to bounce off the walls.

Yelping, Brent jumped back, looking as if he were attempting a two-step. "Oh no! Another one? How many cats do you have in here?"

Christine bit the inside of her lip to keep from laughing. Seeing this muscular, athletic—and six foot three, as she remembered—former football player terrified of her cats was too much. "Only two," She shooed the orange tabby away. "Go on, Pietro! Git!" Then she looked up at Brent's horrified expression. "How about we talk outside?"

He looked relieved. "Great idea."

She pushed the cats toward the back of the store and then followed Brent out to his truck, where he leaned against the tailgate.

"I'm sure your aunt's things will sell quickly."

"Wonderful. I appreciate your help." He held out his hand, and when she shook it, she appreciated the feeling of his warm skin against hers. "And she has plenty more in her basement and attic," he added. "I'll be in touch."

"I look forward to it."

Christine remained on the sidewalk as Brent drove off. Hugging her arms to her chest, she smiled. Then she reminded herself that this was the man who had broken her sister's heart, making him off-limits.

But she did wonder if he'd changed. He seemed so . . . nice.

◆ ◆ ◆

Christine stood in front of the new booth and smiled. After working late the last two nights setting it up, she was pleased with the final results.

She'd moved her extra shelving units in and arranged Midge Marcello's items on each shelf by color and category. The set of vintage flowered dishes sat on one shelf, and a variety of colorful teacups and saucers sat on another one along with a few matching platters. Kitchen gadgets were spread throughout the booth, and the beautiful linens were displayed on a small table she'd also added.

She'd finished decorating with white fairy lights and a painted sign naming the booth Midge's Marketplace. Below that, she'd added a sign that said, "Here you'll find something old yet new to you."

She pulled out her phone and snapped a few photos before texting them to Pam.

Check out my new booth.

Almost instantly, her best friend responded: *I love it! Brent's aunt Midge?*

Yes, and thanks! I decorated and named it, but Brent brought the goodies.

Fantastic!

Now all she had to do was make good on her conviction that the items would sell. She'd just have to make sure her customers knew she had a new booth.

◆ ◆ ◆

Later that afternoon, Christine's nieces burst through the store's front door.

"Auntie! Auntie!" Mila exclaimed. "We have a present for you!"

Maddy sprinted behind the counter. "We made it."

"You did?" Christine gently tugged on one of Maddy's blond braids.

Britney leaned against the counter and dropped her giant designer purse on it. "They insisted we come straight here from day camp. They couldn't wait to give it to you."

"Here." Mila handed Christine a large piece of construction paper and then wrung her little hands in anticipation.

Christine flipped it over and found a colorful drawing. "This is beautiful. Tell me all about it."

"This is you, me, Mila, and Mommy at the beach." Maddy pointed to stick figures standing by wavy blue lines. "And there's Daddy, Nana, and Poppy too."

Mila appeared at Christine's other side. "That's Jake next to Poppy. He likes the beach."

"This is just adorable." Christine's heart filled with love for her sweet nieces as she examined their bright-yellow sun and puffy white clouds in a blue sky.

She pointed to the bulletin board behind the counter. "How about we hang it here so all my customers can see it?"

"Yay!" the girls sang in unison.

Christine attached the drawing with four pushpins, then said, "There. It's just perfect. Thank you so much. I love you both. You're my sweet M&Ms!" The girls giggled as she hugged and kissed them.

"Can we play with the kitties?" Mila asked.

Maddy folded her hands as if she was begging, which she was. "Pleeease!"

"Of course."

The girls reached into a bottom drawer behind the counter and took out two plastic balls with bells and a pink flamingo hanging on a stick before rushing to find the cats, who seemed to be hiding somewhere in the back of the store.

"Wanda! Pietro! Where are you?" Mila called as they scampered away.

Britney shook her head. "I wish I had their energy."

"Me too." Christine leaned her elbows on the counter.

"So what's new, sis?"

"I have a new vendor."

"No kidding! Show me the booth."

Christine led her through the store until they came to Midge's Marketplace. "What do you think?"

Her twin grinned as she touched the creamer that matched the blue-flowered dishes. "Chrissy! This is amazing. The white lights give it a classy look."

"Thanks. I decorated it myself."

Britney's light eyebrows lifted. "You did?"

"Yup. I even painted the signs."

Britney shook her head. "I'm not surprised. I always say you got the talent as well as the brains."

Christine's smile shrank. She loved her sister, but sometimes she still longed to be the pretty one. If only for one moment.

"How did you find the new vendor?" Britney ran one perfectly manicured hand over the lace on a tablecloth.

Christine hesitated. "It's a funny story."

"Oh?" Britney pivoted to face her. "Tell me."

"The vendor is Midge Marcello."

Britney blinked, and then recognition flashed over her face. "Midge's Marketplace. Brent's great-aunt?"

"Right. I stopped by Pam's house to give her a check, and Brent was there. She insisted I stay for dinner, and Brent mentioned that before she moves, his aunt wants to get rid of most of what she's had stored in her basement and attic. Steve suggested she sell some of the items here, and so Brent brought me the first load two days ago. He even paid me to set up the booth for them."

Britney studied her. "Why would you want to get involved with Brent after what he did to me?"

"I'm not getting involved with him, Brit." She lowered her voice as a couple of shoppers walked past. "You know how this works. The vendors pay me booth rent, and I get a percentage of their sales. I can't pay my own rent if I don't have a full slate of vendors, so why would I turn down this opportunity?"

Her sister looked unconvinced.

"He's just a vendor, Brit. That's it." Christine turned toward the end of the aisle and spotted Mila holding out the pink flamingo while Wanda leapt for it. She grinned as she recalled Brent trying to convince her the cat was trying to kill him. "I bet you didn't know Brent is allergic to cats."

"What?"

Christine faced her twin. "When he was here, Wanda was all over him. It was hilarious to see Flowering Grove High's former quarterback pleading with me to get my cats away from him." She chuckled.

"He's bad news, Chrissy." Britney's eyes narrowed with suspicion. "I know he's handsome and can be charming. I was caught in his web too—for years. But he can't be trusted."

Christine dropped her shoulders with a sigh. "Britney, I'm not interested in him that way, and I wouldn't even consider dating him. I would never betray you like that. You're my sister." She shrugged. "It's just funny that he's afraid of my silly cats."

Britney's expression warmed slightly as she stepped out of the booth. "Let me know if you need any help here. I'm volunteering at the day camp only a couple of days a week."

"Thanks." Christine pulled her phone out of her pocket to check the time. "It's almost five." She pointed toward the front of the store. "I need to see if any of the customers still here need to check out, then I'll close up."

She hurried to the front of the store, where the middle-aged women she'd seen earlier stood by the counter. "I'm coming! Sorry about that."

Her sister and the twins arrived at the counter just as Christine handed a receipt to a man with two vintage posters he practically drooled over, then told him goodbye.

Britney looked down at her daughters and said, "Go ahead and ask, Mila."

"Auntie, we want you to come to the park with us."

Christine leaned over the counter and smiled at her adorable niece. "The park, huh?"

"We invited Daddy too," Maddy said as she scooted around the counter, then slipped the cat toys into the drawer. "Will you come with us?"

"Pleeease!" Mila sang.

Christine turned to scan her store. "Well, I have a lot to do here before I can leave."

"We'll help you, right, Mommy?" Maddy asked.

Britney nodded. "Absolutely. What can we do?"

While the twins fed the cats and gave them fresh water, Britney pushed a Swiffer around the store and Christine closed the register before stowing the day's cash in her safe. Then she followed Britney's silver Chevrolet Equinox down Main Street and onto Linwood Avenue to Flowering Grove Park. The twins rushed off to the swings, and when Christine and Britney caught up to them, Christine pushed Maddy while Britney pushed Mila. The girls pumped their legs and giggled as they soared higher and higher toward the clear blue sky.

Hunter arrived, and Britney stepped away from the swings. He kissed her cheek and then beamed at his twins. "How are my princesses?"

"Great, Daddy!" Maddy shouted as she swung up, then back. "Me and Sissy played with Auntie's cats today."

Christine gave Maddy another push. "They also fed them."

"We're good helpers," Mila announced. She turned her head and looked at her mother when she realized her swinging was losing momentum. "Push me, please, Mommy. I want to reach the puffy clouds!"

Britney gave Mila a push and then turned to Christine. "Did you remember I'm on the committee for our ten-year high school reunion? I'm so excited."

"Ten years, huh?" Hunter grinned. "You two are so young. Just babies!"

Britney scoffed. "You're only two years older than we are." She turned her attention back to Christine. "It will be so much fun, and the invitations just went out. You should get yours this week. It's the Saturday after Thanksgiving. The venue and caterer are all set, but now we need subcommittees for things like decorating. You should join us. We could work together!"

Christine frowned. "Oh, I don't think so."

"Why not?"

"Committees aren't really my thing. You know I was never into that." She gave Maddy another push.

"But you're so artistic and creative."

"I'll think about it," Christine said to pacify her sister, but she'd already made her decision. She wasn't going to join a committee.

"It's going to be formal, so we'll get all dressed up. Oh! I can't wait." Britney turned to her husband. "You'll be my date, right?"

"Do I have a choice?" Hunter deadpanned, and Christine and Britney both laughed.

Christine divided a look between her nieces. "Which one of you will be my date?"

"Oh! Oh!" Maddy kicked her feet up in the air. "I'll be your date."

"Will there be cake?" Mila asked.

Everyone laughed again, and Christine's heart felt full.

"We do need to find you someone," Britney said. "You haven't dated anyone for ages."

Christine shook her head. "I'm just fine. I have my M&Ms, my cats, my house, and my store. That's all I need, right, girls?"

"Right!" her nieces said in unison.

Britney frowned. "No, we need to find you a good man. You've been alone for too long."

This again. Christine shrugged as if being alone wasn't a big deal, but deep down she still wondered if she'd ever find anyone to love her.

Then another thought occurred to her. Would Brent come to the reunion? She doubted he'd travel all the way from Virginia for it, and Pam said he'd told Steve he hoped to be back there before Thanksgiving. Of course, he might not even know about the reunion unless his invitation reached him.

But that, like so much else concerning the man's life, was none of her business.

seven

Sitting at her desk in the store's office, Christine made out a check to Maren Marcello, using the legal name Brent had written on the vendor agreement. She clucked her tongue as she looked at the amount his aunt had already earned. Nearly half her items had sold in less than two weeks. The booth was already a huge success, and Christine couldn't wait to see what other goodies Mrs. Marcello had been hiding in her basement. If they were even half as nice as what she'd already sold, she would have a nice profit.

And then there was her attic.

After shutting down her computer and stowing her accounting books, she studied the check. Christine always liked to hand-deliver a new vendor's first earnings, but a wave of anxiety washed over her as she pondered visiting Mrs. Marcello's home. Brent was bound to be there, and what if he thought she'd really come just to see him? Yet if she let him know the booth was half empty now, maybe he'd bring more items to her sooner rather than later, bringing more profit to her store.

If only he hadn't forgotten to give her his number on the vendor agreement, she could have just texted him about all this.

She blew out a sigh. Who was she kidding? She wanted to see Brent, not text him.

Leaning back in her chair, Christine gazed at her tall cat tree and the orange tabby curled up on the top. "What do you think I should do, Pietro? Should I take the check over?"

The cat opened one eye and then closed it again.

"Is that a yes or a no?"

A loud meow sounded, and Christine swiveled her chair to where Wanda sat on the floor blinking at her.

"Was that a yes, Wanda?"

The cat meowed again.

"Well, I'm going to take that as a yes."

After feeding the cats, she noted Midge Marcello's address from the vendor agreement, locked the back door, and left. As she approached the house, the high school football field came into view. The team seemed to be running drills as the coaches stood on the sidelines, and memories flashed through Christine's mind. Sitting in the stands with Pam during the games, watching Britney lead the cheerleaders, cheering when the team won. And witnessing their undefeated team win the state championship under Brent's leadership their senior year.

Brent's truck was in the driveway, and she parked her truck beside his before running her fingers through her hair and taking a deep breath. Then pulling the check and a computer printout from her purse, she bit her lower lip as new doubt swamped her.

Was coming here a mistake?

She shook herself. She'd just drop off the check and invite Brent to bring more items to the store at his convenience. That was it. No ulterior motive, all business. After all, it really was her policy to hand-deliver the first check to her vendors.

Christine grabbed her purse and then made her way to the front door of the one-story brick house. She peered up at the roof and imagined Brent perched there, looking gorgeous in shorts and a T-shirt, hammering on new shingles. And then, determined, she dismissed the image.

She squared her shoulders and knocked on the door.

Brent's aunt appeared a few moments later. "Christine!"

"Hi, Mrs. Marcello."

"Oh, call me Aunt Midge. What brings you here today?"

"I wanted to let you know you've already sold nearly half the items in your booth." Christine handed her the check. "Here's your first payment. I'd love to add more merchandise whenever you're ready."

The elderly woman examined the check, her dark eyes focusing through her turquoise cat-shaped glasses. "Would you look at that."

"And here's what sold." She handed her the list.

The older woman read it, smiling and shaking her head. "Who knew that old stuff would make money? And Brent's father once had the nerve to call me a hoarder! Brent will be so happy to see this. And I like the idea of those things finding new homes!" She beckoned Christine to follow her. "Come on in. You can show this to my nephew yourself."

Christine tried to ignore the flutter in her chest as she stepped into the house, then looked around at the quaint living area furnished with a sofa, recliner, two end tables with lamps, and a coffee table. Some of the furniture looked antique, but she assumed it would move to the condo Brent mentioned.

She imagined him sitting on the sofa in the evening, watching the news or a movie with his aunt, then pushed that image away too.

"I've been meaning to go see the booth, but Brent has been so busy working on my porch that I didn't want to ask him to drive me. Now, I can still drive myself, but my family all say they'd like me to . . . well, slow down."

Christine pulled her phone out of her pocket as they entered the kitchen, the delicious aroma of beef and spices washing over her. "Would you like to see how I decorated your booth, Mrs.—I mean, Aunt Midge? I have photos."

"Oh yes, please! Sit with me here at the table."

Once they were seated, Christine slowly scrolled through the photos.

"Oh my goodness!" Aunt Midge exclaimed. "You set all this up yourself?"

"Yes, ma'am."

"Brent told me about the furniture you so beautifully refinish. You're just as talented and skilled as he said you are."

Christine smiled as a warmth swelled in her chest. Brent had spoken about her work?

"I love the white lights and signs. You need to show these photos to Brent. He'll be so impressed." Aunt Midge paused, then said, "I'm so glad you stopped by. I keep telling Brent he needs to spend time with his friends." A mischievous smile overtook her wrinkled face. "Or someone who's more than a friend, right?" She gently jabbed Christine in her ribs, then stood.

Christine shook her head as she joined her, slipping her phone back into her pocket. "Oh no, no, no. We're just, uh . . . Well, we're acquaintances."

"Nonsense. You've known each other since high school. Come see what he did out here." Aunt Midge took Christine's wrist and led her into a screened-in porch. "Look. First he repaired the roof and painted all the walls. I like this bright white, don't you?"

Christine nodded. "It's wonderful."

"Then he replaced all the screens and installed two new ceiling fans. And he insisted on putting in this new wood flooring."

Christine ran her hand over a nearby screen. "He's quite skilled."

"And handsome." Aunt Midge jabbed Christine in the ribs again. *That's the truth!*

"And so hardworking," she continued. "I have a difficult time getting *him* to slow down. Maybe you can convince him to have some fun. He's working on the commode in my guest bathroom right now."

"Well, I won't bother him. I just wanted to drop off the check and let you both know you have more space in the booth now. Would you please tell Brent I said hello?"

"Nonsense. You need to stay for dinner. I'm making one of Brent's favorites—beef enchiladas."

"Oh no. I don't want to impose."

"There's no discussion, Christine. You're staying." Aunt Midge took her wrist again and towed her back into the kitchen. "I'll finish dinner while you go tell him we're about to eat. He's down that hall-way." She pointed the way.

Christine hesitated, but she wasn't one to disrespect her elders. Her mother had taught her better than that!

She started down the hallway, slowing her steps when she came to a cluster of photos of Brent and Kylie throughout their school years. She stopped and examined each photo of Brent, studying his gorgeous smile and admiring how he'd changed and matured through the years.

When she reached Brent and Britney's senior prom portrait, she took in their perfect smiles. They'd been the most popular couple in high school—the "it couple."

Christine had always wondered what it would feel like to be Britney. Sure, Christine had had her share of boyfriends over the years, but none of those relationships had been serious, and she'd never imagined a future with any of them. Yet there Britney stood in the prom portrait, on the arm of the hottest guy in school. Christine wondered what it would have been like for Brent to send *her* notes, pick *her* up in his car, take *her* out on dates, tell *her* he loved her, promise *her* a future . . .

"I've begged my aunt to take it down, but she says she loves that photo of me. It's just so awkward to have to walk by it every day and see my ex looking at me, you know?"

Christine spun and found Brent leaning against a doorway. Even dressed in faded cargo shorts and an equally faded T-shirt, his dark hair a mess of curls and waves, he was so attractive. Dark stubble lined his jaw again, the jaw that looked as though it had been molded from fine granite. He was just as handsome without the stubble, but the five o'clock shadow gave him that rugged look that stole her breath.

She opened and closed her mouth, her words lodged in her throat.

He stepped into the hallway. "What brings you out this way?"

"I wanted to give your aunt a check. I like to hand-deliver each vendor's first one. You need to see what all sold." She reached into her pocket but then remembered she'd given the list to Aunt Midge. "Oh, right. Your aunt has the printout."

She recited what she could remember, ticking the items off on her fingers. "And I can show you photos of the booth since you haven't stopped by to see me. I mean, it."

Christine internally groaned, realizing how she'd just sounded— like a flirt. Would Brent think she was so desperate for a man that she'd pursue her twin sister's ex-boyfriend? But as he stood at her side while she scrolled through the photos—so close that she breathed in what must be the woodsy scent of his soap—he didn't seem to have noticed her gaffe. Yet she felt a strange stirring in her chest.

Brent grinned. "Wow. You even painted signs. First 'Midge's Marketplace,' and then 'Here you'll find something old yet new to you.' How creative. I love it." He looked at her, his dark eyebrows lifting.

She shrugged. "I'm just hoping she has more to sell. Like you thought."

He frowned, scrubbing his hand over his mouth. "You have no idea, but I don't think she's ready for me to bring you more yet. She's taking her time sorting through it all."

"That's fine." She nodded toward the end of the hallway. "Aunt Midge—she asked me to call her that—took me out to see what you did with the porch. You do such great work."

"You think so?" He seemed pleased.

"Absolutely. Where did you learn how to do all that?"

"I've been working in construction, mostly home improvement and remodeling, since I—well, since I left Chapel Hill."

She wondered why the hesitation, but then he jammed his thumb toward the bathroom behind him.

"I was just rebuilding this commode, but I've had a thought. Could I get your opinion on something?"

She scoffed and pointed to her chest. "You want *my* opinion?"

"Yes, Christine. That's why I asked."

"Okay." She followed him into the bathroom, then felt as if she'd stepped back in time as she scanned the light-blue tile and pink sink, commode, and tub. A toolbox, tools, and a few plumbing supplies sat on the floor. "When was this house built?"

Brent sank onto the edge of the tub. "I would guess in the fifties."

"And your aunt and uncle never replaced any of this, huh?" Christine ran her finger over the sink.

"Would you believe Aunt Midge loves the pink?"

Christine laughed and then spun, leaning back against the sink. "So you're asking my opinion of this bathroom's decor?"

"What would you think about my replacing everything in here?" He swept a hand around the room. "A complete gut. I'd upgrade with a new vanity, mirror, and bathtub and shower combo, along with a low-flow commode." He pointed to one wall. "There's even room for a cabinet over there. And of course I'd rip out the tile and paint the walls. Replace the flooring too." He met her gaze again. "Do you think that's a good idea?"

She tapped her chin, pretending to consider this option. "I don't know. It all sounds good . . . but only if you install avocado fixtures and orange shag carpet."

He laughed, and she enjoyed the deep, warm sound.

"I'm kidding, of course," she said. "It's a great idea to update this bathroom."

"You really think so?"

"Definitely. The more work you do, the less the new owners will have to do, and that makes the house more appealing in the first place." She held up a finger. "And you know, Steve could help with the plumbing."

"I was thinking that." He stood. "It's up to my aunt, of course, but it would certainly help her get a better price for the house. And the truth is the master bathroom needs an upgrade as well. So does the powder room."

"Dinner is ready, you two!" Aunt Midge called.

Brent smiled. "You're staying?"

"I didn't have a choice." She grimaced. "I hope it's okay."

"Of course it's okay." He gave her a knowing look. "Aunt Midge is very persuasive."

"You know it," she said, and they both laughed.

eight

"Aunt Midge," Christine said as she sat across from Brent at the kitchen table, "this is delicious."

Brent dabbed his lips with a paper napkin. "She makes the best beef enchiladas."

"I agree." Christine nodded before forking another bite into her mouth.

His aunt sat a little taller as she adjusted her glasses. "I'm just glad you could join us."

Brent peered at Christine, and she grinned at him. He was taken by how effortlessly beautiful she was wearing jeans and a gray T-shirt with her store's logo, her blond hair—some would call it "dirty blond"—falling past her shoulders in waves. He was certain her pretty face wore a minimal amount of makeup, if any, but she didn't need it. Her blue eyes sparkled, and once again he wondered why he'd never before noticed just how lovely she was.

"I'm certain Brent is tired of my company by now," Aunt Midge continued. "Like I told you earlier, he needs to spend more time with young folks his age."

Brent cocked his head as if to ask when that conversation

occurred, but Christine simply said, "Speaking of our age, Brent, can you believe our ten-year high school reunion is this fall?"

"Yeah, someone sent an invitation to my parents' house." Brent lifted his glass of sweet tea. "But I haven't really thought about it."

"My sister is serving on the reunion committee. Big surprise, right?" She snorted. "She tried to convince me to join a subcommittee, but that's not my thing."

Aunt Midge swallowed a bite of enchilada. "When exactly is the reunion?"

"The Saturday after Thanksgiving."

Aunt Midge pointed her empty fork at Brent. "Well, you'll be here for Thanksgiving, so you can go."

He gave his aunt a look. "I'm hoping to have your house done before then. If that works out, I'll be back in Virginia."

Aunt Midge shook her head. "Nonsense! You and your sister will both be here for Thanksgiving, and you can stay for the weekend and attend the reunion."

"But—"

"Now, now!" Aunt Midge snapped. "I don't know how many more Thanksgivings I'll have, and I want to enjoy the holidays with my precious niece and nephew while I can."

Brent peeked at Christine, who looked as amused by his aunt's insistence as he was frustrated by it.

"Besides, you two should go together." Aunt Midge pointed her fork at Brent and then at Christine.

Christine cast her eyes toward her plate, looking . . . trapped? She wouldn't want to go with him. A woman like her would have much better prospects.

Brent gulped back a groan. Leave it to Aunt Midge to embarrass their guest. He needed to change the subject—fast! "When did you open your store, Christine?"

"Four years ago." Her radiant smile was back.

"What inspired you to open it?"

She looked wistful as she pushed her hair off her shoulders. "My maternal grandmother loved to go antiquing. I started going with her when I was around eight, and we had so much fun. Nana and I would drive to the antique malls in Concord and Charlotte and shop all day. I always saved my allowance so I could buy something. Spending that time with her was special to me, and it was always my dream to open the kind of shop she dreamed of opening herself but never could."

"I bet you enjoyed that." He imagined a little pigtailed Christine holding her grandmother's hand while visiting the booths.

"I cherish those times." She moved her fork around on her plate as if lost in thought. "I miss her so much. I wish she could see the store. I think she'd love it."

Aunt Midge patted Christine's shoulder. "I'm sure she would, sweetie. And I know she's proud of you."

"Thanks."

"Did you work at an antique mall before opening yours?" Brent asked.

"No." Christine set her fork on the edge of her plate. "My parents encouraged my sister and me to go to college, so I earned my bachelor's degree and then a paralegal certificate. I worked in a law office for a couple of years."

"How did you like that?" He was fascinated to learn this about her. He'd never imagined creative, artistic Christine working in an office.

She scrunched her cute nose. "It was a stressful job, and my heart wasn't in it."

"So you quit and opened your store?"

"Not right away." She fingered her napkin. "When my nana passed away, she left my mother, sister, and me each some money. I used a part of mine as a down payment on my little house and the other part to open my store. Not only was it what I'd always wanted to do, but it was also a way to honor Nana. She's the reason I found what I love."

Aunt Midge clucked her tongue. "Isn't that something?" She nodded at Brent. "That's just like you and your great-uncle."

"Really?" Christine's eyebrows lifted.

"Oh yes," Aunt Midge told her. "Sal taught him how to build things. They built my gazebo together and the shed out back too. Brent spent hours with his uncle in his woodworking shop at the back of the garage—when he wasn't on a football field, of course."

Christine seemed to study Brent. "I never knew that."

"Well, it's not very interesting." He shifted on his chair, feeling itchy under her stare. Did he still love what Uncle Sal taught him? He just wasn't sure after . . .

"It *is* interesting," Christine said before taking another bite.

Aunt Midge's smile dimmed a fraction. "And then my husband passed away when Brent was thirteen. We still miss him, right, Brent?"

"Of course."

Christine frowned. "I'm so sorry."

"Thank you, dear." Aunt Midge patted Christine's hand this time, and her expression brightened. "I saw your cute little nieces at the fireworks, and I get such a kick out of them. It's so interesting that your sister had fraternal twins. How are those little darlings?"

Christine beamed as she lifted her fork again. "Oh, they're doing great. I just adore them."

Brent studied her smile as she shared how Britney's children always made her laugh and never ran out of energy. He was struck by how humble and sweet Christine was and how she truly loved her family. She seemed so different from her sister. Britney had always loved to be the center of attention.

He recalled the days when he drove Britney to school. She'd sit in the passenger seat, fretting over her makeup and hair until she was satisfied her appearance was perfect. Then she'd strut around the school's hallways, holding Brent's hand and grinning as crowds actually parted for them. He'd loved being admired too—a football star with the lead cheerleader at his side. But losing his scholarship had put everything into a better perspective.

And then after the breakup with Britney, he'd realized that how people perceived her was all that mattered to her. They had to believe she was flawless. Yet Christine seemed down-to-earth and comfortable in her own skin.

Brent gave himself a mental head slap. It wasn't fair to compare the sisters. Besides, Christine would never be interested in him. He was unemployed and essentially homeless since he'd had to move out of the home he rented in Virginia Beach when his company collapsed. Most of his belongings were shoved into a trailer in Devonte's driveway.

And that reminded him—he needed to contact Devonte to see if he could arrange an interview at the construction company where he worked when Brent got back to town.

After enjoying Aunt Midge's chewy homemade lemon sugar cookies, Brent and Christine cleared the table, and then Christine insisted on loading the dishwasher while Brent wiped down the table and swept the floor.

"I had a really nice time," Christine told Aunt Midge as she and Brent entered the family room once the kitchen work was done. "Thank you for inviting me to stay."

Brent's aunt smiled up from her recliner. "You're welcome here anytime," she said with a wink.

"I appreciate that." Christine gave a little laugh, and Brent was sure she was blushing.

He pulled the front door open. "Why don't I walk you out?"

"That would be nice." She shouldered her backpack purse and waved to Aunt Midge before stepping outside.

As they leisurely walked to Christine's pickup, Brent looked up at the clear sky. Dusk was closing in, and the early August air smelled like honeysuckle.

A loud whistle drew his attention to the football field, where the high school team was once more running drills. The muscles in his shoulders tensed as memories of the hours he'd spent on that field rolled through his mind.

"Do you miss it?"

His eyes cut to hers. "Football?"

"Yes, of course football, silly." She smiled, and his shoulders relaxed.

He shrugged. "I miss the good times."

"There were bad times?"

He folded his arms over his chest. "Oh yeah."

"Like what?"

"When we were in trouble or had to face tougher training after losing. Then we'd run sprints for hours. Or we had to run up and down the bleachers." He closed his eyes. "That was rough."

"It sounds awful. No wonder you all were in such good shape, though."

He snorted.

"Your aunt said you spent time with your uncle when you weren't on the football field, but you were so young when he died. When did you start playing?"

"I started peewee ball when I was in third grade."

She cocked her head. "Surely you had a lot of good times playing football, didn't you?"

"I enjoyed traveling with the team, and I appreciated the brotherhood with the guys."

"I can think of other good times." Christine leaned back against her truck's tailgate. "Like when the team was undefeated in our senior year and you led them all the way to the state championship—and they won." With her coy smile, she was adorable.

He blew out a deep breath. "That was a long time ago." He turned toward the field and then looked at her. She seemed to study him as if trying to figure out a puzzle. "I'll bring you another load of Aunt Midge's stuff as soon as possible, but only on one condition."

"What condition?"

"That you keep those ferocious cats away from me."

"Ferocious?" she squeaked.

"They clearly knew I was allergic to them and tried to kill me."

Christine guffawed, and he couldn't stop his own laugh while enjoying the moment with her. Conversation and laughter flowed easily with her, and he was reluctant to see the evening end.

Christine drew her key fob from her purse and pushed the button to unlock her truck's doors. "You have a good evening," she said as she pulled open the driver's side door. She climbed in, then started the engine before lowering her window.

"Drive safely," he told her.

She smiled. "I always do."

Brent stood in the driveway while she backed out and then waved before disappearing down the street. He turned toward the football field again and took in the sight of the players running up the field and back. If only he hadn't been hurt his sophomore year in college, maybe he wouldn't have dropped out and wound up where he was today.

With a sigh, he ambled back into the house and found Aunt Midge watching the news.

She muted the television and grinned up at him. "We had such a nice evening with Christine."

"Yes, we did." He lowered himself onto the sofa.

"She's just lovely, isn't she?" Aunt Midge asked. "She's so beautiful, hardworking, successful, and *single*." Her smile turned into that familiar mischievous grin. "You should settle down with her before some other bachelor catches her eye."

He threw his hands in the air. "Slow down, now, Aunt Midge! We're barely friends."

"Oh, you're friends. I can tell by how you two look at each other."

He decided to change the subject. "I have a serious question for you."

"What is it?"

"How would you feel if I did some upgrades on the house? I think it would not only sell faster but get a better price."

"What's your plan?"

He pointed toward the hallway. "When I was rebuilding your ancient commode, I thought about remodeling all your bathrooms. I'm sure it would be attractive to potential buyers if the house is move-in ready. They won't have to spend the time and money to do upgrades themselves. I can do the install and pay Steve to help with the plumbing." He rubbed the back of his neck. "It will just take more funds."

"Well, I think investing in the house is a great idea. We can discuss a budget tomorrow."

"Okay. Great." He stood. "You get some rest now."

"I will."

"Good night."

Brent's cell phone dinged as he walked to his room. When he pulled it out, he found a text from Tara, and he rolled his eyes. "What now?" he muttered as he opened the message.

> *Brent, please forgive me. I made one mistake. Just one! Please*
> *call me, and let's talk. I miss you, and I want to make*
> *this right.*

He snorted. As if she could ever make up for cheating on him with his so-called best friend.

He opened his text messages with Devonte and shot off another one.

> *Hey, buddy. Would it be possible to get an interview with*
> *your company when I get back? I still have plenty of*
> *work to do here at my aunt's house, but I'll head back to*
> *Virginia Beach as soon as I'm done. Thanks!*

Conversation bubbles appeared almost immediately.

> *Good to hear from you. My boss would definitely be*
> *interested in talking with you. Let me know when you're*
> *heading this way, and I'll set it up. We have plenty of*
> *work.*
> *Great. I'll be in touch.*

As Brent gathered a fresh pair of shorts and a clean T-shirt, then headed into the guest bathroom to shower, he thought of Christine again and how much he enjoyed spending time with her. He was grateful for her friendship. But knowing they could never be more than friends because of Britney disappointed him. Deep down, he agreed with Aunt Midge. Christine would be a wonderful woman with whom to build a life—if only he had any kind of future to offer her.

He shook his head as he turned on the water, then stripped off his shirt. What did that matter? He was done with love anyway. Done with risking his heart. Tara's betrayal had been the last straw.

nine

Brent slipped the last grocery bag into the trunk of the Camry as the humid evening air seemed to cling to his skin. His aunt was already in the passenger seat.

"Is that Brent Nicholson? All-conference, all-county, and all-state QB, Brent Nicholson?"

Brent pushed the trunk closed, then turned, his back stiffening as Coach Morgan approached pushing a cart full of grocery bags. "Coach. Hi." He lifted his hand in a wave.

"How long has it been, son?" The coach gave Brent's hand a vigorous shake. He looked the same, though his chestnut-colored hair was thinning and turning gray. The lines around his eyes and mouth were also evidence that he'd aged.

"A few years."

Coach had come to Chapel Hill to see him play in a few home games, but then . . . Still, the man seemed glad to see him.

"Are you back for good?"

"No." Brent explained why he was back in town.

The coach rubbed his hands together. "So you'll be here for a while, then. Well, that's perfect. I need a quarterback coach."

"Oh no." Brent shook his head. "I appreciate the invitation, but I'm really busy helping my aunt, and I don't think I'm the right man for the job anyway."

The coach scoffed. "Why wouldn't you be the right man? You led our undefeated team to the state championship and won. I can't think of a more inspiring coach for the kids."

Brent frowned. He was far from an inspiration.

"Come by the school, and we'll talk about it." Coach gave Brent's shoulder a pat. "Take care," he said as he turned to wheel his way across the parking lot.

"You too," Brent muttered before slipping into the driver's seat. "Sorry for the delay," he said as he buckled his seat belt.

Aunt Midge peered at him. "Was that your old coach?"

"Yes."

"What did he want?"

"He just said hello." Brent started the engine, then checked the mirrors.

"Oh, I bet he was thrilled to see you! You're a hero in this town. We're all so proud of you."

Brent pressed his lips together as he turned his head to back the car out of the space, then steered out of the parking lot. He would never go back to a football field. He'd have to face all his failures where they began.

"You know," Aunt Midge said, "I've made a lot of progress with my sorting. When we get home, I'll go through at least one more of those boxes in the basement, and then you can take another load to Christine tomorrow."

"All right."

"You haven't seen her in a couple of weeks. Not since she had dinner with us, right?"

"No, I haven't."

She grinned. "She'll be glad to see you."

The anxiety threading through him began to dissolve. He'd be happy to see Christine as well.

◆ ◆ ◆

A knock sounded on the front door just as Christine zipped up her bank bag, ready to put it in the store's safe. She slipped out from behind the counter and found Brent standing out on the sidewalk.

Her heart skipped a beat as he waved. All during the past couple of weeks, she'd hoped he would stop by—at least to bring her more items for the booth.

"Come in!" she called as she unlocked the door.

He shook his head, looking sheepish as he pointed to Wanda. She was standing on her rear legs and pawing at the door. "See what I mean? Ferocious cat!"

Christine laughed as she picked Wanda up. "Don't listen to the mean man," she cooed. "You're a good girl!"

"Ferocious," Brent repeated, his lips twitching.

"No, she's not. You'll give her a complex if you keep saying that." She shook her head. "I'll be right back."

She grabbed the bank bag and made a beeline for her office. "Pietro! It's dinnertime!"

Her fat orange tabby jogged ahead of her, first joining her in the office and then in the breakroom. She cared for the cats and then gathered a bottle of water and another box of allergy medicine before closing the breakroom door and returning to the front of the store. Brent still stood outside.

She pushed the door open. "I told you to come in."

He pointed to her sign. "But this says you're closed, and I follow the rules."

"You're incorrigible." She handed him the bottle of water and allergy medicine as he stepped inside. "You're just afraid of my sweet, innocent cats."

"Ferocious," he said, supposedly correcting her before popping two pills into his mouth and drinking some water. "Thank you." He gestured toward his pickup truck outside. "I've finally brought you another load. Sorry it's taken this long, but I suspect Aunt Midge spends time cherishing her memories as she works."

Christine took in the contents of his truck bed. "Fantastic." Then she looked him up and down, pretending to size him up. "But the question is whether you're brave enough to carry them into my store. After all, I have these savage cats."

"Hmm." He rested his hands on his hips and pursed his lips. "Well, I think I can take the orange tabby, but it's that female who worries me. She seems determined to rub herself all over me."

"Not to worry. They're locked up in my office."

"Are you sure? You said they were trapped in there before, but that Wanda found a way back to me."

She laughed, enjoying the easy banter between them. She couldn't remember having another male friend who joked with her this way.

"I made sure the door is latched so you won't be mauled." She pushed the allergy medicine into her pocket. "I'll help you carry it all in."

They lugged the half dozen plastic totes inside, then Christine locked the front door again before they carried them all to Midge's Marketplace. It was nearly empty now. Only a few teacups and a vintage tablecloth sat on a shelf.

He scanned the booth. "You weren't kidding when you said this stuff would sell."

"You actually doubted me, Nicholson?" She clucked her tongue and placed one palm on her chest in mock indignation. "I've never been more insulted."

He pivoted toward her, and his warm expression sent a wave of heat over her face. "Now, *you* are someone I would never doubt," he said.

She turned her attention to the totes, hoping he hadn't noticed how he'd just affected her. "Let's see what you brought me." She knelt to sift through the contents, her mouth soon dropping open as she pulled out vintage CorningWare and Pyrex serving dishes, followed by tea sets, candleholders, knickknacks, dolls, and doll clothes.

She pivoted to face Brent. "Your sister doesn't want any of this?"

"No." He shrugged. "We asked her."

Christine ran her fingers over a porcelain teacup. "Brent, this is gorgeous. I have customers who come in hoping to find tea sets like these."

"Aunt Midge used to collect them. She says she has plenty more too."

She set the teacup down, picked up a baby doll, and stood. "And her dolls are exquisite. I feel guilty putting them out for sale."

"Why would you feel guilty?"

"Because if my mother wanted to sell them, I know Britney would want them for her daughters."

He shrugged again. "Kylie isn't planning on having children anytime soon, and if she wanted them, Aunt Midge would find a way to keep them for her."

"Okay." Christine ran her hand over the doll's face. "Well, I'm sure they won't stay in the booth long."

Brent rubbed his hands together. "So what do we do next with all this? Price and then arrange?" When she looked at him with a bit of dismay, he said, "Oh, I thought I'd help this time. But if you have plans, I'll just go."

"I don't have any plans, but I'm sure you do."

"Helping you would be a nice break from remodeling that bathroom."

"So Aunt Midge agreed to that?"

"She did. And to remodeling the other two bathrooms too."

She smiled. "I'll get the Sharpies and tags."

Soon they were sitting on stools, pricing the items and then arranging them on the shelves. Christine tried not to smile each time Brent asked her how much to charge, and she enjoyed spending this time with him.

"How *is* the bathroom remodeling going?" she asked while they placed a vintage rose porcelain tea set.

"Much slower than I'd hoped. It's a lot of work. Steve has already been a tremendous help, but it took a lot longer than I thought just to rip everything out."

"Have you found new fixtures?"

"Yeah." He chuckled. "Aunt Midge is much pickier than I expected. We've taken two trips to Home Depot just to explore vanity and tub and shower options, and she's still thinking about it."

"And I hope the avocado tub wins." Christine grinned.

He laughed, shaking his head. "I can't believe how attached she was to that pink, but I finally convinced her buyers these days want traditional white. We're still debating what color the walls should be, though."

"Definitely burnt umber."

His face lit with amusement. "Where do you come up with these colors?"

She shrugged. "You know me. I'm the nerdy twin."

"I still don't understand why you say that."

Brent paused as though she would tell him, but she merely bent to lift another item. She'd never confessed to anyone how she felt in comparison to her sister, and Brent would probably be the last person she'd tell.

"So . . . what have you been up to besides running the store?" He lifted a tray of teacups and placed them on a nearby shelf. She tried not to stare at his muscular biceps, but that was asking a lot.

She focused on another tea set. "Oh, the usual. Refinishing furniture at home. I've been working on a set of dressers I found at an auction."

"You have a workshop at your house?"

She nodded. "It sits behind the little ranch I bought over on Zimmer Avenue, right across the street from that yellow Victorian with the tower and wraparound porch."

"Oh right. My mom has always loved that house."

"I've wondered what it would be like to live there. I sometimes imagine decorating it for Christmas." She swallowed when she realized she'd probably shared more than he'd ever want to know. "Anyway, that house is magnificent. It looks like it doesn't belong on my street with all the modest homes there."

He snorted. "That's true."

"So what about you?"

"What?" He seemed surprised by the question.

"Do you have a house in Virginia?"

"No." An unreadable expression flickered over his face. "I was renting one, but I moved out shortly before I came here, and now I'm

96

renting a room in my friend Devonte's home. Most of my stuff is in a trailer parked in his driveway." He pointed to another tea set. "Should I mark this one the same price as the others?"

"Sure." Curiosity about his life in Virginia swirled through her mind as he busied himself with pricing the tea set, and she decided to chance another question. "What do you do in Virginia?"

He swallowed without answering.

Had she pushed too far?

"I did own a home remodeling business," he finally said. "With a friend."

"That's amazing, Brent."

He sighed. "It was . . . until he started messing up jobs. He overbooked us and then stopped showing up on time. Before I knew it, we had some bad reviews and business slowed down. By then the cost of supplies and equipment had also gone through the roof, but he'd essentially run us out of business anyway."

"I'm sorry to hear that." She tilted her head. "Was Devonte your business partner?"

"No." He shook his head, and his eyes narrowed for a moment before recovering. "I haven't spoken to my former business partner in quite a while. I have nothing to say to him. Actually, I do have plenty to say to him after what he did to me, but that conversation would turn ugly pretty quick."

Oh, she wanted to know the whole story there! But it was none of her business. "Will you start a new company when you go back to Virginia?"

"I haven't figured that out yet, but I have a lead on a job with the company Devonte works for. I'll start there."

"That's great." But as she said the words, she was sad to hear he really did plan to leave Flowering Grove.

Brent changed the subject to their elementary and middle school days, and when they finished their work, Christine made a sweeping gesture. "Now pull out your phone and take a photo, because most of this will be gone in a week or two."

"It's perfect." Brent stacked the empty containers and slipped the packing paper into a trash bag. "Thank you for your help."

"Well, you've paid me to do it for you, and here you are helping me. But thank you for bringing everything in. You're helping my store too."

Brent lifted the empty containers, and Christine gathered the Sharpies and tags while pondering how to ask him to have dinner with her without sounding desperate for a date. Surely friends could share a meal without any expectations. After all, she'd had a handful of male friends in high school and college, and they hung out together often. And by now she and Brent considered each other friends, right? Yes, she was attracted to him, but he was still the guy who'd hurt Britney, and she'd never let that happen to her. Being friends would have to do.

When Brent's phone rang with a video call, he set the totes back on the floor and answered, grinning at the screen. "Steve. What's up?"

"Where are you?"

"I'm at Christine's store." He turned the phone toward her. "Say hi."

Christine waved at Steve's image. "Hey, Steve."

"Hi, Chris!" he said as he waved back.

Brent turned the screen back toward himself. "We were just putting more of my aunt's stuff in the booth. It's selling fast, but I still think she has enough to keep it stocked for years. What are you and Pam up to?"

Christine left for the office with the supplies and bag of packing paper. She stowed the supplies, then slipped the bag in the recycling bin before heading back to the booth.

"Yeah, that sounds good. Let me just ask Christine," Brent was saying. He met her gaze. "Want to hang out with Steve and Pam?"

"Oh." She hesitated, suddenly self-conscious. Wouldn't that be too much like a date?

"Christine?" Pam's voice sounded through the phone. "Didn't I hear her a few minutes ago?"

"Yes," Steve told her. "They're at her store."

"Brent," Pam called. "Let me see Christine."

Brent turned his phone so the screen faced Christine, and Pam waved. "Chris!" she exclaimed. "I was about to call you. I just found out our neighbor a block away is having a huge one-day yard sale today, clearing out her house before she goes into assisted living. I think she has some antiques, so you might find some great treasures for your store. The signs say she plans to sell until it gets dark, but you need to come before everything good is gone. It's all half price by now too! You and Brent should meet us there." She recited the exact address.

Christine looked past the phone to where Brent watched her. "What do you think? I love perusing yard sales, estate sales, auctions, and flea markets for items I can clean up or refinish to sell."

"I'll drive," he said, his expression hopeful—as though he cared about her business beyond what it could do for his aunt.

"Okay." She met Pam's smile. "Let me just lock up."

ten

After checking on the cats, Christine slipped into the ladies' room at the back of the store, ran a brush through her hair, and applied a fresh layer of lip gloss. Then she made sure the back door was locked before hurrying to the front of the store and clicking off the lights.

Once she'd slipped out the front door and locked it, she joined Brent, who was leaning against the passenger side of his truck. She drank in the sight of his muscular legs and arms before her eyes fell on the scars on his left knee. After he'd rubbed it twice the day he rescued that bookcase, she'd made a point of noticing what must be scars from the surgeries following his football injury. The one the whole town knew ended his college football career.

At least he was still able to pursue his chosen career post–college graduation—home remodeling. She'd had no idea he had such skills. Britney once said he planned a successful career in the corporate world, but finding what you love is more important than a paycheck. She'd learned that for herself.

"I'm ready," she told him.

As Brent drove down Main Street, he peeked at her. "Do you always run the store by yourself? Or does someone help you part-time?"

"I normally run it by myself, but my sister occasionally helps me when she's not volunteering at the twins' school or day camp. My mother helps at times too."

He nodded, but a strange expression had flickered over his face when she mentioned Britney. Oh, how she longed to read his thoughts about her. Did he regret breaking her heart? Or was she merely someone from his past?

"I can't remember the last time I went to a yard sale," he said.

Christine sat up straighter. "I'm excited. I never know what I'll find."

Brent smiled at her, and her heart gave a little kick. But inwardly she cringed at her body's reaction to him. She had to fight this insane attraction to him. He wasn't planning to stay in town, and he *had* broken her sister's heart! He wasn't the man for her and never would be—not even if he had any interest in her.

When they arrived at the sale, Brent parked his truck on the street behind a line of other vehicles. A knot of people milled around the driveway, and Christine could see a rack of clothing and various pieces of furniture as well as folding tables. When she got out of the truck, she saw the tables were peppered with smaller items.

As Steve and Pam approached them, they greeted one another, and then Pam gave Christine a curious expression as she took her arm and steered her away from the men. "You've got to see this vintage jewelry," she said before dragging her to the farthest table. It was covered with bracelets, broaches, earrings—all clip-ons—and necklaces. Then she leaned close and lowered her voice. "Okay, Chris. Spill it now."

"What are you talking about?"

"Don't act all innocent." Pam gave her another look. "I want to know details about you and Brent. Why were you two together at the store when Steve called? Hurry up and tell me now before the guys come over."

Christine glanced to where Steve and Brent stood looking at some tools and then laughed. "They're probably already suspicious since you dragged me off as soon as we got here. And there's nothing to tell. He brought more of his aunt's things to sell. We were pricing the items and arranging them in the booth when Steve called." She shrugged. "That's it."

"That's it? Please. What's going on?"

"Nothing. I guess we're friends, though. Just friends."

"You sure?"

"Yes. Why are you making such a big deal about this?"

"Because I'd love to see you happy."

Christine rolled her eyes. "I'm not Brent Nicholson's type."

"Why would you say that?"

"Because he dated my sister, the supermodel type. Besides, he's not planning to stay in Flowering Grove." Christine nodded toward the jewelry. "I see some nice pieces here." She spotted a wood jewelry box with flower carvings. "Oh, I could get that box and put some of these broaches in it."

Taking the hint, Pam wandered to another table.

Christine picked out a cameo, a beautiful Christmas tree made of rhinestones, and a sparkling bouquet of colorful flowers before placing them in the jewelry box and making her way to the furniture.

"What did you find?" Brent appeared beside her. When his hand brushed her bare arm, she tried to ignore the zip that shimmied over her skin.

Christine handed him the jewelry box. "I can clean this up and display it with the broaches I set inside."

"Nice." He nodded toward the furniture. "Do you like any of those pieces?"

Christine studied the dressers, but they weren't quite old enough for her taste—or for most of her customers. When she spotted a vintage hat rack, though, she smiled. "I do, actually." She ran her fingers over the stand, imagining how she would stain it. "I can definitely do something with this."

"I'll carry it while you keep looking."

The four of them browsed the remainder of the items for sale before paying for the treasures they'd chosen. Along with the jewelry box, broaches, and hat rack, Christine purchased a wood-framed mirror, a quilt stand, and a child's rocking chair. Pam had found a vintage jean jacket that fit her perfectly, Steve had picked up some old baseball cards, and Brent had decided to buy some tools.

After they'd loaded everything into their vehicles, Steve stood beside Brent's truck and looped his arm around Pam's shoulders. "So the first Friday night football game is tomorrow."

Christine turned toward Brent. "Do you think you'll go for old times' sake?"

"Probably not." He shrugged.

"You have to come," Steve said. "My nephew is playing."

Christine clucked her tongue. "I always forget you have a nephew in high school."

"Oh yeah." Pam chuckled, then turned toward Brent. "Steve's dad is on his fourth marriage, and Steve's oldest brother is forty and has a sixteen-year-old son."

"Fourth marriage!" Christine exclaimed. "Wow. I didn't know about that one."

Steve shook his head. "I suppose my dad is determined to finally get it right. Anyway, I'm excited to see Jackson play. He's really good." He pointed to Brent. "You *need* to come. It will be fun."

"Oh, I don't know." Brent dipped his chin as he gently kicked the curb with the toe of his shoe. "I still have plenty to do at my aunt's house, and I didn't get much done today."

Steve frowned. "Give me a break, Brent. You don't need to work night and day. Come enjoy a football game. Have you ever watched one from the stands?"

Brent rubbed a spot on his shoulder, and Christine could almost feel the discomfort coming off him in waves. His back stiffened, and his hands balled into fists as if the subject of football had triggered something in him. If she dared, later she'd ask him why he didn't want to discuss the game. But for now she felt the urge to change the subject to relieve his anxiety.

"Can you believe our ten-year high school reunion is coming up?" Out of the corner of her eye, she noticed Brent's back relax slightly. "Will you two be in town over Thanksgiving?"

Pam nodded. "Yes, we will. We'll all have to go to the reunion together."

"Definitely," Steve said, readily agreeing with the idea. "Unless you still hope to be back in Virginia by then, Brent."

"That's my plan."

"You don't think you'll be back for it?" Pam asked.

"Probably not."

Christine could see Pam working to hide her disappointment, as was she. But then a recognizable determination appeared in her best friend's eyes.

"Well, I guess we'd better get going," Steve said.

As the men walked toward Steve's gray Chevrolet Tahoe, Pam took hold of Christine's arm again and held her back.

"I don't care what you say, Brent is totally into you, and we have plenty of time before the reunion. What are you going to do if he asks you out?"

Christine pulled her arm away. "Pam, how could you possibly get the impression that he likes me when you've only seen us eating burgers and shopping at a yard sale?"

"It's obvious, Chris. He hangs on your every word. He *likes* you."

Christine cut her eyes to the men, who thankfully were engrossed in conversation. "Stop it. He isn't staying in town, and he's my sister's ex. It would never work."

"So what if he's your sister's ex?" Pam's brow pinched. "Just because it didn't work out with him and Britney doesn't mean it can't work out for him and you."

"Look, I'm helping Brent with his aunt's booth. That's it."

But even as she said the words, Christine wondered what it would be like to be more than friends with Brent—and the thought sent a thrill zinging through her.

◆ ◆ ◆

"Thanks for the hangout," Brent said as he shook hands with Steve.

"We need to do this more often while you're here."

"Definitely." Brent pivoted to where Christine and Pam remained beside his truck, looking serious.

Christine looked lovely dressed in jean shorts and a turquoise T-shirt that brought out the deep blue of her eyes. He'd hoped she'd have time to set up the new items in the booth with him so they could spend time together. He relished teasing her about her cats, especially since she easily replied with a playful response and that beautiful smile and adorable laugh.

He grew more attracted to her each time he saw her, and that concerned him. The last thing he needed was a relationship, especially after Tara betrayed him. And besides, he still doubted Christine would be interested in him as more than a friend.

Brent returned to his truck, said goodbye to Pam as she left to join Steve, and then pulled open the passenger door for Christine.

Soon they were on the road heading back to her store.

"I'm so glad we went to the yard sale," she said before shielding a yawn with her hand. "Oh, excuse me. You're not boring me."

He chuckled. She was so cute. "I was wondering, how did Steve and Pam get together?"

"They ran into each other again when they returned home after college."

"I don't remember them dating in high school. Did they?" He gave her a sideways look.

"No, they didn't." She shook her head. "They weren't close back then, but I guess Steve always liked Pam and never told her. He was too afraid of rejection, which is hilarious. Pam is so sweet and never would have hurt his feelings. Anyway, he finally asked her out, and the rest is history."

"Huh."

A comfortable silence stretched between them as he kept his focus on the road.

"*Are* you going to the football game tomorrow night?" she suddenly asked.

Familiar disappointment dug its claws into his shoulder muscles as he opened his mouth to respond, but the words caught in his throat. For some reason he couldn't pretend he might go when he knew down to his bones that returning to a football field—any football field—would be too much to handle. His father's critical words still echoed in his mind.

Without responding, he gripped the steering wheel tighter.

"Brent," Christine began, her tone cautious, "why do you clam up when someone mentions football?"

He blinked, astounded by how astute she was. Were his feelings written on his forehead? Or had she read his mind?

"I'm so sorry," she said in a rush. "Forget I said that. It's none of my business."

Brent steered behind her store and parked his truck beside hers before shutting off the engine and angling his body toward her. "I ran into Coach Morgan at the grocery store yesterday, and he asked me to help out as a volunteer assistant coach."

"That's great!" Her smile was bright with an eagerness he hadn't expected. "The kids would love to have you as a coach. You'd be such an inspiration to them."

He snorted at the same word Coach Morgan had used. "Some inspiration," he grumbled.

"What do you mean? You're a hero. You led our undefeated team to a state championship, and it was the first time since the '90s. You're a local celebrity."

He lowered his gaze and ran his finger over a hole in the bench seat.

"Brent? What is it?" She leaned toward him, and the fragrance of vanilla—her lotion or shampoo?—sent blood hammering through his veins.

He felt something inside of him crack open, and the need to tell her everything erupted in his chest. "Christine, I'm not a hero. I'm far from it. I'm more like a disappointment." He looked up, and her eyes seemed to search his.

"Why would you say that?" Her voice was soft and her tone tender.

"When I went to Chapel Hill, I had the football scholarship and all this promise for a great future. But then I took one bad hit on the field and tore everything in my knee—the ACL, MCL, and PCL—and that was it. I had surgery after surgery, but I never regained the strength I needed. Everyone knows that ended my football career, but they don't know I lost my scholarship. It was based solely on my athletic ability, and I never had the top grades for any other assistance. So I dropped out of school and started working in construction because it was the only thing I knew aside from football. I have no degree."

Christine's expression was warm and genuine. "There's nothing wrong with that, Brent. I went to school to become a paralegal, but I couldn't take the stress. That's why I left the field I'd once believed I was meant to pursue. Just because you didn't earn a degree doesn't mean you're a failure."

"Tell that to my father."

Her brow puckered. "What do you mean?"

"I was the first in our immediate family to go to college. My father didn't even graduate from high school. That's why he's so disappointed that I didn't finish, expecting me to have somehow found a way without a scholarship. He hates that I work with my hands. He considers it a failure." *And so do I.*

"I'm sorry your father hurts you." Her lips turned up in a smile. "But even though I've only seen what you've done with your aunt's porch, I know you're more talented than most people I know."

She reached over and touched his bicep. The feeling of her warm fingers on his skin was almost too much to bear, but he kept his expression blank despite his thrumming nerves.

"You're an inspiration to all the football players at Flowering Grove High, Brent," she continued. "They would want to follow in your footsteps, and I'm sure Coach Morgan could use your help. You should think about what he said."

"I don't know . . ." He tried to smile but failed.

She pushed her door open. "Would you help me load my treasures into my truck?"

"Of course I will, but don't you want to keep them here?"

"No. I'll deal with them at home and then bring them back."

After they'd transferred Christine's yard-sale finds and he'd collected the now-emptied totes from the store, Brent stood with her by her driver's side door.

"Come to the game tomorrow night," she said. "It might remind you of all the reasons you loved to play." Her expression grew coy. "If you do, I'll buy you a soda and some popcorn."

This time he couldn't stop a smile. "Maybe I will."

"I hope so," she said before jumping into her truck. "Good night."

He returned to his own pickup and waved as she backed out of the parking spot and pulled into the street. As he started his own journey home, he was once again grateful for Christine's friendship. Yet deep down—and despite his resolve to protect his heart—he longed for something more with her. But because of his failures, he had nothing to offer her and probably never would.

Besides, Christine would find someone worthy of her love someday.

If only that thought didn't send a spiral of jealousy surging through him.

eleven

Christine tried to keep her disappointment at bay as the Flowering Grove High marching band roll-stepped their way onto the field, their black, white, and light-blue uniforms with white plumes seeming to glow in the stadium lights.

Hugging her arms to her chest, she blew out a puff of air as conversations droned around her and the delicious aromas of nachos, popcorn, and burgers filled the humid night air. The football game was half over with no sign of Brent. She'd hoped her offer to buy him popcorn and a drink had convinced him to join her for the game. After all, he'd given her a bright smile. But she should have realized his vague response was an indication that he was just telling her what she wanted to hear.

She shifted her weight and regretted not bringing the mesh cushion she had to shield her bottom from the hard metal bleachers.

"Maybe he's running late."

Christine turned to Pam beside her. "Who?"

"Brent, obviously. I can tell you're stressing about him not being here, but like I said, maybe he's running late."

Christine pointed toward the street. "His aunt's house is right over there. How could he be running late?"

"I don't know." Pam shrugged. "Maybe he got wrapped up in a big project and wanted to finish it. Steve gets that way when he's focused on something." She nodded toward her husband, who was sitting on her other side immersed in a conversation about the opposing team's strong offense with the man next to him. They were ahead by eight points.

Christine peered down at the concession stand and then stood. She needed to get rid of this foul mood, and some delicious popcorn seemed like a great reason to smile. "I'm going for a drink and snack. Do you want anything?"

"No, thanks," Pam said as the band began playing music from *West Side Story*.

Christine climbed over folks, excusing herself until she reached the end of the row. Then she jogged down the steps while trying to convince herself not to feel so hurt by Brent's absence. He hadn't promised her he'd come tonight. And what did it matter anyway? They were barely friends, and he clearly had no intention of attending a football game with her or anyone else.

Still, as their last conversation echoed through her mind, she had a feeling being here would be good for his soul. It perplexed her that he considered himself a failure, and the pain in his eyes when he told her about his father's disappointment in him had hit her square in the heart. That was why she'd touched his arm.

She bit her lower lip remembering the feel of his firm bicep under her fingertips. Again, she had to find a way to dismiss this attraction she had for him, but that seemed impossible when she felt closer to him each time they were together.

As she weaved through the students and families milling around at the bottom of the bleachers, she tried to put her confusing feelings for Brent out of her mind and just listen to the band's energetic rendition of "Mambo." Then when she took her place at the back of the concession-stand line, Christine spotted the cheerleaders gathered by the fence line clad in their light-blue, white, and black uniforms, each one sporting a large, light-blue bow in her hair. Memories of watching her twin cheering and flying through the air during games came to mind. She'd always secretly envied her sister's athletic abilities.

The line moved forward slowly, and Christine yanked her cell phone from the pocket of her jean shorts to scan her apps for something to keep her mind busy.

"Someone told me the popcorn here is amazing. Do you know where I can get some?"

Christine's head popped up as Brent sidled up next to her. He looked uncomfortable with his arms folded over his wide chest, but why? A faded New York Mets baseball cap covered his curly hair, and she wondered if he was trying to keep a low profile.

"I-I didn't think you were coming tonight," she managed to say. Her pulse galloped as she took in how good he looked in those khaki shorts.

"Neither did I." His eyes scanned the area, and his expression darkened. "The memories are . . . overwhelming."

When his gaze paused in the direction of the cheerleaders, her smile wobbled. Was he remembering the years he and Britney spent together? Did he even miss her? But if he cared that much about her sister, why had he cheated on her?

Brent turned toward her and rubbed his hands together. "So about that popcorn and soda you promised me . . . Is the offer still valid? Or did I miss the deadline?"

"Hmm." She frowned and then checked the time on her phone. "You actually just made it with five minutes to spare."

He swiped his hand across his forehead. "Whew. That was close."

Christine opened her mouth to respond just as three men from their high school class surrounded Brent. She recognized them as members of the popular crowd and athletes who hadn't given her or her friends the time of day.

"Brent Nicholson!" one of them said, pulling him aside.

Another one tapped Brent's arm. "It's the QB!"

"How long has it been?" the third asked.

Christine's happy mood faded. Shoulders drooping, she moved forward with the line. She'd been kidding herself when she assumed Brent would want to be with her once he got here. Not after learning more exciting people wanted to hang out with their former winning quarterback. Why wouldn't he respond to that?

When a warm hand touched her forearm, she pivoted and found Brent with an embarrassed look on his face.

"I'll just be a minute more," he said. "Then maybe we can sit together in the bleachers."

"Yeah. Of course." Her heart gave a kick as he smiled before turning back to the three men, who were staring at her with obvious curiosity.

When she reached the counter, she bought two sodas and a large box of popcorn, then balanced a drink holder in one hand and the popcorn in the other as she approached Brent. But she slowed her pace because he was still talking to his friends.

Embarrassment crept up her neck when all three men turned and peered at her again, a clear look of confusion flickering over each face. Of course they'd question why Brent would choose to spend time with the nerdy twin. She felt so awkward that she considered marching toward the bleachers alone to evaporate into the crowd of spectators.

But then Brent turned toward her, and relief seemed to overtake his face. "Sorry, guys," he said, "but I need to go. I'll see you later." He reached for her drink holder. "Let me carry that for you."

"Okay," she told him before nodding at the three men and falling into step with Brent.

He frowned. "I'm sorry. I had a feeling that would happen."

"Are you really surprised? I told you you're a hero in this town. Everyone will be excited to see you back."

He looked uncomfortable again as he nodded at the people who called his name and waved. "Where are Pam and Steve?"

"About halfway up in the center section."

Brent moved to the side when they reached the steps, allowing her to climb up first. Spotting Pam and Steve, they made their way to their row and then padded past other fans until they reached them.

"You made it!" Steve patted Brent's shoulder.

"I wasn't coming, but then I decided to take Christine's advice. She said it might be good for me."

Pam grinned at Christine as if to say *I told you so*, and Christine shot her a warning look before sinking down beside her.

She'd expected Brent to squeeze in between Steve and the man beside him, but instead he excused himself and maneuvered past Pam before nodding at Christine. "May I sit here?"

"Oh. Of course." She slid closer to Pam before Brent wedged himself between her and a middle-aged woman sporting a "Flowering Grove Cheer Mom" T-shirt.

Brent's left leg brushed hers, sending a shiver dancing up her thigh despite the heat. She took in his sculpted leg and the crisscross of scarring across his left knee, imagining the pain and heartbreak the injury had caused him.

"I assume the Diet Coke is yours, right?"

Her eyes moved to his as he held up one of the cups. "Right. Thanks." She took it from him, and when their fingers collided, she thought her skin might actually burn this time. She had to stop touching this man!

Brent focused his attention on the marching band, now performing the romantic "Tonight."

"I told you he'd come," Pam whispered in her ear.

Christine hissed another warning in reply.

"The band is good," Brent commented before pointing at the box of popcorn. "May I . . ."

Christine handed him the box. "Enjoy."

"Thank you." Brent shook a few kernels into his hand before holding the box out to her. "Would you like some?"

"Sure." She held her breath as he shook some out for her, grateful that their hands didn't touch. She had to get her emotions under control!

The band finished their repertoire, and the audience applauded as they marched off the field.

Brent leaned across Christine and Pam. "Steve, tell me about your nephew."

"Jackson is number twenty-one," he said, talking over the murmur of conversations swirling around them in the packed stands. "He's a free safety on the defensive line."

Brent nodded, looking impressed. "He must be a big kid."

"Oh yeah. Just like his dad, my brother Wyatt."

Christine bit her lower lip. She felt dizzy being so near to Brent. Even if his being here was good for him, it might not be so good for her.

Pam lightly bumped her arm, her expression filled with concern. "You look a little sick. You okay?"

"Uh-huh." Christine took a long drink of her Diet Coke and

then turned her attention to the cheerleaders lining up in front of the stands.

Soon the teams returned to the field, and Brent settled back in the bleachers and faced Christine. "I should have grabbed a blanket or something for us to sit on. These metal seats are so uncomfortable."

He'd said *for us*!

She couldn't stop a smile.

"I thought the same thing." She set her drink at her feet. "*Is* this the first game you've watched from the stands?"

"Yes. But I was on the bench after my injury at Chapel Hill."

"How does it feel to be up here instead of on the field?"

He hesitated as if pondering the question. "Strange."

When the game started again, he seemed transfixed as the opposing team from Glen Rock High School took control of the ball and their quarterback handed it off to a running back who headed toward the end zone.

"Oh no," Brent mumbled as the running back sailed toward the goal line.

Steve cheered. "Get him, Jackson!"

When Steve's nephew tackled the running back, they all cheered, and Christine took in the wide smile on Brent's face. It seemed this game *was* just what he needed to lift his spirits!

They continued cheering when Flowering Grove took control of the ball. Christine couldn't keep her eyes from wandering from the football field to Brent, taking in his grimace when the other team tackled Flowering Grove's running back and then his cheers when the Flowering Grove Falcons scored. By the beginning of the fourth quarter, the Falcons had managed to bring the game to a tie, twenty-one to twenty-one.

The Falcons' cheerleaders punctuated the tie with a rousing cheer before sending three of them flying through the air. Christine peeked at Brent, wondering if he was thinking about her sister.

"This is a good game," he commented as he held the box of popcorn toward her. "Want some more?"

"Thanks." She took a handful before turning her attention back to the field.

The Glen Rock Panthers took control of the ball, but when the team failed to make the fourth down, the Falcons took possession of it. A whistle, a cowbell, and the clacking and crunching of pads sounded through the air.

The entire home section of the stands stood as Flowering Grove's quarterback handed off the ball to a running back, and he took off toward the goal line. Christine clasped her hands as the crowd shouted and the running back continued, dodging linemen and getting closer to the end zone.

"Go, go, go!" Brent yelled before taking Christine's hand in his and raising their arms.

When the running back scored, everyone around them erupted into cheers. Flowering Grove had won the game!

Brent pulled Christine toward him and then wrapped his arms around her. Blood pounded through her veins, and when his muscled arms pulled her even closer, she rested her head against his broad shoulder. She fit into his arms perfectly, and when he placed his hands on the small of her back, a thrill raced through her like nothing she'd ever felt. Being in his embrace was a dream, and she wanted to stay there.

When Brent released her, he leaned past her and gave Steve a high five. "What an exciting game!"

"The best."

As the teams walked across the field, high-fiving each other,

Christine followed Steve and Pam down the bleacher steps with Brent close behind.

"We're going to find my brother and nephew," Steve said when they'd reached the bottom.

Brent shook his hand. "Tell them I said congratulations."

Pam hugged Christine. "You and Brent are too cute!" she whispered. "Invite him over."

Christine grimaced, hoping Brent hadn't heard her. "Good night," she snapped, her words clipped.

She said good night to Steve before she and Brent fell into the flow of the crowd heading toward the parking lot.

"I'll walk you to your truck," he said.

"Thank you."

Several people waved and yelled hellos to Brent as they made their way across the lot. When they reached her truck, disappointment slithered through her. She wasn't ready for Brent to leave.

"Are you in a hurry?" he asked as she fished her keys from her backpack purse.

Hope ignited in her chest. "No. Why?"

"I don't think you're leaving anytime soon." He jammed his thumb toward the line of vehicles waiting to exit the lot. "Why don't we sit for a while?"

"That sounds great."

He lowered the tailgate and then held out his hand. When she took it and he helped her up, a fresh buzz of excitement zapped her. Then he joined her, and they sat side by side, their legs dangling.

As she inhaled lingering scents from the concession stand—and exhaust fumes as well—Christine looked up at the bright stars shining above them. Then she turned to Brent and found him looking out toward the line of traffic as horns blasted and fans called out of the windows of their cars.

"You seemed to enjoy the game." A flush of desire skittered through her as she recalled the hug they'd shared.

He gripped the edge of the tailgate. "I did."

"It reminded me of one of our high school games. So exciting."

He smiled and nodded. "Yeah, I suppose so."

"Did it help you remember your love for football?"

He grinned. "Are you sure you're not a therapist instead of a small-business owner?"

Dipping her head, she covered her face with both hands.

He laughed. "You look mortified, but I'm just teasing you." He bumped his shoulder against hers, and she met his gaze. "It was fun."

"What did you think of our quarterback?"

Brent looked toward the road again, and she wondered if he was avoiding her eyes. "He's good, but I think he needs to work on his confidence. I noticed him hesitate a few times, but when he finally threw the ball, he definitely had power. He just needs to believe in himself."

"I bet you could help him with that."

Now his eyes met hers, and his expression warmed. "I know what you're trying to do, Christine, and I appreciate it. But I still don't believe I'm the right person to coach anyone."

She nodded. She'd let his negativity go for now, but she wouldn't give up on him.

A comfortable silence fell between them, and she relaxed. "What are your plans for the weekend?" she asked.

He brushed his hands over his shorts. "Well, Sunday night is always family dinner." He rolled his eyes.

"Is it that bad?"

He groaned. "You have no idea."

"I'm sorry. I never realized you had this difficult relationship with your dad."

"He was always overbearing, pushing me toward what he still calls my 'potential.'" He made air quotes with his fingers. "But his nagging got worse when I dropped out of college."

"I'm sorry."

"It's okay." He shrugged. "We get along better when I don't live close by, and hopefully I won't be here long."

Renewed sadness overtook her at the thought of Brent leaving Flowering Grove. Even if they'd always be just friends, she'd miss him.

"How are you with your parents?" Brent asked. "Do you get along?"

"We're very close."

"I'm sure you didn't disappoint them at all." When she hesitated, his dark eyebrows lifted. "What could you have possibly done that your parents wouldn't like?"

"Well, let's just say I'm not Britney."

He looked stunned. "And why is *that* a problem?"

"Oh, let's see." She might as well count them off with her fingers. "Besides being the nerdy twin, I'm not married, I don't have kids, and I'm not perfect."

A veil of embarrassment descended when she realized what she'd just said about her sister. She'd never admitted that she felt as though she fell short of her sister's perfection to anyone. Yet this was a burden she'd carried nearly her entire life, and she'd just admitted it to Brent Nicholson, of all people. Surely he thought she was terrible for speaking ill of her twin.

"Oh, I don't mean to sound like I resent Britney," she added, speaking at a quick clip. "I love her. But my mom has always compared us. I remember the times she asked me why I didn't want to go to dance class like Britney or why I didn't want to be a cheerleader like Britney. She couldn't accept that my sister was just like her but I wasn't. Britney and I always had different interests, and the comparisons have grown old over the years. We're as different as two sisters could be, but my mother always seems to think we should be more alike since we're twins. She's just not as obvious about it now."

She ran out of words and awaited Brent's response. But when he didn't speak, she was certain he was lost in memories of her sister—the beauty, the dancer, the cheerleader, the perfect girlfriend. She'd never understand why he threw away a future with her.

Brent leaned against the side of the truck as he stared at the line of traffic still snaking toward the road, silence continuing to fill the space between them. She held her breath. Surely he'd have something to say about the secrets she'd just spilled.

When he finally faced her, his expression was full of empathy. "Christine, I can't imagine why your mother would make you feel bad for being different from your sister. You're a successful business owner and a wonderful person. You're also just as beautiful as Britney is, if not more beautiful because of how humble you are."

She blinked. Had Brent just told her she was beautiful?

"And I'm sure you'll get married and have a family of your own one day, when the time is right for you. Your future husband will be one lucky man."

Their eyes caught, and Christine felt an invisible force pulling them together. She wondered if Brent could feel it, too, but he just said she'd be with someone else one day.

Brent hopped down from the tailgate and lifted his hand. "It's getting late, and the traffic is just about gone."

She placed her hand in his and joined him.

"Be safe driving home," he said before lightly squeezing and then releasing her hand.

"I will. Would you like a ride?"

He chuckled and pointed to his aunt's house across the street. "Thanks, but I don't have far to walk."

"Right. Well, good night."

"Good night. I'm sure I'll have more items for your store before too long."

"I look forward to it," she said before climbing into the driver's seat and turning over the engine.

They exchanged smiles as she waved before steering toward the road. Any hope of more than friendship with Brent seemed ridiculous now. And she couldn't dismiss how he'd treated her sister, making anything more than friendship impossible anyway. Yet she looked forward to seeing him again.

And she wouldn't mind if he hugged her and held her hand again.

twelve

"How was your first week of pre-K?" Christine asked her nieces as she sat between them at her parents' dinner table Sunday evening. The delicious aromas of breaded pork chops, buttery mashed potatoes, and green beans floated around the dining room.

Mila lifted her fork in the air. "It was good. We have six boys and six girls in our class."

"We like our teacher," Maddy chimed in. "Miss Laurie is very nice."

Christine grinned at Britney, who beamed at her girls from across the table. "I'm glad to hear it."

Maddy tapped Christine's arm. "Come see our school, Auntie."

"Yeah!" Mila exclaimed, "Then you can see all the pictures we drew of our family."

"I'll try to stop by one afternoon. I'll talk to your mom about it."

"I heard Flowering Grove won the football game Friday night," Hunter commented as he scooped a pile of mashed potatoes onto his plate.

Christine took the bowl from him and added some to each of the twins' plates. "It was an exciting game."

"You were there?" Mom asked.

123

Christine nodded as she dropped a spoonful of potatoes onto her own plate.

Dad lifted his glass of sweet tea. "I heard Flowering Grove came back in the fourth quarter."

"They did. I told Brent it reminded me of one of the exciting games we had in school."

Britney stilled, her fork hanging in the air as her blue eyes widened. "You went to the game with Brent?"

"Well, not exactly. I was with Steve and Pam, and Brent met us there."

Britney's face clouded with a scowl.

Uh-oh. Christine needed to change the subject fast. "So, Hunter," she began, "how are your folks doing?"

"Great, thanks. Dad is happy we're staying busy at work, and Mom is still volunteering with the animal shelter. She loves it," he said.

Christine smiled, but she could see Britney frowning in her peripheral vision. She was certain she'd have to face her interrogation as soon as they were alone.

After dinner and ice cream sundaes at the twins' request, Dad, Hunter, and the girls' loyal dog moved to the deck to watch the girls out on the swing set Dad had erected for them as soon as spring came. Mom carried drinking glasses to the kitchen while Christine finished stacking plates on the table.

Utensils in hand, Britney came close, her face now contorted in what could only be called a glower. "Chrissy, tell me you're not seeing Brent," she said, practically seething. "Promise me you're smart enough not to get wrapped up with him."

"I'm not seeing him."

"Then why are you spending so much time together?"

"He's good friends with Steve, who happens to be married to my best friend. That's why we sat together at the football game." When her twin continued to look suspicious, Christine set down the plates and held up her hands. "Look, I'm not seeing him or dating him. We're just business partners and friends."

Britney's expression softened slightly. "I just don't want you to get hurt, okay? I know what Brent is like. He's handsome, and it's easy to fall for his charm. I remember how he always held the car door open for me and ran ahead of me to open restaurant doors. He'll act like he'll always be there for you. But then one day you'll discover he's been seeing someone else behind your back, and you'll feel like a fool."

Christine swallowed against the sour lump swelling in her throat.

"I'm just looking out for you, sis. Brent is a cheater. You know what he put me through, and I'm telling you he'll do the same thing to you if you let him."

"I remember what happened, and I'm sorry." Christine touched her sister's arm. "I'm not going to date him, okay?" Her heart ached as she said the words. Her feelings for Brent had grown beyond friendship, but she could never date him no matter how she felt.

Mom appeared in the doorway. "What are you two discussing?"

Britney pinned a bright smile on her face. "I was just asking Chrissy if any handsome guys had come into the store lately. The same question you often ask her."

Mom looked hopeful, oblivious to Britney's lie. "And?"

"Sadly, no." Christine let out a dramatic sigh, playing the game.

"Well, don't give up yet," Mom sang. "We'll get you married off soon enough!"

Christine held back an annoyed retort. Her mother and sister meant well, but she longed for them to accept her life the way it was.

125

❖ ❖ ❖

Brent parked his pickup in the driveway of the small brick ranch house with an attached one-car garage. Then he peered into his rear-view mirror at the butter-yellow Victorian house across the street featuring a two-story tower and sweeping front porch before facing the gold Toyota Tacoma truck beside his.

This had to be the place, then—Christine's house. It was just as he'd imagined it with colorful flowers lining the path leading to the red front door. A black mailbox near the street had "Sawyer" written on the side in large gold letters, another sure clue.

His heart did a funny little dance when he imagined her in the house doing whatever it was she did at home. She'd been a constant thought at the back of his mind during the past week. He couldn't stop recalling how it felt to hold her in his arms at the football game. He'd been so caught up in the thrill of seeing their team win that he hadn't thought twice about hugging her. Yet when he held her, his body had come alive. It felt so natural to embrace her even though they were only friends.

Worse, he'd spent a considerable amount of time trying to come up with an excuse to visit her.

Today he'd finally found one, and he was excited when he learned her store was closed on Mondays as well as Sundays, giving him the opportunity to see her house. He just hoped she'd be as happy to see him as he was to see her—at least as friends.

Brent climbed out of his truck, plodded to the porch and up to the front door, and knocked as the sweet fragrance of the flowers hung in the humid afternoon air. Rocking back on his heels, he waited for the sound of footfalls to echo in the house, but only a siren rang out somewhere in the distance. He knocked again and then rang the doorbell, but he never heard any movement inside the house.

Brent looked at Christine's truck and wondered if she'd gone out with Pam or her sister, but then he remembered she had a workshop behind her house.

He jogged down the steps, and as he rounded the garage, he heard the Go-Go's "Vacation" ringing through the air. Brent smiled, recalling that he'd heard music from the '80s playing in Christine's store too.

He found a small cinderblock building in the backyard along with a wooden swing set, a small utility trailer, and a compact deck with a propane grill, a propane firepit, and a table with six chairs.

The music grew louder as he approached the building. When he came to the open door, he scanned the inside, finding a workbench, toolboxes, and tools strewn about, as well as furniture in various stages of restoration.

And Christine.

She was singing along with Belinda Carlisle and the rest of the Go-Go's while staining a large dresser in the center of the room. Although a mask covered her face to protect her from fumes, she looked adorable in light-blue jeans and a pink tank top, her hair pulled back in a long, thick ponytail with wisps framing her temples and cheeks. The stain dotting both her forehead and clothes did nothing to make her less attractive.

"Vacation" ended, and Madonna's "Dress You Up" started blaring through the speakers.

Christine turned toward the doorway and gasped before removing her mask. "Oh! Brent!" She pressed her hand to her chest and gave a little laugh. "I didn't see you there."

"I'm sorry." Brent lifted a hand. "I didn't mean to startle you."

She set her brush on the workbench, then picked up a remote control and turned down the music's volume.

He came to stand beside her and tried not to stare. She was more than adorable. She was gorgeous. "You like '80s music?"

"I do. Why?" Her little nose crinkled.

"I seem to remember hearing the Bangles, Bon Jovi, and Huey Lewis and the News in your store."

"Oh. Right." She smiled. "This is my favorite satellite radio station."

"Interesting." He grinned as he crossed the room and took in a beautifully finished cedar chest, two oak end tables, a cherry triple dresser, two pine bookshelves, and two matching white end tables and a coffee table. "You did these yourself? Wow. You have a gift."

She blushed as she joined him. "Thank you."

"When will you take them to the store?"

"When Hunter has time to help me move them. He's been too busy with work lately, and I hate bugging him."

Jealousy hit him hard and fast, but he worked to keep any hint of it out of his expression. "Is Hunter your boyfriend?"

She laughed and gave his shoulder a light smack. "No, silly. He's my brother-in-law, Britney's husband."

"Oh." Relief filtered through him, but why had he assumed she had no men in her life? Maybe someone who lived in a neighboring town.

Might as well find out. "Are you seeing anyone?"

"No." She scoffed. "I'm married to my store."

He arched an eyebrow, and they both laughed. He loved her sweet lilt.

Christine pushed a wisp of hair away from her face. "What about you? Do you have a girlfriend back in Virginia?"

"Not anymore."

"Oh." She bit her lower lip, but then just rested her hands on her hips. "Did you stop by just to check out my workshop, or do you have a purpose for this visit?"

"Oh. Right." He snapped his fingers and then pulled the paint chips from the pocket of his shorts. "I need you to settle a debate."

"This is unexpected. What's up?"

He held out the paint chips. "Aunt Midge and I still can't agree on what color I should paint her guest bathroom."

"Uh-oh. Sounds serious. Let me take a look." She studied the two paint chips—one with shades of yellow and the other with shades of teal. "I wouldn't go with either. I prefer magenta."

He guffawed. "You're kidding, right?"

"Of course I am!"

He shook his head. "You've got some stain on your cheek." He reached out, brushing away the stain, and felt a jolt of attraction as he moved his fingers over her soft skin.

Her smile faded, and intensity sparkled in her face as she lifted her eyes to his.

His heartbeat roared in his ears as the urge to kiss her nearly overwhelmed him. But he stepped away, hoping a little distance might squelch the desire.

She licked her lips as she turned her attention back to the paint chips. "Well, since you don't like magenta, I'd settle for this yellow." She pointed to a shade that reminded him of the daffodils in his aunt's garden.

"That's what I chose, but Aunt Midge disagrees." He pointed to the teal she preferred. "She says this reminds her of the ocean, but I think it's too loud for a bathroom."

Christine frowned. "Well, I don't want to get on her bad side, so I need to change my vote. Go with the teal. Then forget I said anything." She handed him the paint chips.

"I'm glad you agree with me, though." He slipped the paint chips into his pocket. "Do you have any cats in your house?"

"No. Why?"

He nodded in the direction of the finished furniture. "Because if you'll give me a tour, I'll help you load all those and take them to the store."

She studied him with suspicion. "Hmm. There must be a catch."

"I promise, no catch."

"Okay. Let me clean up in here, and then I'll give you a tour. But there's not much to see."

After she took care of her brush and stain, he followed her up the deck steps and through the sliding glass door that led to a small kitchen.

"This is where I cook meals." She gestured around the room. "Well, I don't cook as much as I should, but I do enjoy grilling outside."

"It sounds like you need to invite me over for burgers," he said teasingly.

"Maybe." She batted her eyelashes, and he laughed. Then she led him to a small hallway. "I have only two bedrooms, but that's enough for me." She opened a door. "This is the hall bathroom."

He peered in, scrutinized the light-gray walls, and then smirked. "I'm surprised the walls aren't painted magenta."

"You buy the paint, and I'll change them to magenta."

"Is that a challenge?" He lifted his eyebrows.

She laughed and then opened the next door. "This is the guest bedroom, but I never have any overnight guests. I'm hoping my nieces will want to come stay when they're a little older. That would be so much fun."

He stood in the doorway and took in a double bed, triple dresser, and small desk. "It's really nice."

"Well, to me it's just ordinary. I prefer what's in my bedroom." She opened a door across the hall. "This is mine, and that's a small bathroom next to the closet. This bedroom suite was my nana's. I made sure I bought a house with a bedroom big enough for it."

Brent stepped inside and ran his fingers over the mahogany sleigh bed. "This is gorgeous, Christine. So are the dressers and nightstands."

She walked to an antique roll top desk. "Nana gave this to me too."

"It's magnificent."

"I know. I have her favorite wingback chair and love seat as well." She shook her head. "I still don't understand why my sister didn't want any of it, but she was more interested in a few pieces of Nana's jewelry."

Brent smiled at her. "That sounds like Kylie with Aunt Midge's things, and you have great taste."

"Thanks." She started for the door. "You haven't seen the family room yet."

He followed her there, and she pointed out which pieces of furniture had been her grandmother's. He enjoyed hearing her stories. In fact, he could listen to her all day.

They moved to the small dining room. "Was this your nana's too?" he asked as he stepped to the cherry china cabinet in one corner.

"No, that's one of my antique mall finds. I bought it for a song." She pointed to the dishes and teacups inside, which looked like antiques to him. "Most of those belonged to my nana, though." She spun to face him. "So that's it. My little house. Not much, right?"

"I think it's fantastic."

"You're easily impressed, but thank you." She nodded toward the hallway. "I'll get changed and then we can head to the store." She pointed in the direction of the kitchen. "Help yourself to a drink and a snack, and I'll be right with you." Then she hurried back down the hall before he heard a door open and then click shut.

Brent returned to the family room and then crossed to a gallery of photographs hanging on the far wall. He took in a photo of Christine's twin nieces, both grinning in red dresses in front of a Christmas tree. In another photo they wore matching frilly purple dresses while posing in front of Britney and a man with similar blond hair. That must be Hunter, the girls' father.

Beside Britney's family portrait hung a photo of Christine with Britney and their parents that looked as if it was taken when they were in high school. He studied Christine's gorgeous smile and then took in Britney's smile, recalling his conversation with Christine the night of the football game. He folded his arms over his chest while contemplating why Christine's mother would compare her to Britney, making her feel bad for not being more like her twin.

Although he'd once loved Britney, he felt a deeper connection to Christine than he ever had with her sister. Christine was easier to talk to and a much better listener. She was also more empathetic, more in tune with his emotions. Aside from that, she was effortlessly beautiful compared to her sister, who was completely aware of how beautiful she was and had spent so much time ensuring her appearance was perfect.

"Okay," Christine said as she appeared wearing jean shorts and a sky-blue T-shirt. "I believe I got all the stain off me." She looked at the photos and then closed the distance between them. "I see you're enjoying my photo gallery."

"Yeah."

She beamed as she pointed at the twins. "I'm sure you remember Maddy and Mila from the fireworks."

"Of course I do," he said, but he couldn't take his eyes off Christine.

"And that's obviously Britney and her husband." She snickered.

"I always tell her they look like Barbie and Ken, and she tells me to shut up."

Brent snorted. "But you're right."

"I know."

He pointed to a photo of Christine with an elderly woman in front of a historic-looking building. "Isn't that your nana?"

"Yes." Her expression grew wistful. "We're at our favorite antique mall—the Depot at Gibson Mall in Concord. It's one of the biggest antique malls around. We once spent an entire day there. It's huge, and you never know what you'll find."

"We should go sometime." He immediately realized that could be a mistake. "I mean, all of us. You, me, Pam and Steve . . ."

"I'd love that." She jammed her thumb toward the back of the house. "Were you serious about helping me take some furniture to the store today?"

"Absolutely."

"We can't fit everything on my trailer at once, but it will be a great help to take a few of the pieces."

"Christine, we have two pickup trucks here, which means we can take them all."

"Wonderful." She shook her finger at him. "But you need to take some allergy medicine before we go. I don't want you insulting my cats and calling them mean names."

"I already have some in my truck. Just in case."

She looked surprised. "I'm impressed that you're prepared."

"Let's go, then." He brushed his hands together, grateful for more time to spend with her. He just had to keep his resolve—and attraction—in check.

thirteen

An hour later, Brent set the last piece of furniture—a bookshelf—by the rest they'd hauled to the store.

"Would you like me to help you tag them?" he said, glad to make the offer.

"Sure. I'll get the Sharpies and tags." She headed down the main aisle toward her office.

Brent ran his fingers over the impressive pieces and marveled at Christine's workmanship. After several minutes, he pivoted toward the aisle, surprised she still hadn't returned.

"Christine?" he called. "You okay?"

When she didn't respond, he made a beeline for the office, concerned. "Christine?" he asked as he tapped on the partly closed door. "Are you in here?"

"Yeah. Come in." Her voice wobbled, making him worry.

Brent pushed the door open and found Christine staring at what looked like a letter. "What's wrong?"

"I checked the mail and found this." She held it out. "It's from the company that owns this building. They're almost doubling my rent, effective the first of the year."

He took the letter and skimmed it. "I'm so sorry."

Amy Clipston

"They claim it's due to an increase in property taxes, necessary maintenance on the building, and inflation. I've been standing here trying to think of ways I can manage to pay the higher rent, but if I double the booth rent or raise my commission, I could lose vendors. Charlotte and the surrounding area have plenty of other antique malls they could move to, and if I lose them, I'll go out of business."

She dropped into her desk chair. "I don't know what I'm going to do." When she covered her face with her hands, his heart cracked open.

"Hey, it's going to be okay." Brent rested his hand on her slight shoulder, and she placed her hand on his. "What can I do to help?"

She gave him a hesitant smile. "Tell your aunt Midge to find more amazing treasures?"

"You should see what's still in the basement. And we haven't even touched the attic yet."

"Good."

Ignoring the ache radiating in his knee, he squatted in front of her, then leveled his gaze with hers. "I'll help you save your store in any way I can, okay? That's a promise."

"You're so sweet, Brent." Christine touched his cheek. "Thank you."

He took her hand and rubbed his thumb over her palm. He longed to pull her into his arms, unable to deny the overwhelming desire he had to console her. But he had to keep his wits about him.

His phone chimed with a text message, and when he pulled it from his pocket and found a message from Tara, he swallowed a groan.

Brent—I'm so sorry. I shouldn't have hurt you. Please call me. I miss you. We can work this out if you give us a chance. I love you! Call me!

135

Brent shoved his phone back into his pocket as a new level of irritation toward the woman twisted his gut. It was over, and Tara needed to accept that. Would she never get the hint?

When he looked up at Christine, he found her studying him with her brows drawn together. He could almost read the questions sparkling in her blue eyes, but friends or no, he wasn't ready to tell her about Tara's betrayal.

He stood and rubbed his angry knee before holding out his hand. "Why don't we tag the furniture? They're bound to bring in some good income."

"Good idea," she said, allowing him to pull her to her feet.

Christine found the supplies they needed before they returned to the front of the store, then gave him the prices she wanted. He marked half the tags while she marked the other half.

"You okay?" he asked after a few minutes. She'd been keeping her eyes focused on the furniture, seeming deep in thought.

She spun to face him. "Huh?" Then she gave him a smile that seemed manufactured. "Yeah. I was just thinking about my dilemma. At least I have until the first of the year, but that's really not much time. September will be here this week."

She suddenly brightened. "Let me pay you for your time today."

Brent clucked his tongue, insulted. "Are you kidding?"

"No, I'm not. You took time out of your busy day to help me, and your time is worth something."

He studied her with disbelief. "Isn't that what friends are for?"

"Right. What friends are for." Something unreadable flashed over her face.

"I need to get that teal paint at Swanson's before it closes. Do you want to come with me?" He grinned. "I'll pick up a gallon of magenta for your bathroom."

"Oh no, but thanks." She gestured around the store as though she hadn't heard his joke. "I think I'll stick around here and try to come up with some ideas to market the store better, bring in more customers."

He nodded, but disappointment pressed down on his shoulders. "Do you want me to stay and help you think?"

Her expression warmed. "No, but again, I appreciate all you've done today."

"It was my pleasure." He reached into his pocket and pulled out his keys. "Walk me out?"

"Of course."

They ambled toward the back of the building, and when they reached the breakroom, he pointed to the door. "Tell your ferocious cats I said hello."

She chuckled. "I will."

"There's that gorgeous smile," he said before opening the back door for her.

She blushed and strode into the humid air.

Brent's shoes crunched in the gravel lot as he approached their trucks. "Do you need help unhooking your trailer when you get home?"

She slammed her hands on her small hips and narrowed her eyes with phony annoyance. "Excuse me, Brent Nicholson, but I know how to manage my trailer. I am *not* a helpless female."

"Okay, okay." He waved his hands in surrender. "I was just trying to be polite." He jumped into his driver's seat, started the engine, and rolled down his window.

Christine sauntered over and peered up at him. "Have you spoken to Coach Morgan about working with the quarterbacks yet?"

"No." He sighed. "I'm still thinking about it."

"You should do it." She tapped the side of his truck. "Tell your aunt I said hello."

"I will, and I'll see you soon." At least, he hoped to.

As he steered his way out of the parking lot, he looked at Christine in his rearview mirror. He was determined to help save her store. He just had to figure out how.

◆ ◆ ◆

Christine folded her arms over her waist as Brent's truck disappeared from view. Her heart warmed as she recalled how sweet, kind, and thoughtful he'd been, not only helping her haul the furniture to the store but promising his help after she learned her rent would soon nearly double.

As she padded back inside, she allowed herself to wonder what it would be like to have Brent in her life permanently, to be his girlfriend or even his wife, to enjoy his company along with his love and support for the rest of their lives.

But her sister's warnings about him echoed through her mind. Christine was certainly falling for his charms, but one day he could hurt her the same way he'd hurt Britney. And she'd caught a glimpse of that text message he'd received from someone named Tara. Her stomach lurched as she recalled what she'd read—*I love you! Call me!*

Christine groaned. *Ugh!* Brent said he'd had a girlfriend, which meant Tara could be his ex. And if she was still pining for him, he could be pining for her as well. Maybe he'd just ignored the message because he didn't want Christine asking questions. With a history, they could rekindle their relationship when he returned to Virginia.

Not that he was even interested in Christine. After all, when she'd offered to pay him for his time, he'd responded with *"Isn't that what friends are for?"* He'd friend-zoned her for sure and further smothered any hope of a romantic relationship with him.

But her confusing feelings for Brent weren't her most pressing problem. Her shoulders drooped as she stood in the middle of her store and pondered the upcoming jump in rent. She had until the end of the year to figure out what to do, but if she didn't come up with anything other than asking her vendors for more money, she could lose her business for sure.

Pushing open the breakroom door, Christine found her cats loafing on their beds in the corner. "Time to get up, Wanda and Pietro. We need to come up with a way to bring more business into the store."

As if on cue, the lazy cats yawned and rolled over.

"Fine. I'll do it myself," Christine muttered before trudging to her office, powering up her computer, and preparing to brainstorm.

◆ ◆ ◆

"That's insane," Pam said as she sat across from Christine at Bloom's Coffee Shop Thursday evening. Eager for her friend's perspective, Christine had suggested they meet there. "Why would they almost double your rent? That seems unreasonable."

Christine cupped her hands around the warm mug in front of her. "I know. And tomorrow is September, which means the new year will be here before we know it." She frowned. "I did some research and checked into moving to another location."

"What?" Pam's eyes widened.

"I called around and even went to look at a couple of places after I closed up yesterday. One location was too small, and the rent at the other one is just too high. Other than that, I couldn't find anything. So moving the store isn't an option." Christine sipped her decaf

Americano. "I came up with a few other ideas, though. What do you think of a weekly sidewalk sale? I could move some of my own items outside and advertise in the paper and on the local radio station. Of course, I'll advertise on social media as well and hang flyers around town."

Pam smiled. "That sounds great. I could hang some up at the bank too."

"Thanks. I'm trying to think of more ideas that might increase sales. If I had to close the store, what would I do then?" Christine shuddered at the thought of watching her dream go up in smoke.

"Hey." Pam reached across the booth's table and touched Christine's hand. "It'll work out. I'm sure of it."

Christine sighed. "I hope so."

Pam took a sip of her vanilla latte. "So how's Brent?"

"I haven't seen him since Monday." She explained how he'd unexpectedly stopped by her house with the paint chips, asked for a tour of the house, and then helped her move completed furniture projects to the store. She tried not to smile while she talked about him, reminding herself Brent had made it clear where she stood.

Pam pinned her with a knowing expression. "You two make such a cute couple."

"Uh, no, we don't. We're just friends."

"Right. Just friends." Pam snorted. "You two radiate attraction and tension when you're together. It's almost palpable."

Christine shook her head. "There's nothing going on between us, Pam. I'd tell you if there were."

"Why not?"

"Why not what?"

Pam eyed her with suspicion. "Christine, he's handsome. Yes, I married the love of my life, but I will admit it when a man is attractive to me, and Brent is one gorgeous man. And besides that, he's nice and caring. He's proven that by how he's taking care of his great-aunt. And it's obvious he likes you, Christine. It's written all over his face when he's with you."

"Yes, he's hot, but I don't think he likes me that way." Christine shared how he'd friend-zoned her. "But that's okay. I can always use another friend, and I'd rather keep Brent in my life that way than risk losing him by suggesting anything more." *Especially if Tara is his ex-girlfriend and still in love with him.*

Pam pointed a finger at her. "So you admit you're attracted to him."

"Of course I am, but I could never betray Britney by dating him."

"What?" Pam blinked at her. "You're still there? I told you before—"

"Listen, you know Brent and Britney had a rough breakup. He cheated on her their sophomore year in college and broke her heart. Well, I let it slip that I've been spending time with him, and Britney keeps warning me not to get involved, reminding me he's bound to hurt me the same way he hurt her if I do."

Pam looked nearly stricken. "Chris, your sister is living her life, and you need to live yours. Britney is married and has a family. Whomever you choose to spend your time with doesn't need to be her business. Sure, he made a mistake with her, a big one. But that doesn't mean he hasn't changed, that he'll break your heart too. What happened between them was between them. Period."

"I know." Christine took a big gulp of her coffee to avoid looking Pam in the eye as her friend leaned forward.

"Look, I know you love your sister, but you're not her. Britney is great, but she's conceited and all about herself. She's always been that way. I remember how she strutted down the hallways at school

141

surrounded by her popular friends like she was the queen bee. You, on the other hand, have always been down-to-earth and nice to everyone. Britney's narcissism could be the real reason she and Brent didn't work out. But you and Brent make sense, and you shouldn't let your self-absorbed twin ruin that for you."

"Britney means well," Christine said, trying to dispel her best friend's words. "She's just looking out for me."

Pam scoffed, but Christine ignored it.

"Anyway," Christine continued, "it doesn't matter. He's made it clear he's not staying in Flowering Grove. So being his friend is all I can hope to be, and that's fine."

She elected not to mention the text she'd seen from Tara. She didn't know anything about her, and she didn't want Pam asking Steve to pump Brent for information.

"Now, back to the store," Christine declared as Pam took another sip. She was determined to change the subject. "I'll design a flyer and then email my customer base about the sidewalk sale. And like I said, I'll start with my own items, and then if my vendors want to put some of theirs in the next one, that will be great."

"Let me know how I can help."

As Christine turned her focus to her troubles with the store, she tried to push away Pam's insistence that she and Brent made sense as a couple. But a tiny seed of hope took root in her heart, and she had no idea how to pluck it out.

fourteen

Brent crouched on the floor in Aunt Midge's master bathroom and began ripping up the old and cracked orange linoleum. He'd finished the guest bathroom over the weekend, and he was grateful he'd discussed the wall color with his aunt one more time. She'd finally agreed to the yellow after he told her Christine preferred it too.

He smiled when he thought of Christine. He'd missed her during the past week and had considered visiting her more than once, but he'd been too embroiled in finishing that bathroom to make it to the store before closing time. Then when he toyed with the idea of showing up at her house some evening—he didn't have her cell number to call first—he quickly talked himself out of it, certain that might come across as too presumptive. Still, he missed her and hoped to see her sooner rather than later.

Ignoring the pain shooting through his knee, Brent pushed the putty knife under the faded linoleum and yanked. He stopped when he heard a strange noise that almost resembled a loud thump or a crash.

Brent pushed himself up using the side of the bathtub for leverage and then stepped into the hallway. "Aunt Midge?" he called.

He held his breath and listened. When he heard the sound again, he rushed to the kitchen. "Aunt Midge? Where are you?"

"I'm . . . down here, Brent," she called, her voice weak and shaky.

His heart rate ticked up as he loped down the basement stairs, taking two steps at a time until he reached the cement floor. Aunt Midge sat there wheezing, her hand clutching her chest. A metal tray lay beside her, the tool she must have used to alert him.

"I . . . c-can't . . . breathe," she managed to whisper between wheezes. "Need my . . . inhaler. Now. On . . . my . . . night . . . stand."

"I'll find it!" Panic squeezed his chest as he raced up the stairs, then ignored the pain screaming from his knee as he tore down the hallway to her bedroom. He had to get that inhaler to her quickly. He couldn't fathom the idea of something happening to Aunt Midge!

After he found it, he sprinted back to the basement, his heartbeat pounding in his ears. Aunt Midge sat in the same spot, working hard to breathe. He lowered himself beside her and placed the inhaler in her hand. "Here."

She lifted it with a shaky hand and tried to use it, but instead she kept wheezing, then coughed and struggled to suck in air. Fear and panic etched her face.

Alarm gripped Brent as well, but he worked to keep his fear at bay. "Just try again, okay?"

When she once again failed to use the inhaler, reality set in. His aunt needed help—*fast!*

"I'll get some help." His hands shook as he pulled his phone from his back pocket.

She nodded as tears leaked from her wide eyes, her glasses askew.

Brent dialed nine-one-one. When a dispatcher answered, he said, "We need an ambulance. My aunt is having an asthma attack. Please hurry!" he nearly shouted. Then, his voice tinged with dread, he recited the address.

❖ ❖ ❖

Brent turned to the automatic doors leading to the ER waiting room as his parents hurried in nearly two hours later. He was grateful to finally have some company after pacing around the large area, fretting, praying, and agonizing over Aunt Midge's condition. He hadn't heard a word from the hospital staff, and not knowing if she was all right was eating him up inside.

"Mom! Dad!" he called, rushing to them. "I'm so glad you're here."

Mom grabbed Brent's arm, her eyes wide with alarm. "I'm sorry we couldn't get here sooner. We were on our way back from Charlotte when you called. How is she?"

"She was still struggling to breathe when the EMTs loaded her into the ambulance." Brent shepherded his parents to an empty row of bench seats in the corner, where he sat down in a chair across from them.

Mom frowned. "I've warned her over and over to keep her inhaler with her, but you know how stubborn your aunt is."

"I wonder if the dust in the basement finally got her," Dad said.

"I had the same thought." Brent grasped the arms of his chair and took a deep breath, trying to calm his frayed nerves. Aunt Midge had to be okay. He couldn't imagine life without her.

"I would help her sort through those boxes," his mother said, "but I've been working extra hours lately. We had to replace our air-conditioning unit in June, and we're hoping to make double payments on the loan to pay it off early."

"It's fine, Mom. I'll help Aunt Midge with the sorting from now on. You don't need to worry about it."

Glancing across the waiting room, he spotted a young couple holding hands. They looked to be in their early to midtwenties. The woman rested her head on the man's shoulder, and Brent sighed. Once again an image of Christine's beautiful face filled his mind, and he realized how much he missed her—especially now.

If only he had her cell phone number, he could text her. Surely she'd want to know Aunt Midge was in the hospital. He could call the store's number, though, and if she had someone to cover for her, maybe she'd come sit beside him and hold his hand. Having Christine there would do wonders to soothe his nerves.

But they didn't have that kind of relationship.

He leaned forward and stared at the television mounted on one wall. Maybe the news could tune out his rushing thoughts. But the sound was turned so low he could barely hear the news anchor sharing the day's stories. He folded his arms over his chest as frustration pummeled him. What was the point of having a television in the waiting room if no one could hear it? He couldn't concentrate well enough to keep up with the closed captioning.

Brent's phone dinged with a text message, and he swallowed a growl when he found another text from Tara—the last thing he needed today.

> *Look, I know I hurt you. I made a mistake, but I want to make it right. Just call me, and we'll talk it through. We were together almost two years, and we can't just throw those years away.*

It was time to tell Tara she had to let it go, but he wasn't emotionally strong enough to deal with her today. Right now his focus was on his precious aunt.

Now isn't a good time, he typed.

A reply came immediately.

You finally answered me! I'm so relieved. Please let me
explain. You and I had a disagreement, and Doug
was there. I shouldn't have gone to him, and I'm sorry.
Please, please give me another chance.

Brent leaned back in his chair, sighed, and then replied.

Give me some space. We'll talk when I'm ready.

She answered after a few seconds.

Okay. I'll wait. Thank you, Brent.

He slipped his phone back into his pocket and then peered at his parents, who were both thumbing through magazines without reading a word.

"The family of Maren Marcello," a tall man with dark skin called into the room. He wore a white physician's coat and black horn-rimmed glasses.

Brent jumped up from his chair. "We're here!"

"Let's talk privately," the doctor said.

Brent followed his parents to a small conference room and then sat at a table across from them. His right leg nervously vibrated as the doctor folded his hands on the table.

"I'm Dr. Powell," he said, and then Brent and his parents introduced themselves.

Brent swallowed back his angst. "How is she?"

"Much better. Her oxygen levels are just okay, though, so we're giving her an albuterol treatment, and she's responding well."

Brent's mother heaved out a puff of air. "Thank the Lord above!"

"Does she have a pulmonologist?" Dr. Powell asked.

Mom nodded. "Yes."

"When was the last time she had an appointment?"

Brent's parents shared quizzical expressions, and then Mom frowned. "I believe it's been a while."

"I recommend she go in for a follow-up as soon as possible."

"I'll make sure she does," Mom said.

"Perfect." Dr. Powell's expression warmed. "She's had a scare, but as long as she keeps her inhaler within reach, she should be fine."

Brent leaned back as the worry and fear drained out of him. "I'm so glad to hear that. When can we see her?"

"Now," the doctor said as he stood. "Follow me."

◆ ◆ ◆

Brent held Aunt Midge's arm as she made her way to her recliner in the family room. He and his parents had stayed at the hospital until she was released, and then his parents brought her home in their car while he drove his truck.

"I don't need you to coddle me, Brent," his aunt grumbled as she adjusted herself in her chair. "I can manage just fine on my own."

Mom frowned as she set both women's purses on the coffee table. "We're all concerned about you, Aunt Midge."

"I'm sorry, Donna." His aunt gave a resigned sigh. "I should have listened to you about my inhaler."

Dad dropped onto the sofa and gave her a concerned expression. "I know you're determined to clear out your basement, but that dust down there isn't good for you. It's best if someone else sorts through the rest." He glanced at Mom. "Brent says he'll help, but maybe Donna and I can come whenever we have time."

"I know you want to help, Barry, but I don't want you and Donna to feel obligated. You both work such long hours."

Mom smiled. "We don't mind. We can always make time for you."

"I'll figure out a way to get it all done." Brent rubbed his elbow. He had no idea how he could add sorting through the basement to his long to-do list and still get back to Virginia before Thanksgiving, but he'd manage it somehow—for Aunt Midge.

Mom glanced toward the kitchen. "How about I make you something to eat?"

Aunt Midge shook her head. "I just want a grilled cheese sandwich, and my younger nephew can handle that."

"I'm happy to make you a grilled cheese." Brent made a sweeping gesture toward the kitchen. "Mom and Dad, would you like one before you go?"

Dad shook his head as he stood. "Oh no." He turned toward Mom. "We should get going, Donna. Your shift at the store starts soon."

"Oh. Okay." Mom touched Aunt Midge's arm. "I'll call Dr. Jenkins tomorrow and schedule an appointment. And I'll make sure it's for a time I can take you."

"You let us know if you need anything else, Aunt Midge," Dad said.

"Thank you, Barry." She took his hand and squeezed it.

Brent closed the door behind his parents before returning to his aunt. "You gave me one heck of a scare. Don't do that again."

"I'm sorry, sweetie." Aunt Midge patted his arm. "I thought my asthma was under control."

Brent pulled a footstool over and sat in front of her. "What if I bring the basement boxes up here and we go through them together? You tell me what's worth taking to Christine's store and what we should donate or toss."

"No. You have enough to do."

"I'm not worried about having more chores to do. I'm worried about *you*."

Aunt Midge hesitated, and he could almost see the wheels turning in her head. "I have a solution we'll both like. I'll pay Christine to do it. She'll know what's worth selling or donating and what's better off at the dump."

"I like that idea."

Aunt Midge grinned. "I bet you do."

Brent stood, shaking his head. "I'll go make our grilled cheese sandwiches." He started toward the kitchen.

"You should call Christine right now."

He stopped and faced her. "Her store is closed now, and I don't have her cell number."

Aunt Midge looked aghast. "Don't you know how to date?"

He laughed, grateful she still had her sense of humor despite her rotten day. "Yes, I do, and I'm not dating her."

She narrowed her eyes and shook her finger at him as usual. "You should be."

"And you need to rest. I'll call Christine tomorrow."

Aunt Midge scoffed, and Brent chuckled to himself as he continued into the kitchen.

As he prepared their sandwiches, his thoughts centered on Christine. He hoped she'd agree to going the extra mile to help them complete this project. And somehow, he knew she would.

fifteen

"Uptown Girl" by Billy Joel rang through the store speakers as Christine assisted her latest customer. "This is a lovely choice, Mrs. Lambert," she said, ringing up a Tiffany-style lamp featuring a bronze base with a multicolored shade.

Mrs. Lambert pulled her credit card from her wallet and slid it into the reader. "It's just what I was looking for. I often find what I want in your store. This is just lovely."

"Thank you. Would you like me to get a box for it?"

"Oh, no thank you. I have one in my trunk."

Christine handed her a receipt. "Let me help you out." She hurried to the door and pushed it open. "Have a good day."

Mrs. Lambert stepped outside. "You too. I'm sure I'll see you again soon."

Just as the door clicked shut, the store's phone rang, and Christine scooted behind the counter and lifted the receiver. "Thank you for calling Treasure Hunting Antique Mall," she said. "This is Christine. How may I help you?"

"Christine," Brent's voice said. "It's me. Brent."

Christine sank onto her stool, her heart picking up speed. "Brent. Hi."

"I, um, need your help."

"What's up?"

"Aunt Midge had an asthma attack in the basement yesterday while she was sorting through her boxes. I had to get her to the ER. We think all the dust down there caused it."

"No!" Christine cupped her hand to her mouth. "Is she okay?"

"She's fine, and my mom plans to take her to her pulmonary specialist for a checkup as soon as possible. But here's how I need your help. Aunt Midge wants to pay you to finish clearing out her basement and attic so she doesn't risk another attack."

"I'm happy to help. Let me just see if my mom or sister can take over the store today, and I'll come right over."

"I appreciate that, but it's not necessary. Maybe you can come start one evening."

"How about tonight? I'll bring dinner."

"That would be amazing," he said, sounding relieved. "I'm not much of a cook."

"How does Chinese sound?"

"Perfect."

They discussed what she should order, and she wrote it on a notepad before they settled on a time.

She stood. "I'll see you and Aunt Midge around six, then."

"I can't wait," he told her, and her heart stuttered.

"Brent, if you need me to come sooner, please just call, okay? I can get someone to cover the store."

"I promise you we're fine." His voice was deep and smooth, reminding her of velvet.

"Okay. Goodbye, then."

"See you soon," he said before hanging up.

◆ ◆ ◆

Christine stood on Aunt Midge's front porch balancing a bouquet of white daisies, a box of chocolate-covered pretzels, and a takeout bag from Jade Kitchen in her arms. Leaning, she used her left elbow to push the doorbell and then held her breath, hoping Brent would come before everything tumbled to the ground.

The inside door opened, and Brent appeared with a grin lighting his handsome face. He looked good—*really good*—in a pair of tight blue jeans and a faded black T-shirt that fit nicely over his wide chest and muscular arms. His bright, intelligent eyes danced, and his dark hair was the same mess of curls she longed to touch. He also had that stubble she loved on his chiseled jaw.

If only she could ignore all those things.

"Let me help you!" He pushed open the creaky screen door, and she was completely aware that his fingers brushed hers as he took the box of pretzels and takeout bag.

Shaken by his touch, she awkwardly adjusted the bouquet in her hand. "Thank you."

"Come in." He stepped back to allow her to enter, then let the screen door shut behind her.

"How is she?"

"Excited to see you." Brent nodded toward the back of the house. "Aunt Midge! Guess who's here."

"We've been waiting for you!" she called from the kitchen.

"How are you?" Christine asked the older woman when she'd made her way to the kitchen, Brent trailing behind.

Aunt Midge was standing at the counter, drinking water from a glass.

"I'm just fine. I wish everyone would stop making such a fuss." She held out her free hand, and Christine grasped it. "We've both missed you."

Christine tried to ignore how the words warmed her from the inside out. She'd missed them as well.

She held up the flowers. "These are for you."

"So pretty, and that food smells heavenly." Aunt Midge pointed to the bag as Brent set it on the table. "Let's eat!"

Christine chuckled, and when her gaze tangled with Brent's, he blessed her with a smile that made her pulse take on wings.

She found a vase in a cabinet Aunt Midge indicated, and after filling it with water, she set the daisies in it. Brent unloaded the food, and soon they were enjoying their meal.

"Oh, this is the best egg roll I've ever had," Aunt Midge announced. "Thank you so much."

Christine scooped fried rice onto her plate. "You're welcome. Jade Kitchen is a favorite." She turned toward Brent, who'd chosen to sit beside her. "How's your beef and broccoli?"

"Out of this world. And your shrimp and mixed vegetables?"

Christine lifted her glass of sweet tea. "Delicious."

"Thank you so much for agreeing to help clear out the basement and attic, Christine," Aunt Midge said.

"You're so welcome."

"And please use your judgment about what's worth selling, what we should donate, and what we should just toss. You're the expert here, not me."

"I'm happy to help, and I'm grateful you're willing to sell your amazing antiques and collectibles in my store." Christine forked a plump shrimp into her mouth.

Aunt Midge laughed. "One woman's trash is another woman's treasure."

"Oh, your things definitely aren't trash. Your Blue Willow tea-cups are gorgeous, and they're almost all sold already. I can't wait to see what others you might have."

Aunt Midge had a faraway look in her eyes as she smiled. "Sal bought me tea sets for every occasion—my birthday, Christmas, Valentine's Day, our anniversary . . . I enjoyed them so much. He liked to spoil me with gifts, but after he died, I put most of them away. Over these past few weeks, though, I've been able to reminisce over them, and that's made me happy." She looked at Christine as though reading her mind. "Don't worry. I've seen enough. You just do what you think is best."

Christine snuck a peek at Brent and found him gazing at his aunt with such love on his face. Britney's words echoed through her mind. *"You know what he put me through, and I'm telling you he'll do the same thing to you if you let him."* Yes, as a college boy, Brent had betrayed her sister all those years ago. But now? He was clearly a considerate man who cared for this sweet elderly woman.

As Brent met her own gaze again, to the depth of her bones she knew he'd managed to carve out a piece of her heart and she was doomed. Yet she doubted Britney would ever forgive him and acknowledge he'd changed.

A new thought came to her. Could his betrayal have been just a misunderstanding? Might he never have cheated on Britney at all? As unlikely as that was, she wished it were true.

Aunt Midge spent the remainder of dinner sharing sweet memories of her beloved husband and the wonderful times they'd had together. When they finished eating, Christine gathered their dishes and utensils while Brent insisted on escorting Aunt Midge into the family room.

Christine threw away the takeout containers, then rinsed their plates, glasses, and utensils before setting them in the already half-full dishwasher.

She turned to Brent when he returned and leaned against the counter beside her. "I think your aunt enjoyed dinner."

"She loved it, and so did I. Thank you so much for bringing it."

She smiled and brushed off his gratitude. "You're welcome."

Brent grabbed a dishcloth and began wiping the table. "Aunt Midge is settled in for some TV watching now."

Christine poured detergent into the dishwasher before starting the machine, then spun to face Brent. "So do I get to see this magenta bathroom or what?"

"Magenta? You'll be disappointed." He tossed the dishcloth into the sink.

"Uh-oh." She clucked her tongue. "Although your aunt's choice of teal might go better with *avocado* fixtures."

He chuckled, and she enjoyed the deep, rich sound. "Come on, you." He beckoned her to follow him down the hallway, past the photos of Brent and his sister she'd previously admired and into the guest bathroom.

Christine gave a low whistle as she stepped into the remodeled room, taking in the lightly stained wood-framed mirror and matching vanity; white and gray tiles; white sink, commode, and tub with a glass-enclosed shower—and cheerful, bright-yellow walls! She pivoted toward where Brent leaned against the doorframe.

"Well?" he asked. "Do you approve?" He looked hopeful, as if he truly valued her opinion. She found that mind-boggling.

"It's magnificent! You're so darn skilled—and talented. Not only are you great at the work itself but at making design decisions. I have a feeling you influenced Aunt Midge to choose that modern wood stain."

He stood straight and rested his hands on the top of the doorjamb before leaning into the room. "Thanks. Though Steve upgraded the plumbing."

"But how did you convince Aunt Midge to go with the yellow?" she all but whispered in case the woman was all ears.

"Let's just say your opinion made the difference."

Christine laughed before scanning the bathroom again. "I can't get over how gorgeous this is. You need to remodel homes full-time again, start another business. Why don't you do that here?"

Embarrassment overtook her. Had she really blurted that?

"Well, because I don't plan to stay in Flowering Grove," he said.

Christine curled her lips into a smile despite the disappointment plunging through her. "I understand. How's the master bathroom coming along?"

"There's not much to see yet, but I'll show you what I'm up against."

She followed him through Aunt Midge's bedroom to the bathroom, where at least the flooring was gone.

"This will take me as long as a month, counting Steve's work." He held up his pointer finger. "Don't worry. I'll check with you before I buy any paint."

She placed her hands on her hips. "You'd better, Nicholson."

He laughed.

"I suppose I should get to work sorting through your aunt's things."

"I'll show you to the basement. The door is off the kitchen."

Christine was following him down the hallway when Aunt Midge called, "What are you two up to?"

They peeked into the family room, where *Entertainment Tonight* was on.

"I'm taking Christine down to the basement so she can start sorting through your stuff."

Aunt Midge grinned. "Ohhhhh. Well, have fun!"

Brent groaned as they made their way to the basement door. He opened it and switched on the lights.

"What was that about?" Christine asked.

An embarrassed expression appeared on his face. "She's always trying to marry me off."

Christine hoped he couldn't see her cheeks redden. She was always blushing around this man.

When they reached the bottom of the stairs, Christine took in the sea of boxes clogging the unfinished basement. "Wow," she mumbled.

"I know. What you've seen so far was only a dent. This could take you forever."

"I could ask Britney to run the store for a while so I can do it faster. She doesn't mind having the girls with her there when they're not in school."

He shook his head. "I don't want this to take you away from the store. And you're still dealing with your rent increase dilemma, right?"

"Well, yes. And I have some ideas."

"That makes me all the more grateful for your willingness to do this too."

"But remember, Aunt Midge is paying me as well as renting a booth and giving me a percentage of her profits. Every bit helps."

He pointed to a stack of plastic totes. "Use those to organize the items you want to sell, and you'll find trash bags on a shelf over in that corner to gather the items you think we should donate or take to the dump."

"Okay." She brushed her hands together. "I'm ready to work."

"And I'll be in the master bathroom if you need me." He sauntered to the stairs, where he stopped and faced her. "I really do appreciate you taking the time to do this."

"Are you kidding? I feel like a kid in a candy store."

"Great," he said, smiling, then disappeared up the stairs.

◆ ◆ ◆

Christine had been sorting through several boxes of books and knick-knacks from a footstool for at least ninety minutes. She'd smiled when she found classic novels like the Nancy Drew series and works by Ernest Hemingway. But while she'd found plenty of items for Aunt Midge's booth, she didn't feel like she'd made any real headway. Brent was right when he said this project could take a while.

Her phone rang, and she fished it from her pocket. Britney's name was on the screen. "Hey, sis."

"Where are you?" Britney's tone seeped annoyance. Or was it impatience? Maybe both.

Christine balanced the phone on her shoulder and set a figurine in a plastic tote. "Why? What's up?"

"The twins want to see you, so we stopped by your house after meeting Hunter at the diner down the street for dinner. But you weren't home, and I thought you told me you would be. Maybe I was wrong, but they're so disappointed that they've been whining ever since. Are you with Pam?"

"No, I'm not."

"Then where are you?"

Christine hesitated. She considered fibbing to avoid an argument, but then she sat up straight. Her sister had no hold over her. Christine was an adult and had the right to choose with whom she spent her time. "I'm at Midge Marcello's house."

"You're *where*?" Britney nearly shouted into the phone. "Are you kidding me?"

Christine heard a creak. Probably Brent or Aunt Midge up in the kitchen.

She needed to get her bossy sister off the phone so she could get back to work. "No, I'm not kidding, and please stop yelling at me," she snapped. "I'm not one of your children." But then she forced herself to calm despite her boiling frustration.

"I can't believe this! I've warned you to stay away from Brent, but you just don't get it, do you? You're determined to date him and get your heart broken."

"Again, I'm not dating him. I'm just here helping his aunt. Now listen."

She explained how Aunt Midge had suffered a severe asthma attack while clearing out her dusty basement, then asked Brent to engage her to do it instead. She also told her sister about her rent increasing the first of the year, so she had to find ways to offset the cost. "Aunt Midge needs help, I need her items to sell, and the extra money she's paying me doesn't hurt."

"I'm sorry to hear about that, but I doubt Brent will be any help," Britney sniped. "Based on my experience, he only cares about himself. And he has you calling her *Aunt Midge*."

Christine scowled. She'd had enough of her sister's rant about a man who, based on *her* experience, clearly *did* care for more than himself. "Look, I'm here helping his aunt, and that's it. I don't need your permission. Besides, Brent and I are friends whether you like it or not. You can stop lecturing me. It's not a big deal."

"Yes, it *is* a big deal, Chrissy, because you're not listening."

Christine rubbed her eyes with her free hand. "Britney, you've reminded me he broke your heart over and over. But that was a long time ago, and he won't break mine *because we're just friends,* okay?"

"You say that now, but remember that I warned you."

"Are you done? Because I have work to do."

Britney harrumphed. "Let me know when the girls can see you. They miss you, and they're more important than your so-called friend Brent."

"I have to go. I'll talk to you later. Goodbye." Christine disconnected the call and then let out a low groan. When she slipped her phone into her pocket she saw movement out of the corner of her eye. She turned toward the stairs and jumped with a start when she found Brent watching her, his expression unreadable.

Oh no.

"Hey," she said. "I didn't realize you'd come down the stairs."

"I thought you might need a break. Would you like to sit out on the deck?"

"Yes, I would." She stood and followed him upstairs, silently praying he hadn't overheard her conversation with Britney.

But then she remembered that creak.

sixteen

Anger spiked through his chest as Brent poured two glasses of sweet tea. Christine was waiting for him on Aunt Midge's freestanding wood glider out on the deck, but he was so infuriated that his hands shook. He wasn't upset with Christine, though. He was incensed that Britney was telling her sister lies about him. He broke her heart? No. She'd broken his. She'd ghosted him. Just suddenly stopped responding to his calls and texts without any explanation—and after all their years together.

Yet she had the nerve to tell Christine he'd break *her* heart? What reality did Britney live in?

He stepped onto the deck, and the gorgeous, clear evening was a stark contrast to his foul mood. The cicadas crooned their nightly chorus while the stars sparkled in the evening sky.

Christine looked up and gave him a hesitant smile. She looked breathtaking tonight. Her blue eyes seemed brighter, and her thick blond hair hung in waves past her shoulders. Her cutoff jeans and purple blouse fit her just right.

Holding out a glass for her, Brent tried in vain to shove away his exasperation. "Here you go."

"Thank you." She took the glass and sipped. "Did you check on your aunt?"

He sat beside her, and when his thigh brushed hers, his skin tingled. "Yes. She's snoring in her recliner." Attempting to calm his boiling fury, he said, "Tell me about your ideas for the store."

She shrugged and placed her glass on the small table next to her. "I had a sidewalk sale on Saturday, and it went pretty well."

He angled his body toward hers. "That's a great idea."

"Thanks. I thought if folks drive past and see interesting things outside, that might draw them inside. I'm planning another one for Friday. I'd like to run ads in the paper and on the radio, but they're out of my budget. So I'm just posting on social media and asking everyone I know to hang flyers. And I'm buying some balloons at the dollar store too."

"Those all sound good." He ran his fingers over the arm of the glider.

"Thanks." She tilted her head and seemed to assess him. "How are you doing after the scare with Aunt Midge?"

Brent set his own glass on the deck floor, then scrubbed his hands down his face. "I was a mess yesterday. I don't know what I'd do if anything happened to her." He settled back. "I'm beyond grateful she's okay."

"You could have texted me. Maybe I could have helped somehow." She rested her hand on his, and he enjoyed the comfort the gesture provided.

He grimaced. "Actually, I couldn't have."

"Why not?"

"Because I don't have your number."

Christine held her hand out. "Unlock your phone and hand it to me, Nicholson."

"Yes, ma'am," he said as he pulled his cell from his pocket and complied.

Just as Steve had the night of the fireworks, Christine accomplished a number exchange, then said, "Now you can text me anytime, day or night."

"Thank you." He slipped his phone back into his pocket and then lifted his glass.

Silence fell between them as they looked out over the backyard. He stared at the fence and gazebo in desperate need of repair and a paint job and mentally added them to his to-do list. For such a modest home this was quite a backyard. A screened-in porch, a deck, a gazebo . . . And buyers should love the place when it was all spruced up.

He'd been trying to dismiss his frustration with Britney, but it still boiled under his skin. He needed to address the elephant in the room before it ate him alive.

"I overheard you talking to your sister."

Looking horrified, Christine held up her palms. "I'm *so* sorry, Brent."

"No, it's my fault. I thought you heard me coming down the stairs, and then when I realized who you were talking to—and what you were saying—I couldn't bring myself to leave. I'm sorry." He paused. "From what I heard, Britney isn't happy you're here. Is that right?"

She blew out a deep sigh and slouched back on the glider. "No, she's not. She lectures me every time I mention you. She says I need to be careful around you because you broke her heart."

"So I did hear you say that's what she thinks. And how exactly does she say I did that?"

Christine sat up straight, her expression so incredulous he could hardly believe it. "By cheating on her, of course."

His jaw clenched. "That's what she told you?"

"Yes."

"Unbelievable." He snorted. "That's rich."

She studied him, looking as if she were trying to untangle his words. "Don't lie to me, Brent."

He looked deep into her beautiful eyes and took a deep breath. "I'd never lie to you. It sounds like your sister has rewritten history, because the truth is she ghosted me, and as far as I ever knew, for no reason at all." His body vibrated with indignation. "I certainly never cheated on her."

She angled her body toward his, and now her expression seemed open and curious. "Tell me."

"One day she completely stopped responding to my messages, and I was worried something had happened to her. I left voice mails and texted for days, begging her to talk to me. Finally, I was so desperate that I dropped everything, left school, and drove the two hours to see her at UNC Charlotte.

"When I got there, Britney wouldn't even come out of her dorm to talk to me. She had two of her sorority sisters instruct me to leave, and when I told them I just wanted to talk to her, they had a security guard throw me off their property. After that, Britney blocked my number, and I finally got the hint that it was over between us." He took a sharp breath, trying to calm his nerves. "I know she's your sister and you love her. But *she* dumped *me* with no explanation."

Christine studied him as if trying to comprehend his words. "But she's always said you cheated on her."

"No, I didn't. Other women were the last thing on my mind. It was my sophomore year, and it was the worst year of my life. I'd already been struggling with my grades because football was a full-time job, and then I was injured and endured four painful surgeries."

He leaned forward, staring at the floor of the deck. "Our

relationship wasn't perfect by any means, but after all that, things between us grew strained. I admit that was mostly my fault, because after my injury I was in a permanent foul mood. We seemed to bicker more often, and soon we communicated only once or twice a week instead of texting every day. But cheat on her? No. I still hoped we could stay together."

He looked out toward the fence line as lightning bugs swooped through the air like tiny sparklers. "Despite our struggles, Britney was my lifeline. But then she just dumped me without any explanation." He faced Christine. "I thought she was tired of our relationship or maybe had found someone else and then avoided the conflict of telling me. But I never betrayed her."

Christine blinked, looking as if she was working out an intricate puzzle. "But she was told you cheated."

"Who told her that?"

Christine leaned back on the swing. "What was his name?" She squinted her eyes and looked up toward the stars as if they held the answers. "He was on the football team with you. Grant . . ."

"Grant Fahey?"

She spun and pointed at him. "Yes! He said he went to see you at Chapel Hill one weekend, and at a party he saw you making out with a beautiful redhead. When he returned to Charlotte, he went to see Britney and told her all about it. He even made it sound like that wasn't the first time you were pretty intimate with this girl."

"What? That's impossible." Brent's hands fisted, holding on to the truth. "I remember him coming to Chapel Hill, and we might have gone to a party, but . . ." He rubbed his forehead. "Making out with a beautiful redhead?" He searched his college memories for anything that made sense, then snapped his fingers. "I was friends with a redhead named Dina, but I never even flirted with her. She was dating one of my buddies, and there was nothing between us. Nothing at all."

"If that's true, why would Grant say there was?"

He threw up his hands. "Maybe I put my arm around Dina when we were talking, but . . ." He studied her. "Have you ever been friends with a guy? Truly just friends and nothing more?"

"Sure." She shrugged. "I had a couple of good guy friends in college."

"That's what I mean. Dina was just a friend and only a friend. You know, Grant always had a crush on Britney. In high school he once told me he'd get her away from me one day. Well, I suppose in the end he did just that. Did she date him then?"

"No. Not as far as I know."

He blew out a deep sigh as the pieces came together in his mind. "Now it all makes sense." He glowered as the injustice of it all hit him in the face. "Britney's believing him just shows you what she really thought of me, though. She never really trusted me or had enough faith in our relationship, not if she could give up on me after someone she hardly knew made such a horrible accusation. She didn't even give me a chance to defend myself against that snake."

He looked at Christine again. "Do you believe me?"

She nodded. "Yes, I do." Then she studied him, and he could almost hear a question rolling through her mind.

"You look like you want to ask me something. Don't hold back."

She swallowed. "Do you still have feelings for Britney?" Her words were soft and halting, as if she dreaded his response.

"No," he said without any hesitation. "I've been over her for a long time."

She nodded, and when their gazes locked, the urge to confess how he felt about her swelled in his chest. He mustered all his courage.

"The truth is . . . I like *you*, Christine. I mean, I care about you—a lot."

Her expression lit up, and her eyes softened. "I like you, too, Brent."

His heart leapt, and he threaded his fingers with hers, giving her hand a squeeze as happiness ignited inside him. He imagined what it would be like for Christine to be his girlfriend, sitting with her like this often, sharing their deepest secrets . . . His pulse kicked up as he envisioned holding her in his arms and kissing her.

But then reality set in. He had no future in Flowering Grove. He had to settle for being her friend, but at least he would still have the pleasure of her company.

"If things were different and I was going to stay here . . ." He cleared his throat. "I mean, you have your store and your family here, and in my limited experience, long-distance relationships don't work out the way you'd like. I just—"

"Brent. I get it." He caught a glimpse of longing in her eyes before she looked toward the gazebo. "Even though we . . . like each other, it's definitely for the best that we just remain friends." She turned back to face him. "After all, Britney disapproves of even that, and I try my best to keep my twin's drama at a minimum."

"Right. I don't want to come between you and your sister."

When she shifted closer before resting her cheek on his shoulder, he smiled, enjoying the intimacy of the gesture. They were both quiet as only the sound of cars motoring past filled the space around them.

After several moments, Christine lifted her head and looked at him.

"If Britney disapproves of our friendship," he asked, "then why are you here?"

"I like your aunt, and like I told Britney, I want to help her." She bumped her shoulder against his. "I also need to make sure you choose the correct paint colors."

His heart felt light as she grinned, and he was so grateful for his beautiful friend. If only they could be more.

"I'm glad to hear it."

Christine shielded a yawn with the back of her hand. "It's getting close to my bedtime. Let's load the totes I have ready into my truck before I head home." She touched his arm. "I promise I'll be back soon. I'll text you about when."

"Good."

When her truck was loaded, Christine climbed into the driver's seat, and he closed the door for her. She started the engine and lowered the window.

"Have you seen Coach Morgan, Brent? About his offer?"

"No."

"You should. Seriously, I think coaching could help you move past your feelings of failure. Not that I think you've failed, but you've confessed your father's criticism has made an even greater impact on you the last several years."

Not sure he wanted to get into this, he pretended to study her. "Are you sure you didn't major in psychiatry or psychology?"

She smiled but then sobered. "I just think it would be good for you. Trust me, I know a little something about struggling with self-worth. And I have a feeling rekindling your love of football might be one key to your moving forward, just like opening my store was for me."

"I'll think about it."

"Don't think, Brent. Just do." She smiled again. "Good night."

She backed out of the driveway and tooted the horn before heading down the street.

Brent sauntered into the house, and finding Aunt Midge awake now, he sank into the sofa.

She muted the television and gave him a pointed look. "That Christine is special, Brent."

"I know."

"You need to scoop her up before some other man does."

He frowned. If only he could, but he had no stability to offer her, and a woman as beautiful, hardworking, successful, kind, and thoughtful as Christine was deserved the best of everything.

He stood and stretched. "I'm heading to bed."

"Listen to me, Brent. Don't let Christine slip through your fingers. You two would make each other happy, and that's what matters most."

"She deserves better than me." He shook his head.

"That's poppycock. You're a good man, and life is too short to be alone. Take it from me. I miss your uncle every day."

"I know you do. I do too." Brent paused. "What would you think about me helping the football team as an assistant coach? I didn't tell you, but that day in the grocery store parking lot, Coach Morgan asked me to volunteer."

"Oh my." Her dark eyes lit with excitement. "That's a grand idea! You should do that."

"I might go see him, then."

"You should. Now go get a good night's sleep."

As Brent headed to his room, he considered Christine's advice. He'd taken it once, when he joined her at the football game. Perhaps he should take it again and work on finding his love for football again. Watching a game from the stands had been a start, but deep down he wanted more.

seventeen

Friday morning Brent walked down the main hallway at Flowering Grove High School toward the athletic wing. He'd stopped by the office to sign in and receive a visitor pass, and then one of the office assistants called Coach Morgan to tell him Brent was on his way to see him.

Now as he moved through the hallways of his alma mater and scanned the rows of lockers and classrooms, visions of walking these halls surrounded by his football friends and holding Britney's hand filled his mind. Back then life was so simple, but at least he'd had a plan. Thanks to his athletic scholarship, he'd been bound for UNC at Chapel Hill to earn his degree and then live the fruitful life both he and his father had planned for him.

Brent ambled into the athletic wing and recalled the hundreds of hours he'd spent there. Despondency weighed heavily on his shoulders as he stood in front of the trophy case. He found the state championship trophy that sat proudly beside a photo of his team. Then he took in his confident—arrogant?—expression and almost didn't recognize himself. It was as if he were looking at someone he didn't know, someone who no longer existed. Like a ghost.

A plaque beside the trophy boasted his name for earning state records for his accomplishments on the field his senior year—most passing yards and passing touchdowns. Again, that all felt like a lifetime ago, not ten years ago. When he'd been a so-called hero winning awards.

He recalled his fellow players. His brothers. Back then, Brent had been a leader—the quarterback, the team captain—and his team believed in him, depended on him. He couldn't remember how that felt.

"Brent Nicholson. What a wonderful surprise."

He turned as Coach Morgan stepped out of his office and joined him in the hallway. "Coach."

"What brings you here today?" The man looked hopeful as they shook hands.

"I've been thinking about your invitation to serve as an assistant coach."

A smile filled the coach's face. "Is that right? We sure need a quarterback coach, and you are the best man for the job."

"I'm still not sure about that."

The coach snorted. "Are you kidding me? I saw you looking at that trophy. I think all the proof you need is right there in that display case, son."

Christine's words suddenly echoed through his mind. *I think coaching could help you move past your feelings of failure.*

Brent cleared his throat and stood taller. "I'm ready to give it a try."

"Fantastic!"

"I just need you to remember I'm in town temporarily, but I'll be here for the remainder of the season."

"That's perfect."

After they discussed the team's schedule, they shook hands again.

"I'm looking forward to getting started, Coach."

"The guys will be thrilled to meet you. See you at the game tonight."

As Brent left the school, he realized he had a spring in his step.

◆ ◆ ◆

The bell above the store's front door rang, and Christine nodded and smiled as four women entered, all about middle-aged. She didn't recognize any of them, but avid antique-mall shoppers often found her store on day trips.

"Welcome to Treasure Hunting," she called. The women smiled and nodded back before disappearing into the aisles.

As she quietly sang along to A-ha's "Take On Me," Christine peered out the front windows. People meandered past her sidewalk sale display, featuring furniture pieces, a cedar chest, lamps, an antique wagon, and a shelf holding vintage books. She'd included the child's rocking chair, hat rack, and mirror she'd found at the yard sale in Pam's neighborhood and cleaned. She bit her lip, hoping the sale would be a success.

The bell above the door rang again, and her twin pushed through. Her face was twisted in a scowl as she marched toward the counter, looking like a woman on a mission.

Oh no.

"We need to talk," Britney announced with a storm brewing in her eyes.

Christine held up her hand. "This really isn't—"

"I can't let this go. You say you and Brent are just friends, but why are you even giving him the time of day after what he did to me?"

Her sister was seething, and Christine's eyes narrowed as both impatience and anger surged through her. It was hard enough to tell Brent she agreed they should just be friends despite their emerging feelings. She didn't need this too.

"Britney, this isn't the time or the place," she said, her words as measured as she could make them.

Britney tapped one finger on the counter, then looked left and right. "The store isn't that busy, so it's the perfect time."

Her sister was right. The store's only customers were the ladies who'd just come in, and they were lost somewhere among the booths, away from the counter.

"Fine, but keep your voice down," she said, careful to keep her own voice low as she issued the warning. She didn't need customers overhearing her bizarre family drama.

"I've been stewing over this for two days, and Hunter thinks I need to just confront you and get it off my chest."

"You've been discussing this with your husband?"

Britney lifted her chin. "Yes. We have no secrets between us. He knows all about Brent's transgressions."

"So you've been telling Hunter you're upset that your sister is friends with your ex-boyfriend?"

"Exactly."

"Doesn't he find your obsessing over this ridiculous?"

Britney's nostrils flared. "He thinks perhaps I should let it go, but this is *not* ridiculous. I'm concerned about you." She paused. "And I'm offended that you could have anything to do with Brent. Your allegiance should be to *me*." She pointed to her chest. "Not *him*. The man who cheated on me."

Christine blinked as she realized Britney had just admitted the truth. Her sister was upset that she wasn't defending her. She suddenly recalled what Pam said. *"Britney is great, but she's conceited and all*

174

about herself. She's always been that way . . . Britney's narcissism could be the real reason she and Brent didn't work out. But you and Brent make sense, and you shouldn't let your self-absorbed twin ruin that for you."

Christine suddenly felt as if she were seeing her sister through fresh eyes. As usual, Britney was making something all about her, and Christine was ready for something to be about her for once.

Britney looked offended. "Why are you staring at me like I'm some kind of joke?"

"Did it ever occur to you that Brent *didn't* cheat?"

Britney's mouth opened and then closed before she could finally speak. "Why would you say that to me?"

"Because he told me what happened when you two broke up. You were *told* he'd cheated, but it wasn't true."

"Yes, it *was* true. Grant Fahey gave me the whole story. He'd been at a party in Chapel Hill with Brent, who was all over some redhead!"

"Did you ever bother to ask Brent for his side of the story?" Christine tapped the counter. When her sister only stared at her, she continued. "No, you didn't. You didn't even have enough faith in him to ask if Grant's story was true. He had no idea why you ghosted him until I told him the other night."

Britney scowled. "And you believe him over me, your twin sister?" She pointed to her chest again.

"Yes. I don't believe he's the villain you've always made him out to be. If you could see him taking care of his aunt, you'd agree with me. He's a good guy, Brit. You were misled all those years ago, and I think it's time you faced the truth. You're the one at fault. You're the one who never gave the man who'd always been loyal to you a chance to prove Grant was lying."

"I can't believe you're taking Brent's side," Britney hissed. "We always said it was sisters before misters."

Christine shook her head. "You're not listening to what I'm saying. Brent told me Grant once said he'd steal you away from him. It's obvious that Grant made up that lie to convince you to break up with Brent, and it worked." She tilted her head. "Did you date Grant after that?"

"Of course not! He did ask, but I was too heartbroken to trust any guy for a while. I didn't date anyone until I met Hunter about a year later."

"You need to admit you messed up with Brent."

Britney narrowed her eyes. "Chrissy, Brent *cheated* on me, and he's *lying* to you. You're so gullible!"

"Keep your voice down," Christine snapped. "And no, I'm not gullible. Brent was emotional when he told me the story. Genuine. *You* hurt *him*, not the other way around."

"How could you tell he was genuine? You don't really know him."

"I know him well enough. We've become good friends, and we're working together for a common goal—to help his aunt and my store. I already told you about my rent going up. Plus, I enjoy helping Aunt Midge. She reminds me of Nana." She felt a tug at her heart as she pictured her precious grandmother. "Anyway, I'm going back to her house this weekend to continue clearing out her basement."

When her phone chimed, she pulled it from her pocket and found a text from Brent.

I did it. I met with Coach Morgan.

Christine grinned as warmth surged in her chest. Brent had taken her advice!

"Who's that?" Britney asked.

Christine shook her head. "No one."

Britney leaned over the counter and plucked the phone out of Christine's hand.

"Hey! What are we? Sixteen?"

Britney glowered as she read the text. "What does this mean?"

"If it's any of your business, which it is *not*, Coach Morgan asked Brent to volunteer as an assistant coach. Brent wasn't sure he wanted to, but I've been encouraging him to give it a try." She held out her hand. "Britney Sofia Davenport, give me my phone *now*."

Her sister's glare hardened. "Why do you care what Brent does?"

"Because that's what friends do." Christine reined in her temper. She couldn't allow herself to lose it in her store. She had to be professional.

"I think it's more than that. How could you have feelings for my ex?" Britney said, her tone even more demanding.

Christine stared at her sister as the hurt she still carried exploded inside her. She was tired of being in Britney's shadow, and she was ready to break free.

"Not everything is about you, Britney." Her voice sounded raw, and her body quaked with emotion. "I can have a life even though I'm not the pretty one or the prom queen."

Britney's mouth dropped open, and her eyes filled with tears. "So you think I'm awful?"

A ribbon of guilt wrapped around Christine's conscience even as anger still burned her chest. "I didn't say that."

"But now I see the truth," Britney continued, her voice thick, tears forming. "You're choosing Brent over me, and that's because I'm right. You like him as more than a friend."

"I-I never said that."

"You didn't have to. I can tell you want to be with him." Britney sniffed. "You've chosen a cheat over your twin." She lifted a finger.

"Mark my words, Christine. He'll hurt you, and you heard it from me first."

One of the customers who'd been browsing the store appeared at the end of a nearby aisle. "Excuse me. I'd like to purchase a wardrobe I found at the back of the store."

Christine whipped a smile into place. "I'll be right with you, ma'am."

"Thank you," the woman said before dividing a look between the twins and then disappearing back into the aisle.

Christine turned back to her sister, anger boiling in her gut. Britney still thought this was about her. *"So you think I'm awful?"* she'd said.

"I need to get back to work."

"Fine. I need to go anyway." Britney pushed her sunshine-tinted hair off her shoulder before stomping out of the store.

Christine squared her shoulders and trekked to the back, then helped her customer purchase the large cherry cabinet. She was grateful the woman had called her husband, who soon arrived to load the wardrobe into his pickup truck.

When the store was quiet again, Christine texted Brent back. *Sorry for the delay. It's been busy. I'm proud of you.*

Conversation bubbles appeared immediately.

Thanks. You inspired me. Are you going to the game tonight?
Yes.
I'll be on the sidelines with the team, but I'll see you after.
Sounds great.

Christine locked her phone and slipped it into her pocket as another customer entered the store.

"Welcome to Treasure Hunting," she called as she tried to turn her focus back to business, but aggravation with her sister still nipped at her.

Then excitement twined through her. Tonight she'd get to enjoy time with Brent despite what her selfish sister believed.

Britney was right about one thing, though. She *was* falling for Brent, and that scared her. Not only did he plan to leave Flowering Grove, making a relationship nearly impossible, but he was coming between her and her only sibling. Christine closed her eyes as she recalled the hurt expression on her sister's face. As much as she resented Britney's attitude, she couldn't risk losing her, nor her precious M&Ms.

eighteen

"Well, you can't win them all," Steve said with a sigh as the game ended.

Pam frowned. "That's true, but it was still a good game."

And an exciting game. Of course, if Christine were honest, she'd have to admit she spent more time watching Brent down on the sidelines than watching the players. He looked so very good wearing a Falcons light-blue jacket and hat—and like a really, really handsome coach back in his element. Each time he faced the stands, she spotted a smile on his face.

Although she was disappointed that the Falcons lost to the Parkland Pirates thirty-four to twenty-four, Christine was grateful the game was over. Now she could spend time *with* Brent. Taking the last sip of her Diet Coke, she watched both teams jogging past each other on the field, slapping hands.

"We told Brent we'd wait for him by our truck in the parking lot," Pam said as fans filed down the bleacher stairs.

"Okay." Christine pushed herself up from the hard metal seat—having once again forgotten her cushion—then followed Pam and Steve down the stairs, depositing her empty can in a recycling bin as they made their way.

Her phone buzzed as they approached Steve's SUV. She pulled it from her pocket, and her lips tipped up in a smile when she found a text from Brent.

Meet me by the athletic wing entrance instead? Steve and Pam won't mind.

Pam grinned. "Is that Brent?"

"Yes. If it's okay with you, I'll meet him over by the athletic wing." Christine nodded across the large parking lot.

"Sure it is." Steve took Pam's hand. "I'd like to go find my brother and nephew anyway."

Christine texted *See you soon*, and then Pam pulled her in for a hug. "Have fun," she whispered.

Christine gave her best friend a light smack as she laughed. "See you later."

After saying goodbye to Steve, Christine plodded across the lot, dodging groups of fans as well as cars waiting in line to exit the lot. Teenagers called to each other and car horns tooted as the evening air once again held a mixture of exhaust and the lingering traces of food from the concession stand.

As Christine drew closer to the building, she eagerly quickened her pace. She'd missed Brent the last couple of days! Her painful conversation with Britney lingered at the back of her mind, but she tried her best to shove it out. She'd find a way to make peace with her sister—somehow.

As Brent jogged out the building's door, she realized she yearned to talk to him after her argument with her sister. She needed him.

And Britney was right. She did have feelings for Brent. In fact, she was falling in love with him.

She swallowed back a groan. She'd agreed to be just friends, and she had to rein in these feelings. Starting a relationship before Brent returned to Virginia was a ridiculous idea—and Britney's consternation was a nearly insurmountable problem.

Still, deep in her heart, Christine believed her sister's interference was unfair. She'd misjudged Brent.

"Christine. Hi." Brent closed the distance between them and pulled her in for a warm hug.

She wrapped her arms around his waist and drew him closer, closing her eyes and longing to stay in his arms.

When he released her, she smiled up at him. "You look great in the school colors, Coach," she said, gesturing toward his jacket and hat.

"Thank you." Brent jerked his thumb in the direction of his aunt's house. "Would you like to come over to Aunt Midge's for a while?"

"Definitely."

"Great. I want to show you something."

"Okay."

When his smile warmed, her stomach fluttered with the wings of a thousand butterflies. Oh yes, her heart was doomed.

◆ ◆ ◆

"What do you want to show me?" Christine asked as she followed Brent down the basement stairs once they'd said hello to his aunt. She was reading in the family room.

He crossed to the far corner and started looking through the boxes. "I found some paintings the first time I came down here with Aunt Midge, and I remembered them earlier today. I want your opinion on them."

She looked so cute dressed in a pink hoodie and light-blue jeans while subtle makeup brought out the blue in her eyes. And he'd been so happy to see her that it seemed only natural to pull her into his arms. He was grateful she'd allowed him to hug her, but then she'd even wrapped her arms around his waist and pulled him closer.

The truth was he'd like to embrace her as often as possible before he had to leave. He'd also enjoyed their short walk. Any time spent with Christine was a gift. He just had to remember they'd never be more than good friends.

"Do you think your aunt moved them?"

Christine's voice brought him out of his thoughts just as he found the right box and motioned for her to join him. "Here they are. They hung upstairs in the family room when I was a kid." He pulled out one of the paintings and handed it to her.

Christine unwrapped the frame and then sucked in a breath. "This is just gorgeous."

"I know."

After he pulled over Aunt Midge's footstool, Christine sank onto it and turned the painting over. "There's paperwork in a little pocket back here—a certificate authenticating that this piece was painted by a Sonja Deveraux." She peered up at Brent, and her little nose scrunched. "I think I've heard of her."

"The name is familiar." Brent sat on the floor beside her, then retrieved the second painting. "This is a companion piece." He unwrapped the frame, then turned it over as well. "And it has the same paperwork on the back."

"Again, gorgeous. I wonder why your aunt took them down."

Brent shrugged. "I guess she wanted a change. Do you think they're worth anything?"

"Let's find out." Christine rewrapped the painting she held before gently setting it back in the box, then pulled her phone from her pocket. After a few moments she glanced up and smiled. "Come closer. We can look together."

He carefully stowed the second painting and then scooted next to her. She leaned against his shoulder, and he relished her body heat mixing with his.

"Here we go," she suddenly said. "Sonja Deveraux is a well-known American artist, and she passed away a few years ago." She scrolled some more, and her eyes rounded. "Brent, they must be worth a small fortune. Look at this."

He skimmed an article detailing the popularity and rarity of the artist's paintings. "Wow! I think you're right."

"You need to tell your aunt. She might want an art dealer to sell them for her. I wouldn't do them justice in my store."

"Let's go talk to her now."

Brent lifted the box and followed Christine upstairs, where Aunt Midge seemed to be sorting a stack of books on an end table.

"I was just choosing some books to donate to the library. I won't be able to take many with me to the condo." Aunt Midge nodded toward Brent's box. "What have you got there?"

He and Christine sat down on the sofa, and he pulled out the paintings. "I found these Sonja Deveraux paintings you used to hang in here." He unwrapped the first one, then gently placed it on the coffee table. "They were shoved in one corner of the basement."

"Is that where those wound up? I've wondered what your uncle did with them when we redecorated this room. I would have guessed up in the attic."

"Chris and I just researched the artist online, and she passed away a few years ago." He placed the second painting beside the first.

"Is that right?" Aunt Midge pushed herself out of her recliner and studied them as she stepped closer. "She was so talented. Your uncle and I always liked her work, and he surprised me with these one Christmas. I was tickled pink!"

Christine touched the golden frames. "It looks like they could be worth a lot of money."

"Well, they won't work in the condo, so I'd like you to sell them at your store." Aunt Midge patted the edge of the coffee table, then sat in her chair again.

Brent stared at her. "Are you certain? If Uncle Sal bought these for you as a special gift, I'm sure they're still special to you." He shared a look with Christine before returning his attention to Aunt Midge, who smiled.

"Brent, I have plenty of memories more precious than these paintings. Just like with the tea sets."

Christine leaned forward. "But I'm no expert on paintings, and I wouldn't even know how to price them. I suggest you contact an art dealer."

Aunt Midge gestured toward Brent. "Then pull out that fancy phone of yours and find one. There has to be an art dealer in Charlotte."

Brent pulled his phone from his pocket and started searching. When he found what appeared to be a reputable dealer, he looked at Christine. "Here's one. Would you like to go with me if I make an appointment?"

"I'd love to. When?"

He studied the gallery's hours. "They're open tomorrow. I have to be at the school at eight to review game tapes, but I can go in the afternoon."

"I'll ask my mom or sister to run the store for me."

"Great. I'll call first thing in the morning and let you know." He stood. "Did you leave your truck at the school?"

Christine shook her head. "I rode with Pam and Steve."

"So you were planning to ask me for a ride?" He couldn't help teasing her.

She gave him a coy smile he was sure Aunt Midge didn't miss. "Maybe."

"I'd better get you home, then. It's getting late."

Christine said good night to Aunt Midge, and then they walked out to his truck and climbed in.

Once they were on the road, Christine said, "I'd like to ask you something." He glanced at her, and she tilted her head as her expression grew pensive. "How do you feel after your first football game as an assistant coach?"

He turned his eyes back to the road. "That seems like a loaded question."

"Oh, I thought maybe . . ."

He gave her another glance, and now she looked embarrassed. "I'm just kidding, Chris. You seem to know me better than anyone else." And that truth he found surprising. "It was strange to be back."

"Strange how?"

"After my unsuccessful knee surgeries, I never thought I'd be back on a football field."

"And how did it *really* feel?"

He slowed to a stop at a red light and met her inquisitive gaze. "It felt good. I'd forgotten how much I loved the camaraderie."

"Yay!"

She clapped her hands, and she was so adorable that he laughed! Then she took his hand in hers. "I knew it would be good for you. I'm so glad you made that decision."

"You're the reason I did, and I'm grateful."

She smiled and then pointed at the windshield. "The light is green."

"Oh." He motored through the intersection, passing her store before turning onto Linwood Avenue. "How did your sidewalk sale go today?"

She sighed. "I guess it was okay, but I was hoping for better results. I'm starting to wonder if I should raise the booth rent after all. I still don't want to because I'll risk driving my vendors out, but I might not have a choice."

"How is your rent compared to stores like it in the area?"

"I did some research, and it's about average."

Christine told him about some other ideas she'd brainstormed to bring in more revenue, and when he turned onto Zimmer Avenue, he wished he could have found a longer route. He parked in her driveway, then killed the engine, unbuckled his seat belt, and angled his body toward her.

"All we did was deal with those paintings, but I still had a really nice time tonight," he said.

"I did too." She grabbed her purse from the floorboard and then faced him. "I wanted to tell you something earlier, but we got wrapped up—"

His phone was ringing, and he heaved a deep sigh as he pulled it from his jacket pocket. Tara's name was on the screen. Why? She'd said she'd wait until he was ready to talk—though he doubted he'd ever be ready.

He gritted his teeth as he declined the call.

When he lifted his eyes, Christine's brow had wrinkled. "Who's Tara? Sorry, but I could see her name on the screen."

"Someone from my past, but she's not important to me anymore." While he trusted Christine, he'd save the story of how Tara and Doug had humiliated him for another day. "I'm sorry about that. What did you want to tell me?"

"I had a . . . a disagreement with my sister earlier today."

"And you want to talk about it?"

She settled back in the seat and let her purse drop to the floor. "She's still upset that you and I are—that we're friends."

"What happened?"

"She gave me the third degree about being at Aunt Midge's house the other night, once again insisting you're a cheat." She held up her hands. "I told her your side of the story, but she didn't believe it. Then she accused me of choosing you over her."

Guilt swamped him. He'd never meant to cause Christine trouble with her sister. "I'm so sorry."

"Why? You didn't do anything wrong. Britney is the one with the problem."

He rubbed his forehead. "But the last thing I want to do is cause a rift."

She frowned and picked at a seam in her jeans. "It's not your fault. But I've reached a point where I'm beyond tired of how Britney treats me." She paused for a moment, closed her eyes, and then opened them, keeping her attention on her lap. "I'm tired of everything being about her. She was always the prettiest girl in the room—the most popular, the fashionista with all the latest styles, the prom and homecoming queen. And I was always lost in her shadow."

"That's not true—at least it isn't now."

She met his gaze.

"Christine, I've already told you this once. You're just as beautiful as Britney is—if not more so."

The intensity in her eyes sent a sudden rush of desire through his body, and a yearning to kiss her grabbed him by the throat. When he cupped his hand to her cheek, she leaned over the center console and into his touch.

And then he sat frozen as his heart pounded.

Christine straightened her neck, removing her face from his touch. "Enough about my sister. So you'll pick me up sometime tomorrow afternoon? Assuming you've been able to make an appointment."

"Yes." The gravel now in his throat came out in the rasp of his words. He swallowed, working to calm his racing heart. "I'll text you the details."

She fetched her purse and then pushed open the door. "Good night, Brent."

"Good night."

She jumped down from the truck, shut the door, and hurried toward her front porch.

He started the engine but waited until Christine was in the house before backing out of her driveway. Then as he drove home, he pondered his complete shock that she'd perhaps put her relationship with her twin on the line. Aunt Midge was the only other person he'd ever known to go out on a limb for him like that. She'd defended him against his father's disappointed rants, and he was stunned at what Christine had done to defend him to Britney.

She cared about him—truly cared.

Brent merged onto Glen Avenue as he considered how important Christine had become to him. No, more than important. He marveled at how his body came alive when he touched her. He'd never experienced such an intense physical reaction to a woman—not with Britney and not with Tara. He found it mind-bending.

But Christine deserved someone better than him, and that reality tore at his soul. He could never have her as more than a friend, nor could he make the crack in her relationship with Britney even wider by acting on his true feelings. He had to accept that truth.

Still, he would cherish his time with Christine for as long as he had it, at least until he returned to Virginia. After that, he doubted he'd be able to bear staying in touch. It might be better to cut all ties, for her sake as well as his.

◆ ◆ ◆

Brent held the door open for her as Christine stepped out of the art dealer's gallery. "I think that went well," he said as they turned toward the parking lot where his pickup truck awaited them.

"I agree." Christine smiled. She'd love to hold his hand right now, but when he touched her cheek last night, she'd had to pull away before . . .

If only they could be more than friends. But too much stood in their way. The eventual distance between Flowering Grove and Virginia Beach. Her sister. Maybe Tara too. She still wasn't sure Brent's history with that woman wouldn't pull him away.

"Ms. Ramsey seemed impressed with the paintings," Brent said as they stepped into the parking lot.

"And certain that she'd have a buyer soon."

Brent unlocked the truck, then pulled open the passenger side door for her. "It sounds like they'll bring Aunt Midge a nice sum."

Christine climbed in and fastened her seat belt while Brent jogged around the truck.

When he hopped in beside her, he said, "We were so busy talking about the football team on the way here that I never asked you how things were with Britney when she arrived at the store to cover for you today. Did you talk to her about your disagreement?"

She frowned. "I would have, but she brought the girls with her and acted like nothing ever happened. She does that sometimes. It's like she can't handle really talking things through."

He nodded slowly. "She did the same thing to me when we disagreed or even argued. She'd just act like everything was fine, and then we'd move on." He paused. "Are you okay with her not discussing it with you?"

"I guess so." She shrugged. "We're never going to agree about you, so there really isn't anything to discuss. She'll continue believing you're a bad guy, and I'll continue knowing the truth."

"I don't like coming between you and your sister."

She touched his arm. "You're not. Britney and I will agree to disagree. As long as she minds her own business, it will be fine."

"I hope so." He leaned over and touched her cheek—again. "Thank you for coming with me today. I really like spending time with you."

Her heartbeat paused as she took in the heat in his golden eyes, but this time she had no intention of pulling away.

This is it. He's going to kiss me!

Her breath hitched as Brent leaned down, hesitated for a fraction of a second, and then grazed his lips against her cheek. But then he sat up, cleared his throat, and started the truck's engine. "I'm in the mood for coffee. What do you think?"

"Sure," she managed to say.

As Brent steered out of the parking lot, Christine took a deep breath, trying to slow her heart to a normal pace. If this was how a kiss on the cheek affected her, she couldn't help hoping she'd experience a real kiss from him someday.

nineteen

Disappointment flooded Christine as she parked her truck in Midge's empty driveway. She'd expected Brent to be home. When he dropped her off after their trip to Charlotte yesterday, she'd told him she'd be here to work on the basement by noon—with lunch in hand.

She gathered her purse and the bag with the food she'd prepared the night before, then made her way to the front porch. The inside door stood open a crack. After ringing the bell, she turned to peruse the front lawn. Two squirrels chased each other up a nearby tree while a blue jay ate from a black-and-white bird feeder shaped like a lighthouse. Then looking up, she took in the cerulean sky dotted with puffy white clouds and breathed in the fragrance of flowers.

"Come in, Christine!" Aunt Midge hollered from somewhere inside the house.

Christine pulled open the screen door and stepped into the family room. "Aunt Midge?"

"I'm in the kitchen."

Brent's aunt sat at the table flipping through a catalog.

"How are you feeling today?" Christine asked her.

"Just fine, sweetie. Brent's making a supply run. He decided he needed some paint today rather than waiting for Swanson's to open tomorrow. He said to start eating without him. Would you like some sweet tea? I made some earlier."

"I'd love some. How about I pour us both tea and then go ahead and make our sandwiches? I brought chicken salad."

Midge brightened and pushed her turquoise glasses farther up on her nose. "Chicken salad sounds fantastic. What else have you got there?"

"Brownies for dessert."

"Well, then. Let's eat!"

Soon they were enjoying their meal.

"I appreciate this delicious lunch," Aunt Midge said after swallowing a bite of her sandwich. Then she smiled. "I owe you a thank-you for something else as well. Brent has been in a wonderful mood since the football game Friday night and practice yesterday. That just proves what I already thought about you. You, darlin', are a genius."

Christine chuckled. "A genius?"

"Yes." Aunt Midge patted her arm. "I encouraged him to volunteer, but you were the one who convinced him. That was a brilliant way to help him remember how much he loves it here in Flowering Grove. Maybe now he'll decide to stay."

Christine's stomach dipped at the idea, then she lifted her fork to scoop up some chicken that had fallen out of her sandwich. "May I ask why his father is so hard on him?"

"Oh dear." Aunt Midge frowned. "Barry is a good man, but he's always expected a lot from his children, especially when it came to their education."

"Why is that?"

"He never graduated from high school, and with rather low-paying jobs, he and Donna have always struggled to pay their bills. So he wanted both Brent and Kylie to earn scholarships, then degrees, and find successful, high-paying professions. He's disappointed that

Brent not only lost his scholarship but dropped out of college altogether. I understand that he wanted him to earn a degree. Honestly, we all did. But Brent never planned to get injured, and then he made another choice—going into construction and home remodeling, the work he knew best from working with Sal."

Christine fingered her glass. "He needs to forgive Brent for that. He's successful even without a degree—and obviously highly skilled when it comes to home remodeling."

She didn't think she should mention Brent had lost his business in Virginia. For some reason she suspected his family didn't know about that yet.

"Exactly. But Barry's still focused on Brent finishing his education. He doesn't think construction is good enough."

Christine contemplated what Aunt Midge told her as she ate more of her sandwich, then asked, "Is he hard on Kylie too?"

"Not to the same extent. He always leaned more on Brent, including when it came to sports. I guess Barry was never athletic, and he tended to live his football dreams through his son."

Christine nodded slowly. "It sounds like Brent was always close to you and Mr. Marcello."

"With Barry's and Donna's parents gone, Sal and I became sort of surrogate grandparents to both Brent and Kylie. Sal loved spending time with those two, and so did I. We had them over as often as we could, especially Brent."

"He's lucky he has you."

Aunt Midge smiled. "I appreciate that. It's my dream to see him settle down here. I'm determined to convince him."

"I'd like that very much."

Midge wagged a finger at her. "And I know Brent likes *you* very much. He's always happy to see you. Excited, I'd say."

Christine's heart seemed to trip over itself, but she didn't want to let on how she really felt about Brent. "I'm always happy to see him too. We're . . . good friends."

"Uh-huh. Friends." Aunt Midge removed her glasses to clean them on the edge of her shirt. "So tell me about your store. How is it doing?"

As they finished their sandwiches, Christine was glad Brent's aunt hadn't pushed her to admit how she really felt about him, but she did feel close enough to her to share about her rent dilemma and attempts to ramp up business. The older woman was encouraging, just as she'd expected her to be. Then Christine brought the brownies to the table, and when they finished eating, she stored the leftover chicken salad in the refrigerator and placed their dishes in the dishwasher.

"Do you need anything before I get started in the basement?" Christine asked.

"No, thank you. I'll go read in my favorite chair, and you go on and have fun down there."

"Yes, ma'am," Christine said with a chuckle.

◆ ◆ ◆

"There you are!" Aunt Midge announced when Brent stepped through the front door. "I was wondering if you'd run off somewhere and forgotten about me."

Brent grinned. "I could never forget about you, Aunt Midge. You're one of my favorite relatives."

"Ha! I'm your *only* favorite relative."

He chuckled and set his paint can on the floor. "There was a line in the paint department at Home Depot, and then I had to wait to check out too." He nodded toward the basement door. "I saw Christine's truck in the driveway. Is she already at work?"

"Yes, and she brought the most delicious chicken salad and brownies I've ever had. We had a very nice meal—and we talked about you." Aunt Midge gave him a conspiratorial wink.

"Uh-oh." He groaned.

"Nothing bad." She waved him off. "Go make yourself a sandwich."

After depositing the paint in the master bathroom, he returned to the kitchen and washed his hands. Then he made a sandwich and took a bite before carrying his plate and two bottles of water down to the basement. Christine was sitting on the floor, rummaging through a box.

She beamed up at him. "You finally made it back. I was starting to worry you were lost. After all, you've been living in Virginia for a while, right?"

He smirked. "Ha-ha. Apparently, the entire county was at Home Depot today, and they were all buying paint." He held up half of his sandwich. "This is the best chicken salad I've ever had."

"I'm glad you like it."

He handed her a bottle of water and then sank onto the floor beside her.

"I seem to be working faster today, and I have to show you what I found." Christine reached into a container and pulled out a plate with a painted scene featuring a fireplace and a Christmas tree. "Isn't this gorgeous? I found the entire set, complete with serving dishes."

Brent grinned. "I remember these. Aunt Midge used them for Christmas Eve dinner every year when I was a kid."

"They're lovely, and I'm sure they'll sell quickly." She replaced the dish before opening another tote and pulling out a beautiful quilt. "I found four of these. I'll wash them and then display one of them on the stand I found at the yard sale."

"That's a great idea."

She pointed to yet another group of containers. "Two of those have Christmas decorations in them, and the other one has glassware—water glasses, wineglasses, and champagne flutes." She tilted her head. "Did your aunt do a lot of entertaining when she was younger?"

He swallowed another bite of his sandwich. "I believe so. She and Uncle Sal played cards with friends, and she was active in a book club. Most of her friends are widows now, like her, and living where she's going over in Oakboro."

"That makes sense." She stretched out her legs and then crossed them at the ankles before opening her bottle of water and taking a drink. "I also found an incredible record collection—the Beatles, the Monkees, Johnny Cash, Elvis, and Nat King Cole just to name a few. You might want to go through it before I take it away."

He shook his head. "I don't have a turntable or any place to keep records. Might as well sell them all."

"They will definitely sell."

"Good."

As Christine sorted through a box with some sort of porcelain figurines, Brent finished his sandwich. "I need to get to painting walls. I finally got everything torn out of the master bathroom, but I've only painted the ceiling."

"Do you need help?"

He hesitated. "Are you serious?"

"Why not? I've painted before, and I'm pretty good at it, if I do say so myself."

He eyed her with pretend suspicion as he stood. "I don't know,

Christine. You're a risk. For one thing, you might not approve of my color choice. It's not magenta."

"It isn't? Oh no." She pressed her hand to her chest.

He chuckled. "I talked Aunt Midge into a pretty light green."

Christine looked surprised. "Really?"

"Really." He studied her. "And do you really want to help? Or are you just teasing me?"

She popped up from the floor. "I really want to help. I could use a break, and I'm already wearing old clothes."

"Let's go, then," he said before following her to the stairs. "But that T-shirt still looks too nice for painting. Let me see if I have one that will work."

Brent found a faded concert T-shirt he'd stuffed into a drawer, and Christine changed in the small powder room toward the front of the house while he found another paintbrush in the garage. Then they taped off the woodwork and ceiling in the master bathroom and started painting.

Brent silently marveled at what a great team they made, and conversation seemed to flow between them without any stress. Had he ever felt this comfortable with a woman?

When they finished the first coat, Christine stood in the middle of the bathroom, and Brent tried in vain not to stare at her. But he couldn't help admiring how lovely she looked even in her old shorts and his shirt. He longed to pull his phone out of his pocket and snap a photo.

"You know what?" she asked. "I really like this green. It's bright, happy, and cheery."

He feigned relief as he wiped the back of his hand across his forehead. "I'm so glad you approve."

"You're lucky." She shook a finger at him. "If I didn't, I would make you go all the way back to Home Depot to buy another color."

"I really dodged a bullet, then," he quipped before moving into the hallway. "Let's go get a drink. I need one of your brownies too. I worked up an appetite."

"I think I might keep this shirt," she said as they padded toward the kitchen.

"It's yours."

"Really?"

"Yes." He laughed. "It looks great on you."

She blushed and looked down. She was just so cute.

Brent pulled two more bottles of water from the refrigerator and handed her one. "I'll wait a bit before doing the second coat."

"And I should get back to working downstairs."

"Oh no!" Aunt Midge bellowed from the family room. "Work is done for today."

Brent gave Christine a look and then led her to where his aunt sat in her recliner. "What do you mean?"

"You know what day it is, Brent Theodore Nicholson," she snapped.

"Your middle name is Theodore?" Christine whispered from behind him as she opened her bottle of water. "I never knew that."

"Aunt Midge," he began, "I'm in the middle of painting your bathroom. Can't I skip this week?"

Christine sidled up beside him and divided a look between him and his aunt. "What am I missing here?"

"We have a family dinner at his folks' place every Sunday night." Aunt Midge pointed at each of them. "You're both going."

By the sudden look in Christine's eyes, he realized she'd remembered him telling her about those. But did she remember him saying how much he dreaded them?

"I don't want to intrude," she said, probably just making an excuse. He couldn't blame her. Then she added, "I'll just stay here and work in the basement—as long as you don't mind my being here alone."

Aunt Midge shook her head. "You're not intruding."

"But my clothes—"

"No problem. We're a casual bunch, and Barry and Donna won't mind."

Christine turned to Brent, a knowing look in her eyes. She did remember. "You sure?"

"You heard the boss." He winked at her, and she grinned.

Maybe he'd actually enjoy the family dinner with Christine there. But no matter what, he was grateful she'd be at his side.

twenty

Sitting to Brent's right at his parents' dining room table, Christine scanned the paneled walls and took in the wide smile in his high school football portrait. Although his face had matured, Brent was still just as good-looking to her as he'd seemed back then—possibly more so since now she felt as if she truly knew him.

"How are your folks, Christine?" Mrs. Nicholson asked from across the table. "We haven't run into them anywhere for a while."

Christine sat straighter as she set her spoon in her bowl of chili. "They're well. Dad still works for the same IT company and stays busy. And Mom is still a language arts teacher and the cheerleading coach at Flowering Grove Middle School. She talks about retiring so she can spend more time with my twin nieces, but I think she still has a few years to go."

"And how old are your nieces? They're fraternal twins, right?"

"Yes, and they'll be five next month. I can't believe it." She turned toward Brent, and his warm smile sent a spark of electricity through her veins.

Aunt Midge held up her glass of water. "Brent has some exciting news."

He sent her a look of confusion. "I do?"

"Yes, silly," she said. "Tell your folks about your new job."

Mr. Nicholson leaned back in his chair. "So you're employed now?"

Christine reached under the table and placed her hand on Brent's. He gave it a gentle squeeze before threading his fingers with hers.

"What's the job, Brent?" Mrs. Nicholson asked with excitement.

He looked as if he finally realized what his aunt was talking about. "I'm an assistant football coach at the high school, working with the quarterbacks."

Mrs. Nicholson gasped. "You are?"

"I ran into Coach Morgan at the grocery store a while back, and he asked me to consider it." He turned to Christine, and his expression softened. "Christine encouraged me to give it a try."

"That's fantastic," his mother said. "I'm so proud of you."

"Is it full-time?" his father asked.

Brent ran his tongue over his teeth. "No, and it's voluntary. Not all the coaches are paid."

"Oh." Mr. Nicholson's interest returned to his cornbread. "So it's not a real job."

Brent's mother sobered but then beamed. "I think it's wonderful, son."

"Yes, it *is*." Aunt Midge's tone couldn't be much more emphatic. "He's an inspiration to those young men on the team. We should all be proud."

But Brent was frowning down at his chili. The damage had already been done, and sadness swirled in Christine's chest. She gave Brent's hand a squeeze, but he didn't look up.

"You should get a coaching job that pays," Mr. Nicholson continued. "Then you could at least put all those years playing football to good use. What *do* you plan to do after you finish your aunt's house?

When I asked you about work before, you said it was complicated. What does that mean?"

Brent met his father's pointed look with a glare. "I didn't want to get into this, but I no longer have my own business. It didn't work out with my partner. But I do have an interview with a construction company in Virginia Beach lined up. It sounds like the job is mine. I just have to show up." His voice was low and rough, and his shoulders were stiff.

Seeing Brent so upset by his father's lack of support and tone nearly tore Christine in two. So before the man could grill him—the loss of Brent's business no doubt another failure in his father's eyes— she said a little too loudly, "Mrs. Nicholson, this chili is outstanding. I'd love the recipe."

Brent's mom looked surprised. "Why, thank you. I'll give you a copy."

"And did you make this cornbread from scratch?"

"Oh no." She chuckled. "It came out of a box."

"No kidding." Out of the corner of her eye, Christine could see Brent's shoulders relax. She'd managed to take the pressure off him, and she was grateful. "You'll have to show me what brand you buy. It's scrumptious."

Then she pulled Brent's mother into a conversation about recipes, and Aunt Midge joined in. Judging by the twinkle in her eyes, Christine surmised Brent's aunt knew exactly what she was doing. And it worked—although Mr. Nicholson sat with a scowl on his face for the rest of the dinner.

When it was time to leave, Christine gave Brent's mother a quick hug in the kitchen. "Thank you for a wonderful meal."

Mrs. Nicholson held on a moment longer. "Would you make me a promise?" she whispered in Christine's ear.

"Of course."

"Try to get Brent to stay in Flowering Grove."

"I'll do my best," Christine said as she stepped out of the embrace.

"I see how he looks at you, and I think you're the one who could convince him to move back here."

"Oh no." Christine peeked toward the doorway and lowered her voice. "We're just friends."

Mrs. Nicholson smiled. "You won't be for long. You have the power to get him to come home, and nothing would make me happier than to have him here. I'm hoping Kylie will return as well."

"Having them both back would be a blessing."

"Thanks for the chili, Mom," Brent said, suddenly appearing behind Christine. He rested his hand on her shoulder before giving it a gentle squeeze and then stepping where he could see her face. "You ready to go? Aunt Midge is all set, and I need to get that second coat of paint on the bathroom walls."

Christine smiled. "Yes, I am."

When she turned back to his mother, the older woman winked, then said, "I'll see you two again soon."

◆ ◆ ◆

"I'm sorry about my dad," Brent said as they stood alone in Aunt Midge's kitchen. As soon as they'd arrived at the house, his aunt had returned to her favorite chair to read. A romance novel, by the cover.

"Why are you sorry?" She frowned. "Your dad is the one who's wrong—not supporting you."

Brent snorted. "That's putting it mildly." Then he smiled and set his hand on her shoulder. "Thank you for redirecting the conversation."

A thrill raced through her at the intimacy of his touch. "I'm grateful I was there to do it." She nodded toward the hallway. "Would you like help with that second coat of paint?"

"No. I'm sure you're ready to get home."

"Would you help bring up my latest finds, then? Those records are really heavy."

"Nah. You can drag them up the stairs yourself." A grin played on his face as he pulled his hand away and stepped toward the basement door. "I'll bring up all the containers, but you'll have to bring your truck closer to the back door and lower your tailgate. I can't do everything, you know!"

When they returned to the kitchen after loading, Christine bit her lip. "Did you mean it when you said I can have that T-shirt?"

"You really want that old thing? It's completely faded. You can hardly read the name of the band."

She gave him a sheepish smile. "You said it looks better on me than on you, and that's why you should give it to me." Her heart seemed to turn over as she recalled the compliment.

"Of course you can have it. I'll get it and meet you in the family room."

Christine sank onto the sofa across from Aunt Midge's chair. She'd abandoned her book, and a commercial for a local car dealership flashed on the TV screen.

"How is work in the basement going?" Midge asked as she muted the sound.

"Before I took that break to help paint your bathroom, I found some wonderful items for the store. Brent just loaded several containers in my truck, and I separated out other items for him to donate or toss."

"I appreciate it so much. And thank you for being so good to my nephew."

Christine nodded. "You're welcome."

Brent came in and tossed the T-shirt to Christine. "I found it. Enjoy."

"I plan to." She stood and touched Aunt Midge's arm. "Good night, and I'll see you soon."

"I look forward to it."

Brent escorted her out the back door, and she breathed in the cool September air as she gazed up at the dark sky sparkling with stars. It was the perfect evening. She longed to drop the tailgate again and sit on it with Brent, talking until the sun rose. But he had a bathroom to paint, and she had containers to unload at the store.

She swallowed a sigh. This time together had come to an end much too quickly.

Brent leaned against the side of the truck and tapped it with his hand. "Do you want me to follow you to the store and help you unload all this?"

"No thanks. I can handle it with no stairs to negotiate."

"You sure?" He looked unconvinced. "Like you said, those records are heavy."

"I'll use a dolly. You forget I'm an expert."

"Or you're just really, really stubborn." He grinned as he took her hand in his, then pulled her close.

Her breath caught as she looked up at him, feeling the strongest attraction yet. Staring at his lips, she once again imagined what it would be like if they brushed against hers.

Brent's expression grew serious. "Thank you for everything you did today."

"You don't have to keep thanking me," she managed to say.

"I want to." He gave a weighted pause, his lips only a breath away from hers.

She watched his eyes drop to her lips, and her heart pounded. *Kiss me, Brent! Kiss me now!*

But he cleared his throat and then brought his gaze up to meet hers as he took a step back. "Well, I'd better go. Be safe driving home."

Another crush of disappointment surged through her. "Good night."

He waited until she was inside her truck before walking toward the back of the house. Normally he'd wave as she drove away, but tonight he almost seemed eager to get away.

Regret squeezed her chest. Had she done something wrong? Or was he struggling with feelings for her too?

She had no idea as she sighed and started her engine. She might never feel Brent's lips on her own, but she could sleep in his T-shirt tonight and enjoy his familiar scent. And that was something.

◆ ◆ ◆

Christine leaned against the doorframe as she peered into Aunt Midge's master bathroom, the midmorning sun streaming through its small window. She took in the fresh, light-green walls and brand-new commode, towel racks, and gorgeous light-wood vanity with a matching mirror. A pretty white-and-green-plaid shower curtain hung over the new tub, and a new white hamper sat in the corner on top of the luxury vinyl plank flooring.

"You do good work, Nicholson," Christine muttered into the room.

During the past two weeks, she and Brent had spent time together whenever she was here to work on clearing the basement, teasing each other and laughing. She'd also attended an away high school football game with Pam and Steve, and the four of them enjoyed a late dessert afterward. They'd texted nearly every day, and Brent had even been comfortable enough to give her a few hugs or take her hand.

But no more near kisses, not even on the cheek.

She'd enjoyed every moment with Brent, yet she was disheartened that their relationship hadn't progressed even though she'd agreed to just be friends. She still hoped he'd confess that his feelings for her ran deeper and decide to stay in Flowering Grove. But the likelihood of that happening faded a little more each day.

And in her heart she still knew their agreement was for the best. After all, Brent had made it clear he wasn't staying, and she still had the complication of her sister's blatant disapproval of even their friendship.

Her stomach tightened at the thought of Brent walking out of her life forever, and she spun and barreled into the hall, hoping to leave her bleak thoughts behind.

She entered the second guest bedroom, where Brent was spackling holes in the walls. The woodwork was covered in painter's tape, and the furniture was arranged in the center of the room, covered in plastic.

Once more, she took in his physique. Trim waist, muscular legs, sculpted biceps. He was just so gorgeous. When he turned toward her and smiled, her face warmed. Had he sensed her staring at him? Actually, it was more like gawking.

"What's up?" He swiped his arm over his forehead, ruffling a few of his curls.

Christine shifted her weight from one foot to the other. "I just finished sorting through everything in the basement, and I'm ready to take a huge load to the donation center."

"Cool. It's open on Mondays, right?" When she confirmed it was, he said, "Let me finish up here, and then we'll go in my truck."

After they nearly filled his truck's bed with bags, they checked on Aunt Midge and then headed out. Hard-rock music rang through the truck's speakers as Christine rolled down her window and allowed the late-September breeze to fill the cab. Someone was using their fireplace. She loved the smell of burning firewood.

When she stole a glance at Brent, she found him smiling at her. "Why are you looking at me like that?"

"You look so cute enjoying the fall weather in your pink hoodie. It's one of my favorites."

She smiled, warmed by the compliment.

When they arrived at the donation center, Christine climbed into the truck bed, then handed the bags to Brent and the attendant. A few minutes later they motored out of the parking lot, and Brent steered onto Wyckoff Avenue but continued straight instead of merging onto Maple Street toward Aunt Midge's house.

Christine pushed a lock of hair behind her ear. "Where are we going, Brent?"

"You'll see." A spark lit his eyes.

Christine settled back on the bench seat, resting her arm on the door handle as the engine hummed and the music entertained them.

After a short ride, Brent turned onto an unpaved road, and they bounced past a row of trees until they came to a clearing. He parked and then shut off the engine.

"Where are we?"

"You trust me, right?"

"Of course."

"Then follow me."

They met by the front bumper, then Brent held out his hand and she allowed him to pull her down a beaten path lined with a variety of tall trees she was able to name—oak, Bradford pear, yellow poplar, sweetgum, and maple. When they came to another clearing, Christine's eyes widened as she took in the beautiful view. Trees seemed to stretch for miles.

"Brent, this place is beautiful," she gushed. "How did you find it?"

"It was by accident, actually, thanks to a flat tire. But I used to love coming here to think. You should see it when the leaves change. It's breathtaking." He gave her hand a gentle tug. "Let's walk."

Their shoes crunched the already fallen leaves along the path as Christine looked up at the bright-blue sky. Birds sang nearby, and the air was fresh and clean. The humidity had disappeared a week ago. She felt completely transported despite the traffic rumbling in the distance.

She pulled her phone from the back pocket of her jeans, released her hand from Brent's grip, and pulled up her camera app. "Smile."

"Oh no." He grimaced before pushing both hands through his messy hair. "I've needed a haircut since I got here."

"Don't you dare touch those curls. Now smile."

His lips tipped up, and she took a few shots of him before he held out his hand. "Let me take one of you."

"No. I want a selfie with both of us." She handed him the phone and then stepped beside him.

Brent wrapped his arm around her shoulders, pulling her against him, then snapped a few shots. She relished being so close to him.

She slipped her phone back into her pocket as Brent pointed to a small hill.

"Want to sit and enjoy this view for a bit?"

"That would be perfect."

If only they could stay there forever.

twenty-one

As Christine sat next to Brent enjoying the lovely scenery, she hugged her knees to her chest and relaxed.

Brent rested his right elbow on his bent knee and tilted his head toward her. "I'm stunned you finished clearing out the basement. I thought it would take more time."

"I did too." She almost told him she wished it had so they'd have more time together, but that might push the conversation into desperate territory. "If you have time today, maybe we can take all the rest to the store. I'll put what won't fit in the booth in my storeroom."

"We can definitely make time for that."

She studied his profile, longing to read his thoughts. "How's football practice going?"

"It's going well." He picked at a blade of grass. "I'm enjoying getting to know the guys and working with the quarterbacks to help their focus and confidence. It's actually fun." He tossed the blade and then ripped out a few more.

"Could you see yourself coaching long-term?"

"I don't know. That's a big commitment."

"But I'm sure you're making a difference in those young men's lives. That means a lot."

He gave a dramatic sigh. "There you go working your psychology on me again, Sawyer."

She gave his shoulder a gentle push. "I'm just telling you the truth. You're a good man, and those guys look up to you."

He moved the blades of grass through his fingers.

"I peeked in your aunt's bathroom today," she said. "I like it."

"So you still approve of the green walls?"

"Yes, I do. You're both talented and skilled, Nicholson. You do a phenomenal job."

"Thanks." He tossed the grass onto the ground and rested his chin on his palm. "I've decided to paint all the rooms in the house. I'm also considering upgrades in the kitchen. It's just a huge undertaking."

She stared out toward the trees. *But it would keep you in Flowering Grove longer.*

"What's on your mind, Chris?"

She swallowed and decided to just tell him. "Why won't you consider staying here?"

He drew in a long breath. "It's complicated. I have no idea where I would live, and I don't have a steady income so no one would want to rent to me. Plus, I'd have to deal with my father's disappointment in me on a regular basis, and I don't want that kind of stress in my life." He leaned back on his hands. "It's just better if I go back to Virginia and try to rebuild my life there. I still have the rented room at Devonte's."

"But you could start another company remodeling houses here."

"With what money?" He scoffed. "You know what it takes to start a business. The only money I have is from what I sold after I moved out of the house I was renting. It's not enough to buy equipment, supplies, and everything else I'd need. Aunt Midge has offered me my uncle Sal's tools, but that wouldn't be enough."

She nodded despite her disappointment. It seemed she'd never convince Brent to stay, but as far-fetched as that dream was, she still held on to a thread of hope that he might—for her.

"I appreciate the faith you have in me, Chris, but after what I went through, I don't think I'll ever own another business." He sat up and clapped his hands together, wiping off the dirt and grass.

"What happened with your business partner?"

"I told you. He ran our business into the ground."

"You did, but you sounded like more happened there—something personal."

Brent eyed her. "You're very perceptive, Sawyer." Then he frowned. "Doug and I were friends at Chapel Hill. After we both dropped out, he wanted to start a home remodeling business together. We got along well, and he taught me a lot of what I know about remodeling. I trusted him, and at one point I considered him my best friend. But then he did the worst thing possible."

"What?"

"I caught him with my girlfriend." He picked up a rock and tossed it.

Christine gasped. "No!"

"Oh yeah." He flinched. "I'll spare you the details, but it was one of the worst days of my life"—he pointed to his left leg—"aside from when I wrecked my knee, which led to losing my college football career and scholarship."

She began putting the pieces together in her mind. "So Tara is the ex-girlfriend."

"Bingo." He held up his finger and grinned. "You pay attention."

"And she keeps texting and calling you, begging for your forgiveness."

Brent's smile dissolved. "Yes."

"Have you responded to her?"

"No. I've been avoiding her. I texted her back once, on the day Aunt Midge was in the ER, and I said I'd talk to her when I'm ready. She said she'd wait, but she hasn't. I've considered blocking her, but I know how it feels when someone does that. I can't bring myself to do it, no matter what she did to me."

"Do you think you'll forgive her and give her another chance?"

He shook his head. "I could never trust her again, and I don't feel the same way about her anyway." He hesitated. "Besides, it's not the best time for me to get into a relationship. I have nothing to offer a woman—no home, no stability, no real future. Why would any woman want to get involved with me?"

Because I love you. "You have plenty to offer a woman."

He snorted.

"And you'll have that job in Virginia just like that." She snapped her fingers. "But I think you need to start another business. On your own this time."

"We've already been over this. What would I start one with?"

"Your skill. You'd find the money somehow."

He shook his head and bumped his shoulder against hers.

A comfortable silence fell between them as a couple of squirrels raced past.

"Christine, you told me you're married to your store, but did you date much in the past?" he asked, his warm, rich voice breaking through the silence.

She shrugged. "Some, especially in college. But none of those relationships stuck."

"You just never found the right man?"

"I never seemed to click with anyone. So I decided to just concentrate on my store and my family. Especially my nieces."

He seemed to study her, his expression serious. "Do you want to get married and have a family someday?"

"Sure. If I find someone who wants to build a life with me."

Their gazes locked, and her mouth dried as the air seemed charged somehow. She stilled, waiting for Brent to reach for her as goose bumps chased each other down her arms.

But then he stood, and the moment was gone. He wiped his hands down his jeans before holding them out to her. "We should get back, have a quick bite, and then load up my truck with everything for the store. Then if you want, I can stay to help you sort out what you want to put into the booth right away versus keep in the storeroom."

"Okay," she said, trying to calm her racing pulse. "I'd like that." She took his hands, and after pulling her to her feet, he looped his arm around her shoulders and pressed her against his side.

As she leaned into him, she wondered if she'd really never be with this man with whom she longed to build a life. But he planned to leave her, and she knew it.

◆ ◆ ◆

Christine unlocked the store's back door ninety minutes later, then lured Wanda and Pietro into the breakroom with food before meeting Brent at her truck. "The ferocious felines are secured."

"So you finally agree with my assessment of them?" He grinned as he dropped the tailgate.

She rested her hands on her hips and narrowed her eyes. "Did you take your allergy medicine?"

"Yes, ma'am," he quipped before tapping the tailgate. "Why don't you climb up here and push the totes toward me? I'll carry them right to the booth, and then we can get started."

After transporting the containers from her truck and then his, they spent a few hours sorting out the items she wanted to display and pricing them. Then they carried the rest to the storeroom.

They'd just returned to the booth when the back door clicked shut. She spun to face Brent, concern gripping her. "Did you hear that?"

"Yes." Brent stood from where he'd been piling packing paper. "I'll go investigate."

"Hello? Christine?"

"It's my sister." Christine blew out a relieved breath. "Yes. We're back here," she called. "Aisle six." She turned to Brent, and an unreadable expression flashed over his face. He couldn't be happy about this, though.

A moment later Britney and Hunter traipsed down the aisle.

Christine waved at them, hoping both Britney and Brent would be civil. "Hey. What brings you guys here?"

Britney's gaze flickered to Brent, but she didn't react. Perhaps she'd put two and two together when she saw Brent's Virginia plates outside. "We were driving past the store when I noticed the lights were on. I asked Hunter to pull around back to see if you were here, and we saw your truck. But another one was backed up to the door. From out of state." She looked at Brent again and frowned, her "Hello" coming in a mere monotone.

"Britney." He nodded, his expression still impassive.

Christine took a step toward her brother-in-law. "Hunter, this is Brent Nicholson."

"Nice to meet you, Brent." He held out his hand, and the welcome seemed genuine.

Brent smiled as he shook it. "A pleasure."

"What are you two up to?" Hunter asked.

"We're unloading the last of Brent's aunt's things." She assumed he knew all about the project. "We've put out what we could fit in the booth, and the rest is in my storeroom. I'll add it after some of this sells."

Hunter walked over to the tools Brent had rejected as too antique to be of much use. "Check this out, Brit. I love antique tools."

"Oh no," Britney said in a teasing tone. "You know we don't have room for any of that."

Was she performing now? Christine shot Brent an apologetic look, and he gave her a warm smile as though he understood.

Britney turned her attention to Christine. "We were on our way to dinner. Hunter finished a job early, so we dropped the twins off at Mom's and decided to have a date night."

"You should join us," Hunter said. "A double date."

Britney pivoted and shot her husband a look.

Christine cringed. *Uh-oh.* That wasn't what her sister wanted. She'd only planned to catch her with Brent and make her displeasure known to them both.

Brent scrubbed his hands down his work clothes. "Thanks, but I was painting at my aunt's house this morning, and I'm not dressed to go out in public."

Hunter shook his head, ignoring his incensed wife beside him. "Nonsense. We were just going to the Barbecue Pit for an early dinner. Join us. I insist."

Brent turned to Christine as if asking for permission, but was that a spark of amusement in his eyes? It was!

She shrugged, deciding to play. "I'm not dressed the best either, Brent. But you once told me Carolina barbecue is your favorite."

"Yes, it is. And lunch seems like such a long time ago." He smiled at Hunter. "We'd love to."

Britney pursed her lips. "Wonderful," she said, her tone flat.

"We just need to clean up here, and then we'll be ready to go." Christine motioned toward the empty totes, packing paper, tags, and Sharpies littering the area.

Hunter rubbed his hands together. "How can we help?"

After the work was done, Hunter and Britney climbed into Britney's silver Chevrolet Equinox while Brent and Christine took their spots in his truck, leaving hers behind.

"Are you sure about this?" she said as he started the engine. "If you feel uncomfortable, we can come up with an excuse."

He reached over and rested his hand on her arm. "Do I look uncomfortable? I'm fine with it, and it's hilarious that she's not. I just didn't want to embarrass you in these clothes."

Christine grinned. "I think it's funny too. But I'm a little stunned that Hunter insisted we go. He normally does whatever Britney wants, and she clearly didn't want us to go." She paused. "Why are *you* so happy to be going?"

His eyes widened with fake suspicion. "Do you think I just want to stuff my belly with the Barbecue Pit's world-famous pulled pork?"

She snorted.

"Christine." He leaned closer. "I just want to spend more time with you. I'm always looking for excuses to do that, and I don't care if Britney is there too."

He pulled his phone from his pocket and handed it to her. "My password is five-nine-two-two. Do me a favor. Call Aunt Midge and ask her if we can bring her a plate."

Christine's heart warmed as she unlocked Brent's phone. She so admired how he cared for his aunt. He was such a thoughtful and caring man, and she'd be blessed to have him by her side for the rest of her life.

If only he'd give them a chance.

twenty-two

After confirming Aunt Midge wanted a barbecue platter, Christine and Brent had driven to the restaurant to meet Britney and Hunter in the parking lot. While they waited for a table, Christine and Britney talked about the twins, and Brent and Hunter discussed trucks before moving on to their favorite classic car models.

Christine was overcome with the irony of the situation—at how her brother-in-law and Brent were becoming friends, which had to irritate her sister. She tried not to laugh as she considered how even Hunter could see that Brent was a genuine guy, while Britney still insisted he was a cheat who'd wronged her and nothing more.

When their table was ready, they took their seats—each couple across from the other—and all ordered pulled-pork barbecue sandwich platters before the men returned to their easy conversation. Christine tried to find something else to discuss with Britney while pondering why it was easier for these two strangers to talk than for her to talk to her twin.

"What have you done at your aunt's house so far?" Hunter asked Brent after their food arrived.

"I've repaired the roof, remodeled the screened-in porch, and in her two full bathrooms, I ripped everything out and replaced it. The plumbing is upgraded too," Brent said before popping a hush puppy into his mouth.

Christine swallowed a bite of her sandwich. "And the bathrooms are gorgeous. You should see them."

Britney gave her a look before returning her focus to her plate, and Christine swallowed back her annoyance. Her sister needed to grow up. What happened between her and Brent was ancient history, and Brent did nothing wrong!

"Thank you," Brent said. "I'm painting the bedrooms now."

Hunter shook his head. "I don't envy you. Remodeling is a lot of work."

Britney lifted her gaze to her husband. "You did plenty of work to our house before we moved in, and then you remodeled the twins' room before they were born, installing those built-in shelves."

"But I didn't have to remodel our bathrooms. I can't imagine the work that takes, especially the plumbing."

Brent held up a finger. "Steve Barnes did that. I can't take credit for it."

"How is your aunt Midge?" Britney asked, changing the subject. "Christine told me she had a severe asthma attack that sent her to the emergency room."

Christine lifted her eyebrows as she forked coleslaw into her mouth. She couldn't detect whether her sister's motive for asking was born of genuine concern, but perhaps she'd do that growing up sooner rather than later.

Brent swallowed and then wiped his mouth with a paper napkin. "She's okay. She had a good checkup with her pulmonologist right after. She just needs to keep her inhaler with her at all times."

"I always liked your aunt. She's a hoot."

Brent nodded. "She certainly is."

Christine relaxed. Maybe her sister was finally seeing she'd been wrong about Brent and would accept Christine's friendship with him.

"And Hunter told me you're an assistant coach for the high school football team," Britney continued. "How's that going?"

Brent nodded while chewing some of his corn on the cob. "Really well," he said after swallowing, then smiled at Christine. "Your sister convinced me to do it, and she was right."

"Oh yeah? I was right, huh?" Christine said, teasing. "Could I please get that in writing?"

Brent grinned. "Don't push it."

Christine chuckled, but then she sobered when Britney gave her another look that said this might not be over.

"Seriously, though," Brent added, apparently oblivious to the expressions passing between the sisters, "it's been a good experience. I've enjoyed working with the two quarterbacks."

"The homecoming game is in a couple of weeks, right?" Hunter asked.

"A week from Friday." Brent turned to Christine. "You're going, right?"

She laughed. "Of course I am." Out of the corner of her eye, she could see Britney staring at her. "Why wouldn't I go?"

"I don't know. Maybe you'll be too busy washing your hair."

"Oh." Christine lowered her fork and tapped her cheek with her other hand. "Huh. You know, now that you mention it, I just might be." She poked him in the side, and he jumped with a start, which made her laugh again.

Brent turned back to Hunter. "Anyway, we're hoping to pull out a win. We've lost the past few games, but not by much."

Britney suddenly brightened.

"The committee has firmed up the plans for our ten-year reunion two days after Thanksgiving. It's going to be so nice." She glanced at Brent. "You both need to come."

Brent's posture grew rigid, and Christine's happy mood evaporated.

"We're having it at the Flowering Grove Country Club in that huge second-floor room with the balcony overlooking the golf course," Britney continued. "Remember when we went there for Felicia Rhodes's sweet sixteen? She invited everyone she knew just to show her parents could afford to have her party there. They were members too."

Christine nodded, sparing Brent the need to respond. "I remember that. You made me go, and I couldn't wait to leave. I felt so uncomfortable with none of my friends there."

"Anyway, Monique Douglas is on the reunion committee. Do you remember her?"

"Wasn't she one of your cheerleader friends?" Christine asked.

"Yes."

Brent lifted his glass of Coke. "I remember her. One of my football buddies dated her for a while."

"Right," Britney said. "Well, she's Monique Cartwright now and married to a surgeon. She got us a deal on the country club."

Britney lifted her glass of sweet tea as Hunter happily ate his barbecue, clearly unimpressed by his wife's enthusiasm. "The room will look amazing. We're decorating it with fairy lights, and we'll have high-top tables. Very classy. And you can take your drink and hors d'oeuvres onto the terrace and look out over the golf course." She took a sip of her own tea. "We're expecting a good crowd." This time she looked at Brent with a pointed stare.

"You know I'll be there," Christine told her, frantically trying to think of a way to stop what she feared would come next.

"And you'll be her date, right, Brent?" Her tone was measured as if she were daring him to say no. Or was she trying to prove to Christine that he wouldn't be sticking around?

As she divided a look between her sister and the man she loved, Christine's heartbeat nearly galloped.

Brent finished chewing, swallowed, and took a drink. Then he frowned, never taking his eyes off Britney.

"Well?" Britney asked in her most demanding tone. "Are you planning to take my sister to the reunion or not?"

"I won't be here," he finally said.

Christine's patience with her cantankerous twin wore thin. "Britney, give Brent a break."

"No. I want to hear his explanation. Why won't you be here, Brent?"

"I can tell you why. Because he plans to have his aunt's house done and on the market before Thanksgiving so he can return to Virginia. Let's talk about something else, okay?"

Britney glowered and then ducked her head to study her half-eaten sandwich.

"So, Hunter," Brent said, "where are you from?"

Hunter pushed his empty plate toward the end of the table. "I grew up not too far from here, in Oakboro."

As Brent shared that was where his aunt Midge planned to move, Christine lifted her corn and forced herself to take a bite. But her appetite had vanished as she tried to reject not only her exasperation with her sister but her disappointment in Brent. Britney had no right to give Brent the third degree, but Christine longed to hear Brent say he'd stay to take her to the reunion as his date.

No. As his *girlfriend*.

Brent and Hunter spent the remainder of the meal discussing

places Hunter had traveled with his family during summers, and Britney filled Christine's ears with stories of the twins' adventures in pre-K. But even hearing about Maddy and Mila's lives didn't soothe Christine's heart.

She was grateful when the server brought the checks, and after the men paid them, they all walked out to their vehicles together.

"Again, it was nice meeting you," Brent said as he shook Hunter's hand.

Hunter smiled. "I hope to see you again soon, at least before you return to Virginia."

Britney wrapped her arms around Christine and pulled her in for a tight hug. "I'm sorry for being tough on him," she whispered, "but I know he'll break your heart."

"Thanks for the support, sis," Christine hissed as she pushed away. She pivoted toward Hunter. "Give those girls a hug and kiss for me."

Hunter nodded. "I will, Chrissy."

Christine grabbed Brent's arm and steered him toward his truck. "Let's get out of here."

"Was the meal that bad?" he said, teasing her as he hit the button on his key fob.

"No." She sighed. "It's just my sister. She gets under my skin."

Brent pulled her door open and handed her the bag with his aunt's meal. "To be honest, I'm not surprised. You've already told me what she's said about me."

"Tonight she went too far."

Christine climbed in, and once Brent was in the driver's seat, he turned toward her. "Hunter seems like a great guy. He's super friendly."

"He's a saint," she grumbled.

He chuckled. "Don't let Britney get to you."

"It's tough sometimes. I just get sick of how she—" She clamped her mouth shut and rubbed her eyes. If she started complaining about her sister, she might not stop, and she couldn't allow Britney and her stupid comments to ruin her evening with Brent. After all, she didn't know how much time she had left with him, and she wanted to savor every moment.

"Chris?"

His gentle voice was close to her ear, sending a shiver ricocheting down her spine. She swallowed and looked at him.

"Want to talk about it?" His expression was open and sympathetic as he leaned even closer.

"No, but I want Dairy Queen."

He grinned, sat back, and started the engine. "Now you're talking. Let's get some on our way to Aunt Midge's. I'll get her usual. She always said dessert tastes even better when you eat it first."

As Brent drove out of the parking lot, Christine sent up a silent prayer. If only he would start a business in Flowering Grove, maybe time—and her sister—would give them the chance she longed for.

twenty-three

Brent's heart pounded as he stood on the sidelines at the homecoming game. Flowering Grove was pitted against the Ridgewood RedHawks. It was almost the end of the fourth quarter with only three minutes left on the clock, and the Falcons had possession of the ball. The score was tied at twenty-eight to twenty-eight.

The teams lined up, and Brent sucked in a breath as quarterback Eric Maloney shouted out the play. The center, Kent Jordan, snapped the ball to Maloney, who looked out over the field.

"You got this, Eric," Brent whispered. "You got this."

Maloney threw the ball, and it sailed through the air to the far end of the field where wide receiver Connor Tate caught the ball and started toward their goal line.

The crowd in the stands behind Brent went wild as he balled his hands into tight fists. Tate ran, skillfully dodging the RedHawks' defensive players as he glided toward the goal line. When Tate managed to slip past the last linebacker and make the touchdown, the crowd grew louder. The Flowering Grove Falcons had won!

They won! His hometown team, his alma mater, *his* team, had won!

Pride swelled in Brent's chest as he cheered with joy, and for the first time in years he felt connected to the community where he'd grown up. He couldn't take credit for the win, but he had been a part of it, and that felt good—so very good.

The band began to play, and an air horn sounded. The cheerleaders shook their pom-poms while the announcer congratulated the Falcons, and the team gathered in a circle, lifted Tate in the air, and cheered.

After high-fiving the other coaches, Brent faced the crowd in the packed bleachers and searched the sea of faces for Christine, Steve, and Pam. His phone vibrated in his pocket, and he pulled it out, thrilled to find a text from Christine.

Congratulations, Coach Nicholson.
Thank you, ma'am. Can't find you in the stands.

Conversation bubbles appeared immediately.

We're standing in the center section, halfway up. We'll wave our arms.

Brent searched again and spotted all three of them waving wildly. He waved back and then texted.

Meet me by the athletic wing again?
Yes!
I have a surprise for you.
Ooh! I love surprises!
See you soon.

He smiled to himself as he looked back toward the team. He couldn't wait to see Christine's face when he presented his surprise, but first he had to finish his coaching duties.

After walking the line with the team to slap hands with the RedHawks, Brent followed the players into the locker room, where Coach Morgan stood at the front of the group.

"Great job tonight, guys," he said. "You played hard, and your consistency paid off."

Everyone applauded.

"Now go enjoy yourselves, and I'll see you bright and early tomorrow morning to review the game tape."

Brent searched the room for Eric and found him by his locker. A few of the other team members lingered nearby. "Great game tonight," he told them. "Congratulations."

The other young men thanked him and then hurried to the showers.

Brent slapped Eric on his shoulder pads. "Fantastic call out there, QB. You really stood out as a leader. I can see why Appalachian offered you that scholarship."

"Thanks, but I don't think I'm going." Eric peeled off his jersey.

"What?" Brent lowered his voice despite the loud conversations floating around them. "Are you kidding?"

Eric frowned. "No. I don't think college is worth it when I can just stay here and work at my dad's feedstore."

The reasons for Eric to go to college echoed through Brent's mind, but now was not the time or the place to start this conversation. "You're heading to Cook Out with your friends, right?"

"Yeah, we always do after a game. Practically the whole town is there."

"How about you and I discuss this tomorrow?"

"I have a few minutes now, Coach." Eric's expression had grown serious. "Let's talk here."

Brent smiled. He liked when the players called him Coach. He could get used to that. "Why would you give up a scholarship and the opportunity to play college ball?"

"I've really been debating this. I just feel like more school is a waste of time if I can work in my dad's store."

"School is never a waste of time." Brent sank onto the bench beside him. "And if you earn that degree, it can be your ticket to a better-paying job. Or you could even take business classes and help your dad manage his store."

"But I don't like school, which is why my grades have been slipping. I just want to live my life."

"But it's tougher to go to school when you're older and maybe change your mind. You'll have bills to pay, like your mortgage or rent, car insurance, not to mention utilities and groceries. It's easier to get your degree when you're younger, especially when you have a scholarship to help offset the cost."

Eric looked down at the locker room floor. "I just don't know. Right now I feel like I can't do four more years of school." He lifted his eyes to meet Brent's. "How did you do it?"

Brent paused, deciding not to share how much pressure it was to be on a college football team and still keep up your grades. He didn't want to scare Eric out of taking advantage of the opportunity.

"I didn't. I lost my scholarship after my injury, and then I dropped out."

"I didn't know that."

"But I regret not finding a way to finish my degree."

There it was. The truth. Deep down, he was just as disappointed about that decision as his father was. No wonder he felt like such a failure.

"If you could do it again, would you stay in school?"

"Yes. I'd earn a degree somewhere, even if it wasn't at a prestigious university. Since I don't have one, I'm limited as to what I can do." He touched Eric's arm. "But you're staring down a golden opportunity. If you walk away, you might regret it for the rest of your life."

The young man nodded. "That makes sense."

"Think of it this way, Eric. Once you have that degree, no one can take it away from you."

"That makes sense too. Thank you, Coach. You've given me a lot to think about."

"Good." Brent patted his arm. "Be safe on the road, and I'll see you tomorrow."

"Good night."

Brent congratulated a few more players on his way out, and then he stopped in Coach Morgan's office. "Great game tonight."

"Yes, it was." The coach smiled. "I'm so grateful to have you on our team. You're really making a difference in these kids' lives."

Brent stood a little taller. "Thank you. I'll see you in the morning."

"Bright and early."

As Brent headed for the glass exit doors, he could see brake lights shining in the distance as the usual line of vehicles waited to leave the parking lot, car horns blasting. He was grateful the sky was clear, and the chill in the air wasn't too bad for October. The good weather would work well with the plans he'd made for Christine.

He'd texted Steve earlier, shared his idea, and asked him to tell Christine he and Pam weren't available to go out after the game. He'd also sworn Steve to secrecy, asking him to do the same with Pam, and now was the time to put his plan into motion.

"Hey, Coach."

Brent turned to see Christine looking as adorable as ever in a gray winter jacket and matching knit cap. Her cheeks were rosy, and her eyes twinkled in the lights of the parking lot. He picked her up by the waist and spun her around, and she screeched and laughed as she held on to him.

When he lowered her and pulled her into his arms, she rested her head on his shoulder, and he breathed in a scent that was uniquely her. Holding Christine felt so natural—as if she belonged in his arms. And he wished he could hold her close for the rest of his life.

"Congratulations again, Coach."

"Thank you," he whispered against her ear. That familiar yearning to kiss her bubbled up in his chest, but he shoved it away. That was dangerous territory. It would lead to a romantic relationship, and it was better to remain close friends no matter how much his heart protested.

Brent released her and took her gloved hand in his.

"Wait!" She pulled her phone from her pocket. "We need to document this momentous occasion." She pulled off her glove and held up her phone as they smiled for a selfie. Then she slipped it into her coat pocket.

"So do you have any plans for tonight?" he asked as he took her hand in his once again.

"I thought I did with you."

"Good. Did you drive here?"

"No, Pam and Steve picked me up. They said they had to get home, so it's just you and me." She smiled. "So where are you taking me for this surprise?"

"To Aunt Midge's."

She looked confused. "Oh. Okay. Can I have a hint?"

"No. You'll just have to wait."

"Stay here, okay?" Brent nearly whispered as they stood in his aunt's family room. "I'll come back for you when I'm ready."

It was after ten, and the house was dark. Aunt Midge must already be in bed, so they were being quiet.

Christine eyed him with suspicion as she sank onto the sofa. "Okay. But don't make me wait long."

Once in the kitchen, Brent sprang into action, making hot chocolate, filling two mugs, adding whipped cream, and then setting the mugs on a tray beside the box of chocolate-covered strawberries he'd purchased earlier in the day. Then he grabbed two large quilts from the laundry room closet.

Last, he hurried out the back door and plugged in the long extension cord that stretched out to the gazebo he and Uncle Sal had built. It lit up with the white Christmas lights he'd found in a bedroom closet yesterday, which inspired this elaborate plan. Then he carried the quilts and the tray out to the gazebo and placed them on the table he'd set up for the occasion.

Back inside, he found Christine still on the sofa, looking at her phone. "Are you going to stare at your phone all night like a bored teenager?"

"Excuse me?" Christine squeaked, then lowered her voice. "I'm the one who's been sitting here waiting for you to get your act together."

He adored their playful banter and how Christine always had a snappy retort for his teasing. "I'm ready, but you have to put your coat back on and close your eyes."

"Are you serious?" she deadpanned.

"Yes."

She stood and heaved out a sigh, once again reminding him of a teen girl. "Fine!" She made a production of shutting her eyes once she'd donned her coat and stuck her hat in one pocket. "They're closed."

"Good. Now keep them closed."

"Yes, Coach." She folded her arms. "You're awfully full of yourself after winning tonight. I can't imagine how you'll act when you win another state championship."

He took her hands and began slowly walking backward, leading her to the kitchen. "I think we're already too far behind for that."

"Don't give up hope. You're an amazing coach. Just think about what your quarterback did tonight to win. I know that was all you. In fact, he reminded me of you out on that field."

Warmth toward this incredible woman surged in his chest. Her unwavering faith in him blew him away. If only he could be the man she deserved.

He guided her to the sliding glass door that led out to the deck, then stopped walking. "Keep your eyes closed, please."

"Yes, Coach."

Brent slid open the door. "Now you need to step over the threshold."

"Are you really leading me back into the cold? Why did I have to close my eyes if we're just walking outside?"

"Shh. Now step carefully. I don't need to rush another woman to the emergency room."

"I'm going to tell Aunt Midge you said that," she said, her lips quirking.

Once they were on the deck, he closed the door behind her and then stepped to the side. "Okay. Open your eyes."

Christine's eyes flew open, and she cupped her hands to her

mouth. "Brent." She seemed to breathe his name, her tone full of a reverence that sent a thrill rushing through him. "This is beautiful!" She rushed to the railing and leaned over it. "Look at all those lights!"

"I'm so glad you like it. Let's have dessert."

She beamed at him. "What a great idea."

They walked out to the gazebo, and he turned on the LED candles he'd placed on the table.

Christine sank onto one of the patio chairs and smiled up at him. "Brent, this is breathtaking. I'm-I'm overwhelmed."

His heart swelled. "I'm glad you're enjoying this. I came up with the idea when I found the lights. I have hot chocolate with whipped cream and chocolate-covered strawberries."

Christine gave a dreamy sigh. "This is so romantic."

When she shivered, guilt nipped at him.

"It's too cold, right? This was a dumb idea. We can go back inside."

"Are you kidding? It's beautiful out here. Look at that clear sky, those dazzling stars, and the bright moon. It's like this night was made just for us." She wrapped one of the quilts around her shoulders. "Sit with me and have some hot chocolate."

He sat in a chair close to hers, and Christine handed him a mug. Then she draped her quilt over his shoulders as well, and they snuggled while sipping their hot chocolates. She held a strawberry up to his lips and he ate it, savoring the sweet taste. He held one up for her, and she finished it before resting her head on his shoulder and wrapping her arms around his waist.

Closing his eyes, he wished this night would never end. The scent from a wood-burning fireplace somewhere nearby drifted over him, but only traffic in the distance made any sound.

"So, Coach," she said, "how did that amazing win feel?"

"It was just as good as one of the wins from my high school days. College too. It was incredible to feel a part of something again."

"That's what I was hoping you'd say. I'm sure the team was thrilled."

"Yes. They were high on the win for sure." He swallowed a sip. "I had a chance to talk to the winning quarterback after the game, and we had an interesting conversation."

"Tell me about it."

He did, then said, "I just hope Eric considers what I told him. He's so talented, and to let that scholarship go without even giving college a try would be a bad decision."

She sat up to face him, and a knowing expression filled her face.

"What's going on in that beautiful head of yours, Christine?"

She covered his hand with hers. "Brent, this is exactly why I wanted you to take Coach Morgan up on his offer. You have so much knowledge and experience to share with those young men. You're a blessing to them and to so many people. You're the kind of role model Eric Maloney needs."

Brent swallowed against his dry throat as another wave of yearning gripped him, but he couldn't act on it. It wouldn't be fair to either of them. It was a mistake to make such a romantic gesture, yet he couldn't let her go. He loved Christine.

There, he'd admitted it, if only to himself.

She scanned the gazebo. "You and your uncle built this?"

"Yes, when I was about twelve, not long before he died from a massive heart attack. We also built the fence. He taught me the basics of construction. He was like the grandfather I never had since both my parents had lost their folks years earlier."

The temperature was dropping, and Christine's nose was turning bright pink.

"It's difficult to believe it was seventy degrees earlier today, and now it feels like it's fallen as low as the forties," she said.

"That's the fall in Carolina." He rubbed her back. "You look so cold. We should head inside."

She sighed. "I hate to leave this beautiful gazebo, but you're right. I'm starting to shiver despite the warmth of this quilt—and you."

They turned off all the lights, then took the tray and quilts inside before washing the mugs.

As they started the short journey to Christine's house in Brent's truck, she held the leftover strawberries on her lap. Brent wanted her to have them.

Once he'd parked in her driveway, he reached over and touched her hand. She hesitated a moment but then leaned over the console and looped her arms around his neck, pulling him closer. He rested his chin on her head, relishing the moment.

When she pulled away, her eyes sparkled as she smiled. "Thank you for such a lovely evening, Brent."

He touched her cheek. "Good night, Christine."

She exited the truck and then jogged up to her front door. After unlocking it, she waved before disappearing into the house.

Brent leaned on the steering wheel. Despite the risk, this had been the perfect night. He'd cherish every moment he had with Christine before leaving Flowering Grove. Yes, he'd visit his family for holidays—the traditional day or two. But when it came to the woman he loved, he might as well be leaving forever.

twenty-four

The following Wednesday evening Christine knocked on Aunt Midge's front door. It was a typical fall in North Carolina with unpredictable weather—hot one day and cold the next—but tonight the air was warm. It was a stark contrast to how cold it was Friday night when she'd sat in the gazebo with Brent.

She smiled as she recalled that evening. She couldn't remember a more romantic one! It was perfect. Well, *almost* perfect. If only Brent had kissed her. But even if he'd wanted to, his restraint was evident, and she'd done her best to hold her own desire in check.

The door suddenly opened and Aunt Midge stood before her.

"Hi," Christine said.

The older woman smiled and beckoned Christine to enter the house. "Come on in."

She entered the family room, then pulled a check from her backpack purse and presented it. "I have good news for you. You've sold quite a bit more at my store, and here's your next payment."

"Isn't that wonderful? Thank you so much." Aunt Midge took the check and set it on the coffee table. "Brent just got home from football practice." She pointed toward the powder room. "He's working in there. I know he'll be excited to see you." She winked.

The woman wasn't subtle at all, and Christine swallowed a chuckle.

Christine found Brent painting the powder room walls a light gray similar to the color in her guest bedroom at home. "I heard you just got back from practice, Coach."

Brent turned toward her. "Hey there."

"I love this color," she said. "But I think magenta would have brightened this room up a bit more."

"I was thinking more like lime green, but surprisingly, Aunt Midge disagreed."

Christine laughed. "It looks fantastic."

"Thanks. I'm only restaining the woodwork and painting in here. I think everything else still works." He swiped the back of his arm across his forehead. "I finished painting the bedrooms this week."

"You've been busy."

"I still have plenty to do, though." He leaned back on the sink. "Paint the kitchen, family room, dining room . . . I'm not going to remodel the kitchen, though. The Realtor Aunt Midge has engaged says it's hard to know what a buyer will want in there, but I still need to replace the faucet. Then I need to replace a few boards on the deck, restain it, and clean up the yard. Not to mention repairing the fence and painting the gazebo."

"Tell me you'll leave up the Christmas lights," she said teasingly.

"Oh, I think those will be donated."

"No! Aunt Midge is donating her Christmas decorations?"

"She says she'll buy all new decorations for her condo."

Christine smiled despite the sadness creeping into her heart. Brent was nearly done with the house, and they'd have to say good-bye soon.

"So what brings you over tonight?"

"I had another check for your aunt." She hesitated. "I also have an invitation for you."

He brightened. "What is it?"

"Would you like to go to a party with me Sunday afternoon?"

"Darn!" He snapped his fingers. "I left my tux in Virginia," he said, clearly joking.

"You definitely don't need a tux. It's a five-year-old's birthday party. Actually it's for two birthday girls."

"It sounds like a party for your nieces."

"Yes." *Please say you'll go. Surely Britney will behave with our parents there.*

He stood straight. "I would be honored. But if I need to bring a gift or two, I'll definitely need some advice."

"I'll buy the gifts and put your name on them—if that's okay."

"That will be great. Thank you." He held up a finger. "Just remind me about it, okay? I don't have a great memory."

"Of course." Relief filled her. "So would you like me to start on the attic?"

"Sure. But if you'll wait a few minutes, we can start going through it together. I'm almost done with this second coat."

Christine lingered in the hallway, admiring both his skill with a paintbrush and the tautness of the muscles showing across his back from beneath his T-shirt.

When he finished, Brent cleaned his brush and covered the leftover paint, then retrieved some empty boxes from the basement before pulling down the folding stairs in the hallway ceiling. Once they'd climbed into the musty attic—where Brent didn't have quite enough head room to stand at full height—he pulled on a string, and a light bulb dimly illuminated the small space.

Brent plopped onto the wood floor, and Christine surveyed the area and found about two dozen boxes and bags. "At least there's less here than she had in the basement, right?"

"That's true. This shouldn't take too long." Brent pulled his cell phone from his pocket and turned on the flashlight app before opening some boxes. "These are all full of old clothes. I don't imagine they would sell at your store."

She shook her head. "Not unless they're vintage or really unique."

"I see men's sweaters, turtlenecks, sweatpants . . . I assume they belonged to Uncle Sal."

"I suggest donating them if they're in decent condition." Christine opened a box and said, "I found brand-new puzzles. They all feature nature scenes."

"Those must have been Uncle Sal's too. He loved puzzles. Do you think they would sell?"

"They might." She set the box to the side, and they moved on.

For the next hour they sorted through everything there, placing the items for donation to their left and the items to sell to their right. When they finished, they loaded the items for her store into Christine's truck and the donations into Brent's.

After saying a quick good night to Aunt Midge, Christine followed Brent outside. It was disappointing to realize her job there was over. Now she had no reason to visit unless she was specifically invited, and Aunt Midge hadn't said a word. Maybe she'd given up on any hope of Brent staying.

"I guess that's it," she said as they stood by her truck. "My work here is done."

Brent looked toward the high school and nodded, and she was almost certain he was just as sad as she was. He tilted his head when he turned back to her. "Sounds like I'll need to come up with some lame excuses to see you."

"You don't need any excuse."

"That's good to know." He held up his finger. "What if I text you a lot?"

"That works, but I'd like to see you in person too."

"Okay." He smiled. "Thank you again for your help. I'm really grateful."

"It was a lot of fun, and my customers are enjoying your aunt's treasures. Something old to her is new to them."

"Very true." He pulled her in for a hug. "I'll see you soon."

"I hope so."

◆ ◆ ◆

Brent waited in the driveway as Christine backed out and drove off, tooting her horn before she disappeared down the street. Oh, how he wished for more days with her. But he'd be finished with Aunt Midge's house soon, and a job interview was waiting for him in Virginia Beach.

He longed to travel back in time. What if he'd met Christine before meeting Britney? What would have happened if he'd asked her to go to the movies instead? He might have fallen in love with Christine. Then they might have built a life together, had a family, been happy despite his college failure.

She had faith in his skills as a home remodeler, and she believed he'd be successful if he established a new business. He was beginning to have more faith in himself, even though his conversation with Eric made him realize his lack of a college degree had kept him from exploring all the career options he might have had.

But life had worked out that way.

Brent's shoulders sagged as he shuffled up the front porch steps and into the house, where Aunt Midge sat in her recliner in the family room watching a Hallmark movie. Didn't she ever grow tired of those?

"Did you ask her out already? The gazebo night doesn't count, nor does all that time you two have spent with Steve and Pam Barnes."

He sat on the sofa and frowned. "No, I haven't asked her out, and it's not going to happen."

"Brent," she began, her voice vibrating with impatience, "you're my favorite nephew."

"I'm your *only* nephew."

"I realize that, and you're also my most exasperating. You're just as dopey as your uncle once was. He took so long to ask me out that I almost gave up on him. It's obvious you and Christine care about each other. So for heaven's sake, ask her out on a real date!"

Brent flopped back on the sofa. "It's not that simple."

"Why not?"

"You already know why not." He counted his dilemmas on his fingers. "I might have a job soon, but not here. I also have no assets, no home, and no real future. Why on earth would a woman as beautiful, brilliant, and successful as Christine Sawyer want to date a loser like me?"

Aunt Midge's expression warmed. "Brent, those are temporary problems that can be solved. You're quite a catch, and Christine knows that. You two can figure out your future together. That's what couples do. They all face challenges. Do you honestly believe your uncle and I never had hard times? What matters is that you and Christine find a way to work through your hard times *together*, and I believe you will if you love each other enough. She has a problem with her store's rent increase, and you need to get your life together after losing your business in Virginia Beach."

"I can't talk about this now. I have work to do." Brent pushed himself from the sofa and stalked into the kitchen. Resting his arms on the counter, he bowed his head and closed his eyes. If only he *could* get his life together, but right now he had no way to give Christine the future she deserved, and soon he'd lose her forever.

Aunt Midge was wrong, and that truth shattered his heart. All he could do was make the most of the time he had left with Christine in Flowering Grove—*as friends*.

◆ ◆ ◆

Sunday afternoon Brent balanced two huge boxes wrapped in purple paper in his arms as he and Christine strode up Britney and Hunter's driveway for the twins' birthday party. He was grateful for another clear-sky, warm mid-October day, a welcome change from the rain and gray clouds they'd had the day before. The two squirrels he could see happily eating from a bird feeder by the side of the house probably thought so too.

He looked at the two-story brick colonial and nearly grunted. Britney had done well for herself marrying Hunter, but he hadn't expected anything less than perfection in her life.

He turned to Christine. "You only invited me so I could carry these giant boxes for you," he quipped.

She shot him a look. "I could have managed them by myself. But I thought I would be *nice* and invite you."

"Are they both the same gift?"

"Yes. Barbie restaurants."

He stopped walking. "Two of the same?"

"Yes."

"Why didn't you just get one for them to share?"

When she glowered he inwardly groaned. *Uh-oh!* He'd hit a nerve!

"Do you know how many people did that to Britney and me on our shared birthday? Nearly everyone did. One year we received a book—just one. Now, I was delighted, but Britney, not so much. I'm never going to do that to my nieces. Each one deserves her own gift to enjoy. In this case, though, Mila and Maddy both like Barbies."

"I'm sorry. I didn't mean to break any twin rules."

She narrowed her eyes. "And don't you forget it."

"Yes, ma'am," he said, and she smiled.

The inside door stood open, and Christine held the storm door open before motioning for him to enter the house.

Utter chaos reigned as a pack of giggling little girls wearing purple party hats ran around in what appeared to be a family room decorated with purple balloons and streamers. A large banner—also purple—hung over a fireplace with the words *Happy Birthday, Mila and Madison!* When Brent spotted the birthday girls, he wasn't surprised to see they wore matching purple party dresses. Apparently their favorite color wasn't pink.

Groups of adults mingled in the spacious room as well as in the large kitchen he could see through a wide case opening. He spotted Pam and Steve talking with Hunter, and he was grateful to see someone he knew there.

"Girls, please take it outside!" Britney called, her voice already sounding tired as she cupped a hand to her temple. Hadn't the party just started?

Mrs. Sawyer appeared. "There you are, Chrissy! I told your father you'd be along shortly." She turned to him. "Hello, Brent. It's been a long time."

"Hi, Mrs. Sawyer."

"Call me Karla." She pointed to a mountain of gifts near the fireplace. "You can put those boxes over there."

Brent deposited them with the other gifts, and when Christine's father walked over he held out his hand. "Hi, Mr. Sawyer."

The man shook his hand as he said, "Hello, Brent. We can dispense with any formality. Please, call me Bob." He jammed his thumb toward Hunter. "My son-in-law was just telling me you're the quarterback coach for the Falcons."

"That's correct."

"That was a great homecoming game."

Brent smiled. "Yes, it was."

"You made it," Steve said as he and Hunter joined them. He handed Brent a can of Coke.

"Thanks." Brent popped it open and took a drink.

Hunter patted Brent's shoulder. "I was hoping Chrissy would bring you today. So the last football game is Friday, huh?"

Brent nodded. "It is."

"Do you still like coaching?" Steve asked.

"I love it," Brent readily admitted.

Despite the confident front he'd presented to Christine when she asked him to come to the party, he'd thought he might not be comfortable here—especially not knowing how her parents felt about him based on Britney's faulty account of their breakup. He didn't know if Christine had set them straight as well, and he didn't want to ask. But either way, they'd made him feel just as welcome as Hunter had.

Maybe Britney was the only one in the Sawyer family who couldn't let the past go.

twenty-five

Christine smiled as she took in Brent talking with her father, nodding when Dad said something and then laughing. He looked as if he was having a good time, and more importantly, as if he belonged here with her friends and family. As if he were *part* of her family.

If only he could be!

"Why don't we talk for a minute?" Mom said before unceremoniously taking Christine's arm. She steered her into the kitchen, then pulled her into the laundry room before shutting the door behind them.

Christine frowned. She'd known this was coming sooner or later. For weeks she'd imagined her sister grumbling to their mother that her twin was "seeing" her ex-boyfriend who'd cheated on her. Mom had never said anything, but that was about to change. After that dinner at the Barbecue Pit, Britney had probably ramped up her complaints.

"Go ahead and say it, Mom. You're disappointed to see me spending time with Brent."

"*Disappointed* isn't the word I was going to use. I was going to say *surprised*. And I haven't wanted to interfere, but—"

"Brent is a great guy. He's sweet and thoughtful, and he takes good care of his great-aunt Midge. He says he never cheated on Britney, and I believe him." Then she told her Brent's side of the story. "Britney was wrong to think the worst of him and never even give him a chance to defend himself against Grant's lie."

"I see. Well, I'm glad to see you dating again, but I'd still be cautious about dating him if I were you. He was a lovely boy when you were all in high school, but sometimes young people change in college. Your sister is still concerned he could be fooling you."

"We're not dating. We're just friends. And Brent is the same nice guy you knew when we were in high school. He's not trying to fool anyone."

"Well, just be careful. I can't stand it when my girls hurt." Mom touched Christine's cheek. "Now let's go enjoy this party."

Back in the family room Christine joined Brent, and after a while they ate pizza out on the home's enormous deck, Jake watching them as he wagged his tail. Even in their party dresses, the children climbed all over the twins' humongous playset, and their giggles floated around the large manicured yard devoid of fallen leaves.

Christine helped gather all the used paper plates, napkins, and cups before sitting on the family room sofa with Brent. After taking photos of the girls opening their gifts, she convinced Brent to take a few selfies with her, not caring if Britney, her mother, or anyone else objected.

The twins' parents brought out two purple ice cream cakes, and everyone sang "Happy Birthday." Then as Britney and Hunter sliced the cakes, Christine and Mom distributed the pieces. The plates and plastic spoons were purple, of course.

"Chrissy, would you please find the party napkins?" Mom asked. "They're in the kitchen, and they're purple."

"You didn't need to tell me they're purple, Mom." Christine

chuckled as she entered the kitchen and searched the counter, where she found a bag from the local party store and pulled out the napkins.

When she felt a hand on her shoulder, she jumped, then spun to find her best friend smiling at her.

"Sorry. I didn't mean to scare you," Pam said. "I wanted to talk to you alone." She looked toward the family room, then lowered her voice. "You and Brent seem to be getting awfully close. I haven't seen you for a while. How are things going?"

Christine decided to be forthright. "We've been spending a lot of time together." She quickly told her about their romantic evening in his aunt's gazebo and how Brent often held her hand and hugged her—had even kissed her cheek. "Everything feels so natural with him. When he hugs me, it's like I'm supposed to be in his arms. But every time I'm certain he's about to kiss me for real, he doesn't."

"Don't give up on him. I think it's going to work out."

Christine searched her friend's eyes as hope rose in her chest. "Why? Has he told Steve anything?"

"Not that I know of, but it's so obvious you two are into each other. I just have this feeling you'll eventually be together."

"I don't think so."

"Why not?"

"Because every time I mention the idea of his staying in Flowering Grove, even starting a home remodeling business here, he tells me no, it's not possible. Says he doesn't have the resources. But if he wanted it to work out between us, he'd find a way." She paused. "I love him, Pam."

Christine cleared her throat against a swell of grief. She couldn't allow herself to get emotional here. Not at her nieces' party.

Pam touched her shoulder. "Chris, I think he loves you too. Maybe he just needs to wait to tell you how he really feels until he has a plan he thinks will work."

Mom suddenly burst into the kitchen. "Did you find the napkins, Chrissy?"

"Yes." Christine handed them to her. "Sorry. We were in the middle of girl talk."

Shaking her head, Mom marched back to the family room.

Pam looped her arm around Christine's waist. "I think you and Brent will make a great couple. Just give him time."

Christine nodded, but time was running out.

◆ ◆ ◆

"Did you mean it when you said you had a good time at the party?" Christine asked as Brent parked his truck in her driveway later that evening.

He unbuckled his seat belt and faced her. "I did. It was fun and even interesting."

"Interesting how?"

"I've never seen so much purple in my life."

Christine burst out laughing, and he joined in. "Would you believe their room is purple too?"

"Yes, yes, I would believe it. Good thing they share that at least." He rested his arm on the back of the seat. "How are things going at the store?"

She frowned and shook her head. "I took a long look at the books yesterday, and it's not good. The sidewalk sales haven't made much difference, and I'm running out of time before my rent goes up. I'll have to raise my booth rent at least 10 percent."

Despondency crawled onto her shoulders as she studied her jeans and flicked away a piece of lint. "I asked my parents for a loan last night. I despise doing it since I've always done my best to be self-sufficient, but I don't have much choice. Raising the booth rent won't be enough, but I've decided raising my percentage of sales would be going too far. I keep trying to think of a way to increase business, though, and I'm hoping something works out."

Christine brushed away more lint and then lifted her eyes to Brent's warm gaze. "I'm wondering if I need to add something like a coffee bar, but what do I know about coffee? And how could I afford to have someone build a coffee bar? And then how do I find the money to buy all the coffee supplies and pay someone to run the coffee bar? That would all add to my expenses, and I don't want to ask for another loan if I can't even afford to pay off the first one." Her heart raced as anxiety wrapped around her chest.

Brent began massaging her shoulder. "It's going to be okay, Christine. I have faith in you and your amazing store. I'll try to come up with a solution too. No matter what, I'll do my best to help you. Remember, I promised, and I do keep my promises."

She turned toward him, his caring touch and offer relieving some stress as she lost herself in the depth of his honey-brown eyes.

Stay in Flowering Grove, Brent. Tell me you love me.

When Brent's fingers moved to her neck, a quiver of desire danced down her spine, and she longed for him to kiss her as he traced his fingers over her cheek with a feathery touch.

"I'd better let you get some sleep," he said, pulling his hand away. "I have to get up early tomorrow and finish painting the hallway. After that, I still have a lot to do."

She lifted her purse from the floorboard and pushed open the door. "Good night, then."

"See you soon."

As she hoofed it to her front porch, she realized the promise of Brent's kiss was just a dream.

◆ ◆ ◆

Friday morning Brent walked into the kitchen through the back door and found Steve with Aunt Midge.

"There he is," she announced. "We were just talking about you."

"Hey, Brent," Steve said as he shook his hand.

"Well, I'll let you two get to work," Aunt Midge said. "I'll go see what's going on with *Days of Our Lives*. There's always something exciting happening in Salem!" She headed back to the family room.

"Thanks for coming over," Brent said. "I'm sorry I didn't hear you drive up. I was in the backyard looking at the fence."

"It's no problem. I had a nice discussion with your aunt. And I'm glad I had a cancellation and could help you. I picked up a new faucet for you with my discount."

"I appreciate that."

They set to work removing the cleaning supplies under the sink before removing the leaking faucet.

"So what's going on between you and Christine?" Steve asked.

"We're . . . friends. Why?"

Steve scoffed. "Please, Brent. Chris told Pam about the gazebo thing, and then you two seemed awfully cozy at her nieces' birthday party. Don't try to play it off like it's nothing. I know you both better than that. It's obvious you care about each other, and Pam and I think it's great. We'd love to see Christine settle down, and it would be great to have you back here for good."

"Whoa. I just knew she'd enjoy the gazebo all lit up like that, and we're *not* dating."

"You could've fooled me."

Brent shook his head and turned his attention back to their work.

"Brent, I know you think there's a life for you in Virginia, but you can also build one here. You looked so happy when you were talking to Hunter, Bob, and me about coaching. Why would you want to give up Christine and coaching when you seem to love them both?"

Brent swallowed. He'd known he loved Christine the night he surprised her with the lights on the gazebo, but that didn't change his circumstances. "Let's get this faucet changed out."

They worked in silence, and soon the faucet was installed and working. Steve set his tools back into his toolbox and stood. "Why are you so afraid to take a chance with Christine?"

"I need to rebuild my life before I can even think about getting into a relationship." Brent leaned back against the counter and studied his friend. "I've wanted to ask you a personal question."

"Shoot."

"How did you find a way to believe in love and marriage after witnessing your father marry and divorce so many times?"

Steve shrugged. "That's an easy one. I'm not my dad. And I found my soul mate and snatched her up before I missed the opportunity. You should do the same."

Brent pushed off the counter. "Let me get you some money from my wallet."

As he made a beeline to his bedroom, he tried to leave his friend's words in the kitchen. But they followed him, latching onto his heart.

◆ ◆ ◆

Brent trudged toward Coach Morgan's office Friday night as excited conversations echoed throughout the locker room. The Falcons' last game had just ended, and they'd managed to pull off one more win, beating the Montclair Mavericks thirty-four to twenty-eight. Brent had been proud as Eric once again threw the winning pass.

It had been a bittersweet game and evening because now it was time to say goodbye. Brent dipped his chin to look into the shopping bag holding the hat, jackets, and shirts he was ready to return, then knocked on Coach Morgan's open office door.

"Come in, Brent," the coach said when he looked up from his desk. "Heck of a game, huh?"

"Yes, it was. And since I'm heading back to Virginia soon, I thought it would be best to resign now. Thank you for the opportunity to work with this incredible team. Here's my gear." Brent set the bag down on a chair.

"I'm sorry to hear you say that." Coach Morgan frowned as he stood and rounded his desk. "I was hoping you'd changed your mind about leaving."

"I enjoyed my time here, but I have an opportunity in Virginia, and I need to follow up on it."

The coach pulled the hat from the bag and handed it to Brent. "Keep this to remember us. There will always be a place for you on this team if you come back to Flowering Grove. And come see us when you visit your family."

"Thank you." Brent slipped the hat on his head.

Brent stepped out of the office just as Eric rushed over. "We did it, Coach," he said as he gave him a high five.

"We sure did."

"I was hoping to talk to you for a minute." Eric motioned for Brent to follow him farther down the hallway. "I've decided to go to Appalachian."

"That's wonderful! I'm so proud of you."

"I've been doing a lot of thinking, and you're right. I can't miss out on this opportunity. My parents agree. So thank you for the helpful advice."

"You're welcome." Brent felt his smile slip. "I'm glad you found me. I wanted to let you know I'm leaving town soon. I'm returning to Virginia Beach for a job opportunity."

"Aw, that's a shame. I thought you were staying. My little brother is coming up from middle school, and I was hoping he'd get a chance to work with you next fall. I've been telling him what a great coach you are."

Brent swallowed back the unexpected emotion swelling in his chest. "It's awfully nice of you to say that."

"I mean it. You're one of the best." Eric held out his hand, and Brent shook it. "Good luck in Virginia. We'll miss you."

As Eric walked away, Brent wondered why leaving Coach Morgan and this team hurt so much.

But he knew. His love for football had never gone away. It was just buried—for far too long.

twenty-six

Christine breathed in the crisp November air as she sat beside Brent on the high-backed bench on her deck. Her propane firepit provided warmth as they gazed out over her small backyard, and she couldn't think of a better way to spend a Sunday evening.

Despite having a source of heat, Brent pulled her against him and rested his hand on her waist as they both looked up at the twinkling stars. Christine reclined her head on his shoulder and closed her eyes, relishing his nearness.

"The tilapia was delicious," he said, his voice rumbling in her ear. "You just had to outdo my hot chocolate and chocolate-covered strawberries, didn't you?"

She raised her head and shook it. "Our dessert in your aunt's gazebo was better than fish. Honestly, I just wanted to try something different, so I pulled out my nana's favorite cookbook and checked out the seafood recipes. Parmesan tilapia sounded delicious, and I'm glad you liked it."

"I loved it."

"But our view with the Christmas lights was much better than the one we have here. All we have is the stars."

"The lights were pretty, but your outdoor furniture is more comfortable. And your firepit would have kept us warmer."

Christine yearned for time to freeze—or at least back up a month or two. How had November snuck up on them?

When Brent heaved a sigh that sounded like it had bubbled up from his toes, a foreboding took hold of her. She closed her eyes and gnawed on her lower lip, dreading whatever words were about to come out of his mouth.

"I finally finished all the indoor painting, including that empty room above the garage and the laundry room," Brent said. "Now I just have to repair the deck and fence and paint the gazebo before cleaning up the yard." His lips flattened. "My aunt's Realtor is coming on Thursday to look things over, and the house should be listed by the weekend. She's already told us the new windows Aunt Midge had installed a few years ago will be a selling point."

Christine's eyes focused on the dark backyard as they stung with tears. *Don't cry, Christine. Hold it together!*

Brent's fingers moved over her spine, and she tried in vain to relax the muscles bunching in her back and shoulders.

"So you're leaving soon," she whispered, her voice faltering.

"I don't know exactly when, but I'm ready to tell Devonte it won't be long. I just need to make sure everything's set for Aunt Midge before I go."

Her throat stung, too, and she struggled to keep her emotions at bay. "Hey, I sold that set of Christmas dishes your aunt had."

"Good."

"The last of those quilts went too."

She babbled on about her store, her nieces, anything she could think of while trying to ignore how much she dreaded the day he'd leave her.

◆ ◆ ◆

Brent stepped into his room, pulled his phone from his pocket, and plopped onto his creaking bed—one of Aunt Midge's furnishings that had seen better days. He'd spent the ride home from Christine's trying to come up with a plan to keep her in his life. At one point he almost drove back to her place to ask her to move to Virginia Beach. But that was the stupidest idea of all. He couldn't ask her to give up her store. Just proposing it would be preposterous!

Then he considered applying for construction jobs near Flowering Grove, but once again, he had no place to live. The notion of living in his childhood bedroom tied his stomach into a knot. How humiliating! What would people think if they heard Brent Nicholson, star quarterback who'd had such a promising future, was back living with his parents?

For a brief moment he pondered asking Steve and Pam if he could rent a room from them, but he despised the idea of invading their space. After all, they'd been married for only a couple of years, and he'd no doubt put a cramp in their style.

By the time he'd parked in Aunt Midge's driveway, he'd convinced himself that working and living with Devonte in Virginia Beach really was the only practical option open to him. Then he'd mulled over the notion of a long-distance relationship with Christine, but what made him think the five-hour commute with only calls, texts, and video chats between visits would work? Their relationship would fizzle after a couple of months, and that could be more painful than leaving her behind in the first place.

Those were all the reasons he had to ignore the pain expanding in his chest and stay the course of starting a new life in Virginia. But if this was the right plan, why did the idea of leaving slice through his soul?

Opening his texts he found his last conversation with Devonte and started typing.

> *Hi! I'm finishing up my aunt's house. It's going on the market this weekend, and I should be there soon.*

After a few moments Devonte responded.

> *Awesome! I was talking to my boss about you today, and he was wondering if you could send some photos of your work. Can you do that?*
> *I'll take some tomorrow. I have some before shots too.*
> *Perfect. I'll let you know what he says. We have a big remodel starting right around Thanksgiving. I'm sure we'll need help with it.*
> *Thanks so much. And for keeping your spare room for me.*
> *Absolutely, buddy.*
> *I appreciate you. Talk to you soon.*

Brent locked his phone and dropped it next to him on the bed. Then, scrubbing his hands down his face, he wondered how he'd ever get over losing Christine. It seemed impossible.

◆ ◆ ◆

Tuesday morning Brent parked in front of Christine's store and then pulled two paint chips featuring shades of lime green and magenta from his pocket. He'd pocketed them at Swanson's Hardware when picking up more supplies for Aunt Midge's deck and fence. When he saw them, he immediately thought of Christine and smiled as he imagined presenting them to her as a joke.

With two allergy pills already in him, he climbed from the truck and shivered. The sky above him was a blanket of rolling gray clouds, and the air smelled like rain. He should have worn a jacket.

Bon Jovi's "Livin' on a Prayer" sounded through the store's speakers as he pushed open the front door, and just as it clicked shut behind him, Christine's gray tabby raced over and immediately rubbed his shins as if she'd been expecting him.

"Hey, Wanda," he said. "Could you please go bother someone else?"

The kitty blinked up at him, then meowed before continuing her harassment.

Brent pivoted toward the counter and opened his mouth to ask Christine for help, but Britney was there instead, glowering at him.

"May I help you?" she asked, her voice dripping with disdain.

Great. He resisted snarling a snarky response as he approached the counter. "Where's Christine?"

"Running errands. She's planning a big Black Friday promotion, and she's delivering flyers throughout the downtown area."

"Oh." Brent felt something on his thigh and looked down at that determined cat, now standing on her back legs and tapping him with her front paws. "Wanda, please go visit some other customers, okay?"

"She must like you for some stupid reason."

Brent's lips twisted. "How about we try to be civil to each other, Britney?"

"How about we don't?" She reached into a drawer under the

counter and held up a container of cat treats. "Wanda! Come here, girl." Then she hissed *psst, psst, psst* and held up a handful of them.

The cat snapped its attention to her, jumped up on the counter, and nearly inhaled the offering as Brent backed away.

"Thanks," he mumbled.

Britney still glared at him. "Do us all a favor and stay away from my sister. I know you're going to hurt her just like you hurt me. Christine is an amazing woman, and she deserves so much better than you—a cheat." Her tone was as icy as her expression.

"I never cheated on you, Britney," he said, his voice vibrating with frustration. "Why did you ever believe Grant Fahey? You and I were together for six years, and I was *never* unfaithful to you, not once." He pointed to his chest. "When did I ever give you a reason not to trust me? What he told you isn't true. The only redhead I knew at Chapel Hill was my friend Dina, who dated one of my football buddies. She was like a sister to me. I might have given her a hug, but that's all. What Grant told you was a lie."

Britney snorted.

"Don't you see it was a plot to break us up? He was always obsessed with you, and he wasn't shy about it." He rubbed his forehead while attempting to gather himself. "But who cares? None of that matters anymore. I've been over you for a long time. Now you need to get over yourself and move on."

"How *dare* you talk to me like that!"

"Look, you need to get rid of that chip on your shoulder. Please tell Christine I stopped by."

Turning, he charged out of the store and got into his truck, then let his head smack the back of his seat while forcing himself to face the truth. What upset him the most was that Britney was right. Christine did deserve better than him, but that didn't change the fact that he was madly in love with her.

His phone rang, and he pulled it from his back pocket to find Devonte's name on the screen.

"Hey," Brent said.

"I just spoke to my boss and showed him those photos you sent. He's eager to get you started here. Can you be any more specific about when you'll come?"

Droplets of rain sprinkled his windshield as Brent tried to tamp down the anguish radiating through him. "The week of Thanksgiving." He'd make sure he was gone by then, avoiding both a frustrating family dinner and that reunion Britney was so thrilled about. "I just need to tie up a few more things here."

"Perfect. He was hoping you could get here by then. I told you about that big job, right?"

"You mentioned it."

"Well, we're starting it the Monday before Thanksgiving. We're completely remodeling a huge three-story house in downtown Norfolk. The owner wants it done by March, so we need to get going."

While Devonte gave him a few more details, Brent studied the front windows of Treasure Hunting Antique Mall, trying to memorize every detail. This might be one of the last times he saw it.

◆ ◆ ◆

"Anything interesting happen while I was gone?" Christine asked when she returned.

Britney wrinkled her nose as if she smelled something foul. "Brent was here."

"He was?" Christine's pulse ratcheted up. "What did he say?"

"He wanted to talk to you, but I was direct with him."

Anger flashed through Christine. "What did you tell him?"

"That he's a cheat. And then I warned him to stay away from you because you deserve better."

Christine's whole body shook as she glared at her sister. "I'm a grown woman, Britney, and I don't need you to protect me."

Britney's face softened. "But I care about you. I can tell you've fallen in love with him, but he's going to hurt you, Chrissy. I just know it."

Christine pulled her keys from her purse. "Can you stay here for a while longer?"

"Sure." Britney shrugged. "I have a while before the twins get out of school."

Christine hurried out to her truck, her heart pounding the whole way to Aunt Midge's house. When she arrived, she heard what sounded like hammering in the backyard, and she found Brent installing new boards in the wood fence. She pulled the hood of her wool coat over her hair and zipped up the front as a mist of rain kissed her face.

"Why are you working out in the rain?" she asked as she sidled up to him.

He stood to his full height and turned to look at her. "I'm trying to work off some frustration."

"I suppose your source of frustration is that talk with my sister."

"That's one." He seemed to study her. "But I didn't expect you to come here because of it."

"I want to know why you stopped by."

He shrugged. "It wasn't a big deal. I had a couple of paint chips to give you as a joke."

The rain picked up, pouring down in angry patterns from the sky, and she shivered as it began to soak through her hood and coat.

Brent pointed his hammer toward the back door. "Do you want to go inside?"

"No." She shook her head. "I want to hear you say it."

His expression grew guarded. "Say what?"

"That you're going to leave me."

He hesitated, then squared his shoulders. "Christine, I told you I was going back to Virginia from the beginning. It shouldn't be a surprise."

"But I know you care about me. You told me so that night we sat right here on your aunt's deck, after you told me the truth about you and Britney. It's written all over your face right now, and I can feel it when you hold my hand, when you hug me, when you kiss my cheek. Don't tell me we're just friends. I know I mean more to you than that." Her words came out like chipped rocks, and she wiped the rain from her face. "Don't lie to me, Brent."

His Adam's apple bobbed, but he remained silent.

"So my sister has been right all along. You *are* going to hurt me. You're doing it right now." She looked at the ground as tears spilled from her eyes.

"But it's because I have nothing to offer you." His voice was gravelly now.

"All I want is you," she whispered.

He just stared at her, and the truth reared its ugly head. Now she knew what he couldn't offer her. The one thing she wanted most from him.

"I was a fool to think you could actually love me," she croaked as her heart fractured. "Why would you? I'm not Britney. I'm just Christine, the inferior twin. I'll never be good enough for you."

He looked pained, and she was certain she spotted tears filling his eyes. But that didn't mean she was wrong.

"You're not the problem, Christine, and you've got to stop comparing yourself to Britney." He pointed to his chest. "I never said I don't love you. I'm the loser. I don't have a career or a home, and I have little potential to do much more than support myself. Why would you want someone like me?"

She reached toward his chest but was careful not to touch him. "Because I know you, the real you. I know your heart. I know the kind of man you are, but you believe what your father tells you, not all the other people who love you. Aunt Midge, your mother and sister, Steve and Pam . . . me."

"I know what I am, and you deserve better."

She snorted. "You know that's not true, but you refuse to see what's right in front of you. A woman who loves you no matter what. And now I'm walking out of your life forever, because if you loved me too—" She nearly choked, and, turning on her heels, she stomped through the rain to her truck.

Once she was locked inside, her sobs broke free. It was over.

twenty-seven

Christine wiped her eyes with a tissue as she sat at her desk in the office at the back of the store and dried out. When she arrived after leaving Aunt Midge's house, she managed to ask Britney to run the store a little longer and then hid with her precious cats, her wet coat hanging on a hook by the door. She was grateful Wanda had decided to sit on her lap and offer some sympathetic purrs while she doused her heartache with a hot cup of tea, wrapped in the warm shawl she kept close for chilly days.

Her conversation with Brent kept echoing through her mind, and she pondered what she could have said to convince him to stay. But she just kept coming to the same agonizing conclusion. Britney had been right all along to say Brent would hurt her. He loved her, but he was giving up on any chance they had, unable to overcome the lack of self-worth his father had inspired. And that truth cut her to the bone.

A soft knock sounded on the door, and Christine drew in a long breath. Now she had to face her twin and have the conversation she'd been dreading ever since she'd returned.

"Come in," she called, hoping she sounded more confident than she felt.

The door squeaked open, and Britney gave her a concerned look. "Are you okay?"

Christine tried to swallow, but her heart was caught in her throat. "Yes, and I don't want to talk about it."

Britney remained in the doorway, studying her.

"Fine!" Christine threw her hands up in the air. "You were right. Brent never cheated on you, but he did hurt me. There. I said it. Now please leave." She sniffed as fresh tears trailed down her hot cheeks.

Britney closed the distance between them. When she bent down and pulled Christine in for a hug, Wanda leapt off Christine's lap and joined Pietro on the cat tree in the corner.

"I'm so sorry," Britney whispered in her ear. "Deep down, I wanted him to prove me wrong. I really did."

Christine disentangled herself from her sister's embrace and wiped her eyes with a fresh tissue.

"I've been meaning to tell you Hunter has this cute friend, Tony, who works with him. He's single, thirty, and has his own house." Britney leaned back on Christine's desk. "He's quite a catch, Chrissy."

"Brit, I know you mean well, but I'm not interested. I need some time to grieve. Just back off, okay?"

"But you don't want to miss out on this guy."

Christine groaned. When would her sister ever listen?

Britney snapped her fingers, and Christine could almost see the light bulb go on in her head. "We'll invite you over for dinner and have him there too. How does that sound?"

"Like torture," Christine deadpanned.

In her weakened position all she could do was sigh. But her heart pined for Brent, and it would for a long, long time.

◆ ◆ ◆

Rain drenched Brent's hoodie and jeans, yet he kept replacing boards in the fence, hoping the motion would stop the soul-crushing pangs of grief.

He'd lost Christine, even as a friend. If only he'd found a solution to avoid it. Now he couldn't stop replaying the pain in her beautiful face when he told her Britney had been right to say Christine deserved better than him. The tears racing down her cheeks had been too much for him. He'd hurt her deeply, and he would feel the sharp sting of regret for the rest of his life.

He'd wanted to tell her he loved her, needed her, and wanted to build a future with her, have a family with her. But he couldn't make those dreams come true, and he had to let her go.

"Brent Theodore Nicholson, what on earth are you doing working out here in the rain?" Aunt Midge's voice rang out behind him.

He turned to face her confused expression. She wore a yellow raincoat, yellow rain boots, and a large yellow rain hat, all while holding a bright-pink umbrella over her head.

"I'm trying to get this done."

"In the rain? Have you lost your mind?"

Possibly.

"Come inside. Now!"

He deposited his supplies in the dry garage, then followed his aunt into the kitchen, where she grabbed a clean towel from the dryer in the adjoining laundry room and handed it to him.

"I saw Christine was here briefly," she said as she hung her wet gear on hooks by the door to the deck. "She looked upset. Did you two have an argument?"

He dried himself while debating a response. "It's nothing to worry about," he finally said.

"I'm not stupid. I saw the look on your face too." She pursed her lips, then said, "You're making a huge mistake letting her go."

His phone rang, and he was grateful for the interruption. But when he found the art dealer's name on the screen, he was disappointed. He'd hoped it was Christine. But who was he kidding? She'd never call him again, and that truth drove a nail into his heart.

"Hello," he said. "Ms. Ramsey?"

"Brent, yes. Hi. I have exciting news. I have a buyer for your aunt's paintings, and he's considering a very generous offer. He's coming to look at them in person next week."

"Fantastic."

"I'll be in touch soon with more information."

"We'll look forward to hearing from you." Brent disconnected the call and found his aunt watching him. "Someone is interested in buying your paintings."

"That's great, but what are you going to do about Christine?"

"It's over, Aunt Midge." He considered that statement. "Actually, we were never a couple, so there's nothing to be over."

She harrumphed. "You could've fooled everyone who saw you two together. You're the one who refuses to admit that you just lost a woman who loves you deeply. And you also refuse to admit that you love her just as much and you're meant to be together."

Brent slipped past her. "I'm going to take a hot shower."

He made his way down the hall and tried to put his aunt's words out of his head. But he knew the truth. He'd always regret what he'd just done to the woman he loved. Still, what choice did he have?

Thursday afternoon Brent stood in his aunt's driveway and studied the For Sale sign on her front lawn. Aunt Midge and her Realtor, Elena Wolfe, stood next to him.

"You did a tremendous job updating this house, Brent," she declared, then turned toward his aunt. "I predict you'll have a bidding war over this place once we start accepting offers. But we'll wait a while to build interest. I also don't think it will be on the market long, so you'd better start packing."

"I will," his aunt said, her eyes bright with anticipation.

Elena hit a button on her key fob, and the doors on her black Cadillac Escalade unlocked. "Thank you again for your business. I'll be in touch." She shook Aunt Midge's hand, then climbed into her SUV and backed down the driveway.

Aunt Midge rubbed Brent's arm. "I can't thank you enough for your hard work."

"You're welcome. I'm going to finish the fence now."

"In the mud? All that rain has made a mess back there. And you look tired. Why don't you come inside and watch a movie with me? You can finish it tomorrow."

"No, I need to get this done if potential buyers are going to start coming. Call if you need me."

He retrieved his supplies from the garage and then tramped through the mud to the fence. While he worked, he tried to dismiss the raw anguish that had kept him awake for two nights. He felt gutted after losing Christine, and he couldn't stop doubting his decision to leave her. Yet he still had no viable solution for not only staying in Flowering Grove but making a life with her.

Despair continued to plague him as he worked his way around the yard, replacing the last of the rotten boards in the fence. He was nearly done when footsteps sounded behind him. He kept working, hoping his aunt would go back inside without imparting more of her wise gems. They would only make him feel worse.

"Son," his father's voice said, "you do fantastic work."

Brent blinked and did a mental headshake. He had to be dreaming. No way would his father actually bless him with encouraging words. Especially not about his remodeling work.

"Did you hear me?" Dad asked.

Brent closed his eyes for a moment and then opened them before spinning to face his dad. "I did. But I must have heard you wrong." He held his breath, preparing for an argument, but to his surprise his father smiled. Had the entire world gone crazy?

"Your aunt just gave your mom and me a tour, and we can't get over the improvements you've made. The house looks great." He hesitated. "I never realized how skilled you are."

"Thanks," Brent managed to say.

Dad cleared his throat. "Listen, I'm sorry for pushing you toward my dreams, not listening to what you needed and wanted—especially after your injury."

Brent studied his father, wondering again if he was dreaming. "Why are you suddenly supporting me now?"

Dad massaged the back of his neck, looking nervous—or maybe embarrassed. "Over the last few weeks your mom has made me realize I've been blinded by my own failures. She's been telling me that for years, but I believed I was being a good father by pushing you to do better than I did. Now I understand how wrong I've been, and I want to make amends with you—if it's not too late."

Brent's eyes burned as confusion churned in his gut. His mother had been defending him for years, and now his father saw his own mistakes? This was too much to comprehend at once!

Dad nodded toward the house. "Your mom brought a lemon cake, and your aunt is making coffee. Come inside and join us."

Brent considered refusing his father. After all the years he'd nagged and berated him, this apology seemed like too little too late. But then something inside him snapped apart. He needed his family, and maybe today his father had become the loving, supportive dad he needed.

He cleared his throat and nodded. "Sure."

◆ ◆ ◆

Christine tried to stay calm as she examined her books, but while the loan from her parents had helped, it wasn't enough to solve her problem long-term. She still had no choice but to start charging the higher booth rent next month. She'd emailed her vendors, and so far none had threatened to leave, which was a good start. But this was only Thursday, and the weekend might tell another story. No matter what, though, she had to find a way to bring in more revenue in order to afford her own higher rent.

But what was weighing so heavily on her shoulders wasn't finances. She slumped back in her desk chair and rubbed her eyes as grief once again wrapped around her heart. Wanda and Pietro were snoring on their cat tree, and she longed to be that relaxed without a care in the world.

She folded her arms on the desk and rested her head on them. Replaying her devastating conversation with Brent on a painful loop, her mind had been taunting her for two days. And each time, she wondered if he would have admitted he loved her and decided to stay if only she'd said the right words.

When her cell phone rang, she jumped with renewed hope. But

after she dug it out from under a stack of receipts, her posture wilted when she found not Brent's name on the screen but her mother's. She silently berated herself. She was grateful for her mom.

"Hey," she said, hoping she sounded chipper.

"Chrissy. How are you holding up?"

Christine sat back in her chair. "Why do you ask?"

"I'm at your back door. Please let me in."

"I'm not home. I'm at the store."

"So am I. Let me in, please."

She met her mother at the back door and then invited her into the office, where Mom sat on the love seat across from the desk as she returned to her chair.

"Your sister shared what happened." Mom's tone was gentle and sympathetic. "I'm so sorry, sweetheart. Why didn't you tell me?"

"I didn't want to hear you say 'I told you so.'"

Mom shook her head. "I'm not here to tell you that. I'm here to listen and offer my support."

"Thanks." Christine's voice cracked. "But I assumed you still disapproved of Brent even after I explained the truth about him at the twins' birthday party."

"I believe what you told me. I watched him there, and he seems like a nice man."

Christine sniffed. "He is." She ran her fingers over the edge of her desk. "But in the end, he's returning to Virginia. I think he loves me, but he's given up on us. He claims no woman would want him even though he knows I do. As if it matters to me that he doesn't have the life he'd hoped for." She told her mother just enough for her to understand where Brent struggled. "I think he should have given us a chance to work things out together, but he wouldn't. And that hurts."

Christine rested her elbow on the desk and her chin in her hand.

"I thought I was making a difference, but now I keep wondering what I did wrong."

"I don't think you did anything wrong, Chrissy. And from what I saw at the party, he does care for you, perhaps deeply. But whatever he's going through, he must have to work it out on his own."

Christine sighed. "Truthfully, I think I was fooling myself into thinking I was good enough for him."

"Why would you say that? You're beautiful, intelligent, hard-working, and you own your own successful business. Why would you ever imagine that you aren't good enough for any man?"

Christine felt a wall crack inside her and then crumble. "Mom, I always felt stuck in Britney's shadow. She was the perfect, popular, beautiful, sophisticated twin while I was the invisible wallflower. When we were growing up, she was the one who always had a boyfriend. She and Brent were prom queen and king, homecoming queen and king, the most attractive and popular kids at school, the 'it couple.'" She made air quotes with her fingers before going on.

"You had Britney in dance classes and on cheer teams—just like you were when you were growing up. That's fine, but when I didn't want to participate, you acted as if something was wrong with me. It drove me crazy." Christine's voice sounded reedy to her own ears as her emotions bubbled up. "Britney was the one you paraded around, and I was the one in the background, trying not to choke on my jealousy as you and everyone else compared us."

"Oh no." Mom's blue eyes glittered. "I'm-I'm so sorry. I never meant to do that."

Christine pushed away a niggle of guilt. "I'm sorry, Mom. I didn't mean to make you feel bad."

"I wish you'd told me sooner." She pulled a tissue from the box on the desk and wiped her eyes. "I never realized you felt that way. I love you girls equally, and I never meant to compare you or make you feel inferior because you had different interests. I'm proud of you both. You're as special as Britney is."

Christine sniffed. "It's okay." She took a tissue from the box and dabbed her nose. "I'm just feeling broken after losing Brent."

Mom came around the desk and pulled Christine in for a hug. "I'm so sorry, sweetheart. I adore you. And I'm sorry Brent broke your heart. Someday you'll meet a man who will treat you right and love you the way you deserve to be loved. Don't give up."

Christine closed her eyes and savored her mother's support. But she was ready to put a cover over her heart and give up on love. Maybe she was better off alone. After all, she had her family, her cats, and her store. That was all she really needed.

If only she could stop yearning for Brent.

twenty-eight

Christine tried to keep her expression pleasant as she sat in her sister's dining room. Tony Wallace gave her a warm smile from across the table, and she returned the gesture before focusing on her roast beef.

She'd considered turning down her sister's dinner invitation since she was aware it was a veiled excuse to introduce her to Hunter's coworker. But as much as Christine dreaded her twin serving as a matchmaker, the thought of seeing her sweet nieces warmed her aching heart. So she'd reluctantly agreed to not only come but bring a cheesecake from the bakery across from her store.

When Christine arrived, Tony was already there, laughing as the twins danced around for him. He seemed kind and patient with the girls. He was also attractive with short, light-brown hair and kind gray eyes. He was fit and tall and friendly and outgoing as he asked about her store and seemed interested.

But he wasn't Brent.

Christine was grateful when the girls took over the dinner conversation, sharing detailed anecdotes about their adventures in pre-K. Yet as much as she usually enjoyed listening to her nieces, her thoughts were stuck on Brent. She missed his smile, his laugh, his teasing, their talks. She longed for the feel of his hand holding hers, his strong arms embracing her, and his lips brushing her cheek. A hollow ache radiated in her chest.

"Auntie Christine?"

Her eyes flicked to Maddy sitting beside her. "Yes?"

"You look sad." Her niece reached up and touched her cheek. "Are you okay?"

Christine's heart seemed to turn over in her chest. "Yes, sweet girl. I'm just a little tired." She peeked at her sister, who also looked concerned.

She rubbed her hands together. "Who's ready for chocolate chip cheesecake?"

"Me! Me! Me!" the twins sang.

"I'll get it, then."

Britney jumped up from her chair. "And I'll make a pot of coffee."

Between them, they were able to clear the table with one trip to the kitchen. Christine rinsed dishes and placed them in the dishwasher, and Britney gathered mugs, dessert plates, and cream and sugar on a tray before she moved as close to Christine as she could get. "Isn't Tony nice?" she asked quietly.

"Yeah." *Here it comes.*

"And he's handsome too."

"Uh-huh."

"Chrissy, look at me," Britney said, her tone insistent.

Swallowing a sigh, Christine turned toward her sister. "What?"

"Do you like him?" Britney looked too eager, too excited about the prospect of Christine's moving on from Brent.

"Brit, it's been exactly six days since I had my heart broken." She held up her hands, the correct number of fingers displayed. "So would you please back off a little?"

Her sister frowned. "Oh. Right. Sorry." She cleared her throat. "You should get his number so you can call him when you're ready to go out, though. Like I told you last week, he's a great catch."

Christine choked on the urge to scream. Would Britney *ever* respect her wishes?

Mila scampered into the kitchen. "Do you need help?"

"Would you please get six small forks from the utensil drawer, sweetie?" Britney asked.

"Yes, Mommy." Mila yanked it open.

Christine lifted the cheesecake from the bottom shelf of the refrigerator as Britney carried the tray into the dining room.

"Auntie Chrissy," Mila said.

"What, honey?"

"Where's your boyfriend?"

Christine set the cake on the counter and fingered the box. "I don't have a boyfriend."

"Your friend Mr. Brent," Mila said. "He came to our party. Where is he?"

Christine blinked as her hands shook. "Well, Mr. Brent and I are just friends, and he's going back to his home in Virginia, so we won't see him anymore."

"Oh." Mila frowned. "I liked him." She closed the drawer and rushed back into the dining room with the forks in her hand.

Christine looked down at the cheesecake box as a fresh pang of sorrow overcame her.

Britney appeared in the doorway, her brow knitted. "Are you coming?"

"Yeah. I just need a minute."

Once Britney left, Christine hugged her arms to her chest. Then, closing her eyes, she took a deep breath to steady her nerves. She had to get herself together and find a way to move on without Brent. She was strong. She could do this.

She removed the cheesecake from the box and set it on the serving plate Britney had left on the counter. Then she located a knife and cake server before squaring her shoulders and carrying the dessert into the dining room.

"All right," she announced. "Let's enjoy this scrumptious cheesecake."

◆ ◆ ◆

After reading her nieces a bedtime story and kissing them good night, Christine descended the stairs and peered out a window to find the other three adults sitting around the wood-burning firepit on the deck. Joining them—and unwilling to appear rude to Tony—she took the open seat next to their guest on the patio sofa. The night air was chilly, and the scent of burning wood floated all around her as she took in the clear sky.

Memories of enjoying that romantic evening with Brent in the gazebo hit her hard and fast, and she took yet another deep breath, hoping to keep her emotions under control.

"Did they behave for you?" Britney asked.

"Of course they did," she said, hoping to keep her voice steady. "They always do."

Britney and Hunter looked at each other and laughed, then Hunter lifted his mug. "That coffee hit the spot."

"Would you like more?" Britney's expression suddenly brightened. "Or how about some hot chocolate? That's always perfect on a cold night."

Hunter smiled. "That sounds great. What do you think, Tony?"

"I never turn down hot chocolate. How about you, Christine?" Tony angled his body toward her, his expression . . . eager?

She pasted a bright smile on her face. The last time she'd had hot chocolate, she was with Brent. "Sure." She looked at her sister. "I'll come help."

"Hunter and I can handle it." Britney stood and gave her husband's arm a gentle smack.

Oh no. Christine grimaced. She knew exactly what her twin sister was up to. Britney wanted to get herself and Hunter out of the way so Christine and Tony would have time to talk alone.

Britney and Hunter disappeared into the house, and Christine stared at the fire as it snapped, popped, and hissed.

"Your nieces are adorable," Tony said. "I wish I could bottle their energy."

Christine nodded. "I've had the same thought many times."

"It sounds like your store keeps you busy."

"It does." She folded her hands in her lap. "But I'm planning a Black Friday sale to try to generate more business. I could use it."

Christine inwardly groaned. Why had she told Tony she needed more income?

An awkward silence stretched like a giant chasm between them. Britney and Hunter needed to return soon. She couldn't keep the conversation going on her own.

"Christine," Tony finally said, "it's obvious that Hunter and Britney are trying to set us up. They haven't been at all subtle about it."

She rolled her eyes. "Subtlety is not my sister's strong suit."

"No, it's not." He chuckled, and Christine joined him, feeling as if the ice had broken between them.

"You have a very pretty smile." His tone was gentle. "Listen, I know we're strangers, but I would like to get to know you better."

Christine frowned. "Tony, I need to be honest with you."

"Please do."

"I just got out of a—well, a relationship, and I'm still licking my wounds. All I really need right now is a friend."

"I completely understand, but it would be nice to have another friend."

"Thank you," she said as relief relaxed her shoulders.

The sliding glass door opened with a *whoosh*, and Hunter returned to the deck balancing a tray with four mugs.

Britney followed him holding a tin. "We not only have hot chocolate but some snickerdoodles!"

"I don't think I can eat another bite after that delicious cheesecake," Tony muttered.

Christine shook her head. "Neither can I."

Hunter distributed the hot chocolate, and Britney opened the tin of cookies but then set them on a side table.

"Can you believe Thanksgiving is next week?" Britney asked. "And our reunion too! I'm so excited. Aren't you, Chrissy?"

Christine nodded before taking a sip of her hot chocolate. But the idea of attending the event without Brent made her eyes sting.

She'd get through it, though. She just didn't know how.

◆ ◆ ◆

"The paintings sold so fast!" Aunt Midge said as she sat beside Brent in her Camry. "I know Ms. Ramsey could have mailed the check, but like I told you, I want to cash it right away so I can give you the money before you leave on Sunday."

Brent shook his head as he navigated the heavy Friday afternoon traffic on Interstate 485 on their way back to Flowering Grove. "No,

Aunt Midge. Those were your paintings. Uncle Sal purchased them for you as a special gift, and you've already paid me for my work. I can't take this money."

"You can and you will," she said. "I don't need it, Brent. I've told you. Your uncle saved and invested well, and the money from the sale of my house will be more than enough to buy my new condo and help pay my retirement-community fees. In fact, I've already made the deposit on the exact condo I want. And speaking of the house, I can't believe how many people have seen the house and shown interest. It's all because of the work you did to spruce it up."

He pushed one hand through his mess of unruly curls and tried to banish the bereavement that had gripped him ever since Christine left him in the rain. He'd thrown himself into hauling Aunt Midge's unwanted furniture to the donation center, finding her moving boxes, keeping the place clean, mowing the lawn, and taking her out for coffee or ice cream whenever her Realtor scheduled a showing. But none of that had helped his battered heart.

"You need this money, Brent. Use it to restart your life, maybe even start a new business. Now take me to my bank. Normally they'd want me to wait for a check this large to clear, but let's just say I made an arrangement."

His aunt's words had broken through his mental tirade, and he knew better than to question what arrangement she might have made. "Yes, ma'am," he muttered. No use arguing with her. After he deposited the money into his savings account, he'd keep it there in case she needed it one day.

They drove on with only the sound of oldies music and road noise filling the car. Then while Aunt Midge took care of her business inside her bank, Brent stared out the car's windshield. Thoughts of Christine invaded his mind in a fog, his anguish as sharp as a blade.

When Aunt Midge returned, she said nothing until he'd parked the car in her driveway. "Here," she said, pressing the thick bank envelope into his hand. "I won't take no for an answer."

"Thank you," he whispered. Her generosity was overwhelming.

Aunt Midge smiled as she cupped her hand to his cheek. "You deserve to be happy, Brent. And giving you this money makes me happy."

As they walked into the house, he considered what to do with this influx of funds if he did decide to spend it. The possibilities were endless. And if he could just get on his feet again, maybe Christine would give him another chance.

But then an idea smacked him in the face, and after quickly formulating a plan, he was determined to act on it the very next night.

◆ ◆ ◆

Brent sat in his truck and studied the darkened front windows of Treasure Hunting Antique Mall. A banner boasted Christine's upcoming Black Friday sale in large, neon-colored letters, and by the light of a streetlamp he could just make out the sign asking customers not to let the cats out no matter what they said. He smiled weakly. Allergies or no, those cats weren't so bad. And Christine loved them.

Brent opened his center console and pulled out the thick envelope. Earlier he'd scrawled "Christine" across the front with a Sharpie before writing a note on an index card and slipping it inside. Now closing his eyes, he tried to imagine Christine's face when she found the envelope Tuesday morning, following her two days off. He'd made a promise to help her save the store, and this was how he could keep it.

He'd considered delivering the gift in person, but he was afraid he might change his mind about staying in Flowering Grove if he faced her. Returning to Virginia Beach was still the best choice, and he'd be back there tomorrow.

He got out of the truck and made his way to the storefront, where he dropped the envelope through the mail slot and listened as it *thump*ed to the floor inside. Then as he drove away, seeing the precious store in his rearview mirror, his heart gave in to despair. Leaving Christine was the hardest thing he'd ever had to do.

◆ ◆ ◆

Christine flipped on the sound system in her store, and "Wake Me Up Before You Go-Go" by Wham! rang through the speakers as she crossed to the front door. Wanda and Pietro trotted behind her, singing a chorus of meows as if telling her the details of their two days spent alone.

"I know, I know," she said. "I'm sorry I didn't stop by to see you, but I left you plenty of food and water like I always do. I also scooped your litterbox and refilled your bowls as soon as I came in this morning, so there's no need to keep haranguing me. I am a good cat mommy despite what you seem to think."

She bent to gather the small mountain of envelopes and catalogs strewn about the floor below the mail slot, then dropped it on the counter as she sank onto the stool behind it. Flipping through the pile, she tossed the catalogs and ads into the recycle bin. But when she came to a thick, plain manila envelope with her first name written neatly in black Sharpie, she narrowed her eyes. She turned the envelope over in search of a return address or some kind of note but found it blank.

"That's strange," she whispered.

She opened the envelope, pulled out a stack of cash, and gasped. Then she found three more stacks. Her pulse rocketed as she set the money on the counter, then tipped the envelope hoping for a letter, a note, anything to explain the mystery. An index card with the same neat block penmanship slipped out. *Use this to save your store. It's not a loan. It's a gift.*

Her elbows dropped to the counter, and a small cry of shock escaped her throat as she examined the cash, finding thousands of dollars. What this money could mean cycled through her mind. She could repay her parents, pay her building rent months in advance, add upgrades to the store.

But all that seemed too good to be true, and she pinched the bridge of her nose as she speculated who on earth would give her such a large and generous gift—and why. If it were Britney and Hunter or her parents, they would tell her outright. And Pam and Steve didn't have that kind of money.

After running the names of almost everyone else she knew in Flowering Grove through her mind, Midge Marcello's popped up, and then she pictured the paintings Brent found in her basement.

The pieces fell together. She'd shared her worries about her store with Aunt Midge, and she must have sold the paintings and then decided to give her the money. Who else would have that kind of cash to give, let alone do such a generous thing?

"Oh, Aunt Midge," Christine whispered as tears filled her eyes. "How can I ever thank you enough?"

Christine slipped the money back into the envelope before securing it in her office safe. Then, glancing at the clock on the wall, she realized it was time to open the store. She returned to the front door and flipped the Closed sign to Open. She'd visit Aunt Midge later today.

But then her thoughts turned to Brent. Why hadn't Aunt Midge given the money to her nephew? He could have used it to start a new business. Then again, maybe she had and he'd refused it.

Christine shook her head to clear it. Not only was Brent's business not hers, but he'd made his choices, especially when it came to her. She doubted Aunt Midge's money would have made a bit of difference.

twenty-nine

Brent placed his keys and wallet on the dresser in Devonte's spare room and then dropped onto one corner of its twin bed. He yawned and rubbed his eyes before flopping back on the mattress. Every muscle in his body ached from working on one of the bathrooms in the elegant Victorian home he and his new coworkers were remodeling in downtown Norfolk. And it was only Tuesday, his second day on the job.

When he'd first laid eyes on the home, he'd cringed. Although it was gray instead of yellow, it reminded him of the Victorian across the street from Christine's house. It had a similar sweeping front porch and two-story tower. But being there felt worse when he learned the new owner had decided to gut and modernize the home rather than preserve its glory. That went against every fiber of Brent's being. When he'd worked on historic houses for his own company, he'd always taken their original charm and style into consideration.

In fact, he'd very much resented the work today as he disposed of a flawless, vintage clawfoot bathtub to replace it with an ordinary, modern garden tub. And he'd had to bite his tongue as he watched two other workers remove the custom, hand-carved wood stair railing and swap it for a sleek metal one.

But that wasn't the worst part of his day. He was still drowning in agony after leaving Christine behind. She'd become a permanent fixture in the back of his mind during the day, and she haunted his dreams at night. He constantly lost himself in memories of their time together—laughing and teasing, holding hands, hugging each other close, sharing their deepest secrets. He longed to call her to hear her sweet voice, ask her how she was doing, and recount the details of his day. Regret and doubt had become his constant companions as he pondered his choice to leave Flowering Grove without even telling her goodbye.

His jaw tightened. Coming back to Virginia Beach felt like a mistake. Life without Christine was miserable, and each day without her seemed worse than the last.

When his phone rang with a video call, he pulled it from his back pocket and found his sister's name on the screen. "Kylie!" he said as he answered.

His younger sister glowered at him. "Why am I home for Thanksgiving and you're not? Aunt Midge told me you left on Sunday and said you're not coming back. Are you deliberately avoiding me, big brother?"

Brent chuckled. He loved how Kylie always got straight to the point.

"You're laughing at me? I'm annoyed, and you're *laughing*?" Her lips were twitching.

"I'm not avoiding you. I just had to get back here to start my new job. You know how it is."

"Speaking of work, you did an amazing thing here, Brent." Kylie pivoted, showing him one freshly painted family-room wall in their great-aunt's house. "I can't get over your skills."

"Thank you. How's Aunt Midge?"

His aunt appeared on the screen. "Hi! How's Virginia Beach?"

"Cold." He folded his free arm behind his head.

"And how's the new job?"

"It's—well, it's not what I thought it would be."

Her brow furrowed. "What do you mean?"

"I didn't realize we'd be updating an old Victorian to turn it into an Airbnb." He frowned. "It's not the kind of work I want to do. It just feels . . . wrong to disrespect an elegant house like this."

"Oh. I'm sorry to hear that."

"How are things with you?" he asked, desperate to change the subject.

"My Realtor is accepting offers starting Friday, and she still thinks we may have a bidding war."

"That's good news."

Kylie appeared on the screen again. "So why aren't you coming home for Thanksgiving?"

"It's a long drive, and I have to work both tomorrow and Friday. I would get there, have dinner, and then just have to leave again."

Kylie looked annoyed. "But we want to see you. And who works the day after Thanksgiving?"

Brent sighed. "This is a big job, and it has to be done by March."

"It's only November!"

"Trust me when I say it will take until March. Plus I have a new boss to impress."

Aunt Midge appeared again. "But you'll miss your reunion, and Christine will be there." Her look was rather pointed.

"Come back, Brent—if only to get Christine," his sister said. "Aunt Midge told me you have a thing going with her, and she's more important than a job. You can get another one."

He frowned and shook his head. "There's no *thing*."

Amy Clipston

"Only because you messed it up," Aunt Midge said.

"I need to go, you two. I'll call you on Thursday to wish everyone a happy Thanksgiving."

Both women said what sounded like disgruntled goodbyes before he disconnected the call.

He opened his photo app and scrolled through the selfies Christine had taken and sent him. He came to the one of them sitting on the hill, and he took in her beautiful smile and gorgeous blue eyes. Then he stopped when he came to a photo of Christine laughing with her nieces at their birthday party. He cherished how much she loved those two little girls.

He swiped to another photo of the two of them, and this time they were snuggling under the white Christmas lights in the gazebo. They looked so happy—like they belonged together.

Brent closed his eyes as his heart constricted with missing her. He admired how kind, thoughtful, giving, and loyal Christine was. He loved everything about her—her smile, her laugh, her teasing. How she listened to him, supported him, and always had faith in him no matter what.

Aunt Midge was right. He had messed up. But he still had no idea how he could build a life with Christine, let alone make things right after abandoning her.

Was she okay?

He opened his last text conversation with her, but his fingers merely hovered over the keys. What could he possibly say that would make her respond? Besides, he didn't want her to suspect the money she surely found with her store mail that morning was from him. He didn't want her to know, at least not for sure. If he had, he would have signed the note.

He locked his phone and dropped it onto the bed beside him.

289

He had to find a way to evict Christine from his mind. But how could he when he loved her so?

◆ ◆ ◆

Christine parked her pickup truck in the driveway behind Aunt Midge's red Camry and a white Ford Escape. She'd stayed late at the store to start getting ready for her Black Friday sale three days from now, and then after a quick bite at home, she'd headed here to thank her friend for such a generous gift.

It had occurred to her to return it, but not only had Brent shared that his aunt was financially stable even without selling the paintings, but she thought Aunt Midge might be hurt if she didn't put the money to good use. *We all love your store,* she'd said that day over chicken salad sandwiches. *"It's good for this community, and whatever I can do to support you, I will."*

"Looks like she has company," she mumbled to herself as she stepped out of the truck. When she spotted the For Sale sign on the front lawn, her heart felt heavy. It seemed like only yesterday that she and Brent were working to clear out Aunt Midge's basement and attic. That time together had passed too quickly.

The front door swung open, and Kylie Nicholson appeared.

Christine grinned. "Well, hi!"

Brent's younger sister was just as lovely as Christine remembered. Her light-brown hair was pulled back in a long, thick French braid, and her golden-brown eyes, so like Brent's, were accentuated with just the right amount of makeup.

Kylie yanked her into a warm hug. "Aunt Midge and I were just talking about you."

"Uh-oh. I hope it was good."

"Of course it was. Come in and have some tea and cookies with us."

"That sounds heavenly." Christine followed Kylie to the kitchen, where Aunt Midge sat at the table.

"Oh, Christine! I've missed you," Aunt Midge said as Christine leaned down and hugged her. "I'm so glad you stopped by."

Christine shucked her coat and hung it on the back of a chair before sitting down. "I missed you too. You look well. Have you had many folks looking at your house?"

"It's been like Grand Central Station! We must have had a dozen couples here since that sign went up. My Realtor is expecting more than one offer starting this Friday. She's had such good feedback."

"That's because of Brent's work," Kylie said as she poured hot water from a kettle into a mug with a tea bag.

Christine's heart gave a little bump at the mention of his name. "Aunt Midge, I have another check for you." She fished it out of her purse and pushed it across the table.

"Oh my goodness! I see sales have been good," Aunt Midge said.

Christine nodded and chose a sugar cookie shaped like a turkey from a plate in the center of the table. "These look delicious."

"Aunt Midge was telling me about your store, Christine. I want to stop by before I leave on Sunday. Will it be open this weekend?" Kylie brought the mug to the table for Christine.

"Thank you," Christine said. "Yes, I'm having a Black Friday sale that will span both Friday and Saturday."

"Wonderful!" Kylie sat beside Christine and looked at her aunt. "Maybe you, Mom, and I can go on Friday." She selected a cookie shaped like a pumpkin with orange icing.

"Oh yes! You know I love to shop." Aunt Midge clapped her hands, but then her expression grew more serious. "How's it going with the store, Christine? I hope you don't mind I told Kylie a little about your struggles."

"No, I don't mind, and it's going to be fine. But I have you to thank for that. I found the envelope of money mixed in with my store mail this morning. I figured out such a gift could only be from you. I assume you sold the paintings, and I honestly don't know how to thank you properly." She took a sip of her tea.

Aunt Midge hesitated but then smiled. "Sweetie, you're right that the money came from the sale of my paintings, but it's not a gift from me."

"What do you mean?"

"I gave the money to Brent so he could start a new life. But the day he left for Virginia, he told me he'd secretly given it to you to keep his promise to help you find a way to save your store. I wasn't supposed to tell you, but I think you should know. And I'm glad he did it."

Christine stared at Midge, speechless and astonished.

"That sounds like my big brother, taking care of everyone else instead of himself." Kylie shook her head.

Renewed grief hit Christine like a wall of water, stealing her breath as she looked down at her tea. "I miss him so much," she whispered, her voice hoarse. "I keep hoping he'll show up to tell me he can't live without me."

She swallowed a groan when both Kylie and Aunt Midge gave her sympathetic expressions. "I'm sorry. I shouldn't have said that out loud." She lifted her mug and straightened her shoulders. "I'm grateful Brent's given me this money, and more than ever I know he cares about me. I just wish he'd stayed. We could have worked out any problem—together. Mine. His. Instead, he chose to fight his battles on his own."

Kylie rested her hand on Christine's arm. "My brother is a doofus, but I think he'll soon realize he made a mistake."

Christine sighed. "I'm sorry. I don't mean to whine about how Brent broke my heart. Let's change the subject. Kylie, tell me about your master's degree program and work with children."

"Oh my goodness. They're both so demanding, but I love every minute."

Forcing herself to pay attention, Christine enjoyed Kylie's stories as they ate a few more cookies and drank their tea. When she looked up at the clock on the wall, it was almost nine o'clock.

"It's getting late. I should go." She carried her mug to the counter and then pulled on her coat.

Kylie stood. "We need to do this again before I leave on Sunday."

"I agree!" Aunt Midge announced as she pushed herself up from the table.

"I'll see you at the store on Friday?" Christine asked her.

"Yes, you will, sweetie." She touched her cheek. "And don't give up on my nephew. He'll come to his senses in time."

Christine smiled and hugged her. "Have a wonderful Thanksgiving."

"You too."

Kylie walked with Christine to the front door. "Brent is stubborn and hardheaded, and sometimes he has tunnel vision. He doesn't see the obvious because he's so focused on some goal he believes is out of his reach. But Aunt Midge told me how happy he was whenever you were together. Just keep the faith, okay?"

Christine hugged Kylie goodbye, and as she walked to her truck, with all her heart she hoped both women were right about Brent. She needed him. The money would save her store, but only the man she loved could save her heart.

◆ ◆ ◆

Christine had tried her best to enjoy the Thanksgiving feast with her family, but her thoughts were stuck on what Kylie and Aunt Midge had told her. And she was still stunned to have learned Brent had given her the money. She'd considered reaching out to thank him, but she couldn't bring herself to do it. He'd made his decision and left her behind.

Yet she found herself impatiently checking her phone for missed calls or texts, hoping Brent might use the holiday as an excuse to reach out *to her*. But so far he hadn't, and the day was half over.

Delicious aromas from the remnants of their traditional meal—including turkey, stuffing, sweet potatoes, and green bean casserole—hung in the air as Christine set the last hand-washed serving platter in a cabinet, Mom finished loading the dishwasher, and Britney slipped the last of the leftovers into Tupperware.

Her sister seemed quiet today, but maybe she was just tired.

She padded into the family room, leaving her mother and Britney in the kitchen as they discussed plans to hit the Black Friday sales early. Her stomach twisted as she stared at the football game her father was watching on TV. Memories of Brent standing on the high school field's sidelines, looking happy while proudly wearing Flowering Grove Falcons attire, assaulted her mind.

"You okay?"

Christine turned toward her father. "Yes." She scanned the family room. "Where did Hunter and the girls go?"

"The twins begged him to play catch outside. He said he'd try to get back before the fourth quarter so he can watch the end of the game, but we'll see. You know how those girls are when they want to play." Dad's eyes twinkled. He loved those children as much as she did.

Christine came around the sofa and sat beside him, clasping her hands. "Sorry to interrupt, but I want to talk to you about something—alone." She pulled a check from her pocket and handed it to him. "I'm grateful that you and Mom gave me the loan, and here's the entire amount."

Dad took the check and stared at it. "We told you to take your time, Chrissy. Why are you giving the money back now?"

"I received a gift from a benefactor, enabling me to not only pay you back but make my new rent and install upgrades to the store while I work to grow my business long-term."

"A benefactor?" Dad's hazel eyes searched hers.

Christine took a deep breath, then explained what Brent had done and asked that he and her mother keep this news to themselves. She doubted Brent would want anyone else to know.

Dad's brow pinched. "So Brent gave you money to save your store." He said the words slowly as if trying to process them.

"Brent did *what*?"

Christine spun to see her sister standing in the doorway. *Great. So much for keeping his gift a secret!*

Mom came up behind her, looking confused.

"Where did he get the money?" Britney plopped into a chair across from Christine. "And how much did he give you?"

Mom padded over and placed her hands on her hips. "What's going on?"

Christine held up her hands like a traffic cop. "Slow down. I'll explain it again." She retold the story, leaving out the amount Brent had given her. No one else needed to know that.

"So he gave you money and then returned to Virginia," Britney said. "Huh. That's something."

Mom's brow crinkled. "I'm still confused. Brent cared enough to help you save your store but then left you? Why didn't he stay?"

Christine hugged her arms to her waist and swallowed back what must be the truth. *Because although he's a good and generous man who cares about me, I've been kidding myself to believe he loves me.*

Mom's expression was sympathetic when Christine didn't respond to her question.

"What will you do with the money?" Britney asked.

"I just paid Mom and Dad back for a loan they gave me, and now I can pay the higher rent without raising my vendors' booth rent. Then I'm not sure, but whatever I do, it will serve to grow my business and make it sustainable."

Britney leaned forward. "Chrissy, the man really cares about you."

"He left me, Brit." Christine gave a humorless laugh. "If he cares so much, then where is he?"

Dad patted her arm. "Judging by what Brent did to help you, I agree with your sister. And not only does he care about you, but he loves you."

Christine slumped back on the sofa and shook her head. *He was just keeping a promise to help a good friend, nothing more.*

Mom sat beside her and patted her knee. "Sweetheart, your dad and sister are right. I think Brent will be back—and sooner than you might imagine."

"That's what his sister and aunt told me, but I still doubt it. He hasn't reached out to me since we"—she took a trembling breath as their devastating conversation in the rain filled her mind—"parted ways two weeks ago."

Britney stood, then sat on the coffee table directly in front of Christine, her expression full of empathy. "Chrissy, I've wanted to talk to you all day. I've been doing a lot of thinking, and I owe you a huge apology." She paused as if gathering her words. "I'm sorry for not supporting you when you and Brent were together. Now I see he's a genuine and loyal man, and I had completely misjudged him when I ghosted him. He didn't break my heart. If anything, I broke his."

"You mean that?" Christine wasn't sure she should believe her ears.

"I do. I never gave Brent a chance to explain his side of Grant's story." She scoffed. "Worse than that, I never even asked him if what Grant said was true. I just assumed the worst about him, even though he'd never given me a reason to doubt him. He was loyal and always thought of me before he thought of himself."

"That's how he treated me too."

"I know, but I've been blind. Or maybe I refused to admit the truth. I've been so focused on myself that I haven't realized how much I've hurt other people, especially Brent."

Christine stared at her.

"But the worst part is the pain I've caused my own twin." Britney's words vibrated, and her blue eyes glistened with unshed tears. "I never supported you the way a sister should. You tried to tell me how much you were hurting after Brent confirmed he was leaving, but I didn't listen. I was focused on trying to set you up with someone I believed was better than him. I was meddling in your personal life instead of acknowledging your pain. But Hunter made me realize how wrong I was to insist on pushing my own agenda when you just needed me to be a sister to you."

She took Christine's hands in hers, then inhaled a shaky breath. "I'm so sorry. I've been a lousy sister for years. I hope you can forgive me."

Christine pulled her twin in for a tight hug. "Of course I forgive you, Brit." Tears trickled down her cheeks as she sniffed. "Thank you."

"I promise to do better."

When Christine heard someone else sniff, she pulled back and divided a look between her parents. They were both wiping their eyes. "This has been an emotional holiday, huh?" She laughed.

Mom passed around a box of tissues. "I'm just happy to see my girls bonding. No matter what, you need to be there for each other."

Britney nodded as she wiped her nose. "I know." She turned to Christine. "Do you think you'll come to the reunion Saturday?"

"I have no idea, Brit. It's the furthest thing from my mind right now."

"I understand, but I hope you will. It wouldn't be right without you." She took Christine's hands in hers again. "You won't be there alone. You'll have me and Pam by your side. I promise."

Christine appreciated her sister's love and support, but attending the reunion without Brent sounded like a nightmare. She couldn't let Britney or Pam down, though. She'd just have to power through and endure it.

thirty

Sitting in his truck, Brent pulled out the ham and cheese sandwich he'd packed earlier in the day. Then he frowned as he took a bite and stared at the home they'd been renovating all week, excluding Thanksgiving Day. He couldn't escape his conviction that destroying the Victorian's historic integrity was just wrong, and he dreaded spending the afternoon ruining another exquisite bathroom, taking it down to the studs.

His thoughts turned to the yellow Victorian across the street from Christine's house, and he wondered what it would be like to buy it for her and help decorate it for Christmas as she'd always longed to do.

And just like that, Christine's beautiful face filled his mind's eye for what seemed like the thousandth time this week. He nearly groaned as the familiar regret pounded him like members of an opposing football team determined to get their hands on the ball.

"You okay, man?" Devonte asked from the passenger seat. He pushed one hand through his thick dark hair before retrieving his own sandwich from a maroon zippered lunch bag.

Brent was grateful for his friend. He'd not only helped him find this job but charged him only the rent he could afford right now. "I'm fine."

"Thinking about her again?" Devonte took a bite.

Brent sighed. "Yeah." He'd given Devonte an abbreviated version of what happened between him and Christine yesterday, right after they'd shared a delicious Thanksgiving dinner with a few friends at the house. But it didn't feel like Thanksgiving without Aunt Midge keeping everyone laughing with her stories.

He missed his family.

And Christine.

When his phone rang, he pulled it from the pocket of his coat. His aunt's name filled the screen, and apprehension slammed through him. "Aunt Midge. Are you all right?"

"Of course I am! Why wouldn't I be?"

Brent heaved a sigh of relief as he turned toward Devonte, who chuckled. Apparently her voice carried enough that his friend could make out every word.

"Oh good. I was worried for a second."

"Don't be silly. So I have some news."

"Okay . . . Is it all right that my friend Devonte is here and can hear you?"

"Of course! Anyway, I just accepted an offer on my house."

"That's fantastic—and fast." He shifted in his seat and set his lunch bag on the center console. "I hope it was a fair one."

She laughed. "Oh, Brent, you have no idea. My Realtor arrived midmorning with the four best offers."

"Four?"

"Yes, four. And two of the buyers were so afraid of a bidding war that they offered high. The one I accepted is well over the asking price."

"No kidding." Brent caught a glimpse of Devonte raising his eyebrows.

"*And* I want you to use the difference."

Brent leaned his head back on the seat. "Aunt Midge," he began slowly, "I know you think you'll have plenty of money even after you buy the condo and move, but—"

"Don't talk to me like I'm a moron, young man!" she snipped. "I haven't lost it yet!"

"Yes, ma'am," Brent said, rolling his eyes as Devonte covered his mouth to shield a chuckle.

"This offer means I'll have cash to spare. I offered Kylie some of it, but she wants you to have it."

"But—"

"Now listen. You already know Elena Wolfe was impressed with the upgrades you made to my house. Well, now she's suggested a business flipping homes in Flowering Grove. She's offered to find houses with potential and then negotiate the best purchase price, and then you'll make all the necessary renovations. After that, she'll help sell the houses for a nice profit, and—"

"Whoa, Aunt Midge!" Brent raised his hand as if she were standing in front of him. "Slow down. Are you saying you want *me* to start a remodeling business there?"

His aunt clucked her tongue. "Isn't that what I just said? Now who's acting like the moron? But just listen to the rest. Until you're up on your feet, I'll be your silent partner, cosigning on the initial mortgages. Now you need to get your behind back here pronto so we can do this."

Brent's jaw dropped.

"You told me the truth," Devonte whispered. "She *is* feisty!"

"Are you still there, Brent?"

"I'm here," he managed to say. "I'm just in shock." He paused, trying to wrap his brain around what his aunt just told him. "You're serious about this."

"Of course I am! You belong in Flowering Grove, and it's time you admitted that."

Brent gulped against his dry throat as his mind whirled. His aunt was offering him a solution for not only returning to Christine but leaving a job he loathed. This past week had made him realize home remodeling was what he was meant to do, what he *wanted* to do. And didn't he deserve to do it on his own terms? He'd just had no idea how to pull that off after losing his first business. But now . . .

"Christine was here, Brent."

"She was?"

"She came to thank me for the money she thought I'd given her. I set her straight."

His stomach seemed to drop. "What did she say?"

"She was shocked. And she misses you, hon. She loves you just like you love her. Now come home! You can stay with me until the closing on the house and help me pack. Then once I'm in my condo, we'll start our business."

Excitement coursed through him. "Okay. I'll do it."

"Isn't your high school reunion tomorrow?"

"Yes."

"Well, then! Get here in time to go and apologize to Christine. Now get off the phone, pack your things, and call me when you're on the road."

"Yes, ma'am." He grinned. "And thank you."

"You'll thank me by coming home."

"I love you, Aunt Midge."

"I love you too. Now get moving. You have a lot to do." She disconnected the call.

Brent stared at his phone as his thoughts raced like a running back dashing toward the end zone. In just a matter of a few months, his life had done a one-eighty. He'd traveled from the brink of ruin to the opportunity to own another company.

And most importantly, Christine Sawyer loved him! There was still a chance he could get her back, and he wanted that so desperately he could taste it.

"I wish I had my own Aunt Midge."

Brent turned toward Devonte. "I'm still in shock. I don't know what to do first."

"Well, since it sounds like you need to be at that reunion, I suggest you find out how to buy a ticket. Then tell our boss you're quitting before you go home and pack."

Brent frowned. "I'm sorry to just pick up and leave like this."

"Why?"

"Because you've done so much for me."

Devonte shrugged. "Just remember me when you're ready to hire some folks. Maybe I'll move to Flowering Grove and work for you."

"Deal." Brent shook his hand. "And thank you."

After they finished their sandwiches, Brent picked up his phone and searched for Steve's number. He'd need his and Pam's help for his next plan.

◆ ◆ ◆

Christine rested her elbows on a high-top table and tried not to frown as she glanced around the venue for the reunion. Pop music pulsated from large speakers near the DJ while members of her class, all dressed to the nines, boogied on the country-club dance floor.

Britney and her committee had outdone themselves decorating the large room with white fairy lights, silver tablecloths, silver and white balloons, and white votive candles. A long table with food, punch, and a fancy ice sculpture sat in the corner beside a cash bar.

It was a lovely venue, but Christine would rather be just about anywhere else. She spotted her sister in the far corner talking with her cheerleading friends while Hunter stood nearby with a group of men who must be their husbands or dates. Although Britney had been hovering, offering her support, Christine insisted she visit with other people. She appreciated Britney's empathy, but she knew she'd miss reconnecting with other members of their class if she focused only on her.

Everywhere Christine looked she spotted happy couples—laughing, talking, dancing, holding hands—even kissing. Their bliss made her stomach curdle. As much as she tried to push Brent from her mind, he remained front and center, and seeing couples enjoying each other rubbed salt in her deep emotional wounds.

Christine peered down at her short, cap-sleeved, sequined black dress and three-inch black heels, then inwardly groaned. Yesterday Pam had suddenly become overly excited about the reunion, reminding Christine of their senior prom. Her best friend had called the store and announced that she'd made salon appointments for them to get their hair and nails done this afternoon. Christine still wondered how Pam managed to get them in with so little notice. She'd also arranged for Christine's mom to run the store in her absence even though she'd have to manage the second day of her Black Friday sale.

Now Pam looked adorable in a long dark-green dress with lace sleeves, her dark hair styled in a perfect French twist. But she'd insisted Christine don this dress she'd originally bought to wear herself, saying it looked better on her because of her "long, beautiful legs."

Christine, however, felt ridiculous in the fancy—no, absurd!—dress. And at Pam's insistence, her face was covered with more makeup than she ever felt comfortable wearing, not to mention cramming her feet into such uncomfortable shoes. She now towered over not just her sister but Pam and almost every woman there. Pam said she looked like a model, but she didn't feel like one. She felt like a buffoon, or more accurately, an imposter. She even felt odd with her hair pulled back and falling past her shoulders in spiraling curls.

Pam appeared and bumped her shoulder against Christine's. "You're way too lovely to look so depressed at this fun party. I'm telling you that dress never looked that good on me." She turned to her husband. "Doesn't Christine look fantastic tonight?"

"Uh . . ." Steve rubbed his neck as his cheeks blushed bright red. "Will I get in trouble if I answer your question honestly? Because if so, I'd rather lie." He looked as uncomfortable as Christine felt.

Pam laughed. "I know Christine is a knockout. She looks *perfect*." Then she and Steve seemed to share a look. They'd been acting as if they had a secret all evening, and it was wearing on Christine's already thin nerves. She'd had enough of this horrible event.

She picked up her black sequined clutch. "I want to go home. But since you two wouldn't let me drive myself, I'm stranded." She met Steve's hesitant gaze. What was going on? "Would you please take me home? You can come right back."

Now concern flashed over his face, and he looked to his wife . . . for help? "Um . . ."

"You two have been acting suspicious all evening. What are you keeping from me?"

Pam touched Christine's arm. "Just be patient, okay?"

"Patient? Why? I didn't even want to come tonight, but I didn't want to let you and Britney down. Now I'm just ready to go home."

Steve's eyes focused on something behind Christine, and his expression brightened. "Finally," he mumbled.

Pam turned to look, then squeaked. Christine turned as well, and her knees nearly buckled when she saw Brent standing in the doorway. He was drop-dead gorgeous in a three-piece charcoal-colored suit, coupled with a white shirt and darker-gray tie. His face was clean-shaven, and his hair was short, his unruly curls transformed into waves. How could he cut those glorious curls?

His eyes were bright as he scanned the room as if in search of someone. Why was he here? Christine suddenly felt off-kilter and gripped the edge of the table to steady herself, then divided a look between Pam and Steve. "You knew he was coming and didn't tell me?"

"Don't be mad." Pam touched Christine's arm as her face filled with contrition. "Brent asked Steve to keep his coming quiet, and—"

"Hey! It's the QB!" someone called.

Several of Brent's former teammates surrounded him, trading high fives and patting him on the back as he grinned and nodded. Christine's heart sank as she took in the scene. Brent seemed so happy, and his renewed love of football had to be the reason he'd come. The surprise was for his former teammates, not her. He might be glad to see her too—kind and cordial. But that didn't mean he'd changed his mind. He'd be back in Virginia soon.

The room started closing in on her. She had to get out of there before she fell to pieces in front of her graduating class. She longed to call her father and ask him to pick her up, but she would have to strut past Brent and his friends if she tried to leave.

"I need to get some air alone," she told Pam. "Please don't follow me."

She looped her black wool wrap over her shoulders, slipped her clutch under her arm, and made for an open doorway that led to the terrace. She could hide there until she had a chance to slip away unnoticed.

A wall of chilly air hit her when she stepped onto the wide

balcony. Grateful that only a few couples were gathered at the far end of the railing, she moved to the opposite end of the terrace and gazed out over the golf course. It was a lovely evening with the clear dark sky dotted with bright stars that seemed to mock her somber mood. She hugged her wrap closer to her body and wished she'd opted for a dress with long sleeves.

A minute later, she decided she would call her father, ask him to come, and then find a way to escape unseen. But after pulling her phone from her purse, she merely opened her photo gallery.

When a selfie of her and Brent at her nieces' birthday party filled the screen, her heart lurched. She studied his bright, electric smile, and when her bottom lip quivered, she closed her eyes.

Keep it together, Christine! You're in public!

"That was the best day."

Christine's eyes flew open, and she craned her head over her shoulder to where Brent stood behind her.

"I still can't believe all that purple, though." His expression was hesitant yet . . . what? Hopeful? "May I please talk with you?"

She faced him and placed her phone and clutch on a table next to her. "Go ahead. Talk."

"Thank you." He cleared his throat. "First, you look stunning."

She ran her hands down the dress. "I feel ridiculous in this."

"You could never look ridiculous. You're the most beautiful woman I've ever known."

She folded her arms over her chest as if to shield her heart from more hurt. "What do you want to talk about?"

Brent took a step closer. "I'm so sorry for hurting you, Chris. I'm a complete doofus, as my sister so eloquently told me earlier today. I was wrong to walk out on you. Away from *us*. In fact, I was a coward, and I'll regret causing you such pain for the rest of my life."

He reached for her arm but then pulled back. "You've had a profound effect on my life, and I can't put into words how much you mean to me. You never stopped believing in me, even when I had so little faith in myself. But because of you I finally believe I'm not the complete failure my father led me to believe. I'm able to use what I learned playing football to help kids the way I helped Eric Maloney, and not only is there nothing wrong with a career in construction, but it's what I was meant to do all along."

He paused. "More importantly, I've realized what I want, and I'm ready to go after *all* my dreams."

"And what are they besides realizing your chosen career and calling?" Her voice was quaky as she looked deep into his eyes.

"The most important one is building a life with you. Someone told me I'd need to snatch up my soul mate when I found her, making sure I didn't miss the opportunity for a love like no other. And that's what I intend to do. You've had my heart for a long time, and I was a moron to push you away because of my insecurities." His voice was rough as his eyes glimmered. "I'm back now, and I can't lose you again."

She closed her eyes for a moment and tried to think, then opened them. "But, Brent, you said you didn't want to build a life here in Flowering Grove. You said you belonged in Virginia."

When he moved even closer and gently took her hand in his, she relished his touch. But she had to know if this would work. Flowering Grove was her home.

"I was wrong, Christine. I was so focused on running away from my past that I completely missed what was right in front of me—you. You're everything to me. You're my best friend and the love of my life. I want a future with you, and I want it to begin right here in Flowering Grove and right now—if you'll give me a chance."

She stared at him as tears sprang to her eyes. Was she dreaming? "Christine?" he whispered. "Do you feel the same way about me?"

"Of course I do, but I'm still confused. You told me you had no future to offer a woman. No job, no home. Then when I told you all I wanted was you, that we'd work it out somehow, you still left me. So then I thought the truth was you didn't love me and that was the real reason you wouldn't stay. Are you sure this is what you truly want?"

"Yes, I'm sure." He released her hand. "I have some news, but right now I want to give you something." He reached into the pocket of his trousers and then placed a small vial of magenta model paint in her hand.

She laughed. "What's this for?"

"I want to paint walls magenta with you." He grinned. "I was going to bring you a whole gallon, but I figured it wouldn't look good with my suit."

His expression became a simmering stare. "I love you, Christine, and if you'll let me, I'll spend the rest of my life trying to prove that to you."

She gave a little laugh as she set the vial by her purse. "I need to say something first."

"What?"

"Thank you for the money. I was so overwhelmed when your aunt Midge told me it came from you." She searched his eyes. "You kept your promise to help me save my store, and you put my needs before your own. You're the most loyal, generous, thoughtful man I've ever known, and I'm deeply and completely in love with you. So, yes, I will let you prove you love me. I love you too."

He cupped his hands to her cheeks, and then, leaning down, he brushed his lips over hers. Her body relaxed, and when he deepened the kiss, she wrapped her arms around his neck and savored the thrill of his mouth against hers. She felt as if she were floating on a cloud as the world around them fell away. Kissing Brent—the love of her life—was like nothing she'd ever experienced.

When he released her and smiled, she tried to slow her galloping heart.

"Have I told you how ravishing you look tonight?" he said, holding one of her curls between his thumb and forefinger.

"And you look like a super-hot model in that suit, but I have a bone to pick with you, Nicholson."

His brow puckered. "What?"

"How dare you cut your hair! I loved those curls."

He touched his head. "I figured I needed to clean up to wear this suit. It was either cut it or pull the curly mess into a man bun. I'm not really a man-bun kind of guy."

"Well, I miss those curls, so you'd *better* let them grow out again."

"Yes, ma'am." He rested his hands on her hips. "But only on one condition."

"What condition?"

"Agree to go into business with me."

"What do you mean?"

He smiled again as he pushed a lock of her hair behind her ear. "That's my news. Aunt Midge sold her house, and she and I are starting a remodeling business right here in Flowering Grove. I'm going to flip houses—a lot of them historic restorations, I hope—and she'll be my silent partner."

"I'm so happy for you. But how can I help?"

"I need you to stage the houses once I've finished the renovations. After all, you're an expert on antique furniture . . . as well as evaluating paint chips."

She laughed. "I'd love to. Maybe I can hire someone to help me at the store part-time so I can ensure you choose the correct colors for the walls."

"I was going to suggest that."

"Will you return to coaching too?"

"Yes. Coach Morgan gave me an open invitation."

"I'm glad to hear it." She rested her hands on his broad shoulders. "So you're back in Flowering Grove for good now? You don't have to go back to Virginia for anything?"

"I'm not going anywhere. Everything I own is in a trailer parked in Aunt Midge's driveway. I'm staying with her until she closes on the house, and then I'll find a place to rent and we'll start our company."

He paused. "When Aunt Midge proposed this plan yesterday, I'd already realized what you've been telling me all along—that I need to do the work I'm called to do. And this is it. I have nothing to be ashamed of. I have skills and the ability to succeed. Besides, Aunt Midge is a more reliable partner than my last one."

He grinned, then leaned down to kiss her again, sending her stomach into a wild swirl.

When he broke the kiss, she rested her head on his shoulder and let out a happy sigh. She felt safe and protected in his arms.

"I missed you so much," he whispered, rubbing her back.

"I missed you too. More than I can say."

When George Michael's "Careless Whisper" came through the speakers, Christine squealed, then looked up at his confused expression. "Eighties music! Dance with me, Coach!"

"Yes, ma'am."

He chuckled as she slipped her phone and the small vial of paint into her clutch, grabbed his hand, and yanked him back into the party room. She tossed her wrap and purse onto a table where Pam and

Steve stood, relief on their faces as Christine towed Brent to the dance floor.

He pulled her into his arms and kissed her head as they began to sway. "I love you, Christine. I hope you won't mind hearing that a few dozen times tonight."

"I won't. And I love you too," she whispered as she rested her cheek on his shoulder again. She closed her eyes and smiled. The love of her life was finally where he belonged—and so was she.

epilogue

Six months later

Christine parked her truck in the driveway beside Brent's pickup at the large, two-story brick home he was renovating, then breathed in the warm air through the open window. The fragrance of fresh grass and May flowers washed over her, making her smile.

Britney had taken over the store for the rest of the afternoon so Christine could help Brent paint. She considered the whirlwind she'd experienced since his return the day of the reunion. Quickly falling into the comfortable routine of seeing each other nearly every day, they shared meals at her house or Aunt Midge's, and Brent had even started helping her out at the store from time to time with the understanding that she had to keep Wanda away from him. It was apparent that the cat had a crush on him. She refused to leave the man alone.

And honestly, Christine couldn't blame Wanda for her feelings. After all, she fell more in love with Brent each day. She'd never been so happy, and she felt closer to him than anyone else in her life.

After Aunt Midge closed on her house in early January, Christine and Brent helped her move into her new condo, and Brent moved into the cottage he'd rented only a few blocks from Christine's home.

Aunt Midge gave him the money she'd promised, with Brent using a portion of it to set up Nicholson Remodeling. He'd told her about his father's change of heart, and it was evident when she'd seen the pride on the man's face when Brent told him the company would bear the family name.

Then with Elena Wolfe's help and his aunt's financial ability to cosign his mortgage, he'd purchased a small two-bedroom home to renovate in a town just outside Flowering Grove. In three months he'd remodeled the bathroom, replaced the hardwood floors, restained the kitchen cabinets and replaced their hardware, painted all the rooms, and added some landscaping. When it went on the market, it sold within a week, and they had their first successful sale!

Now Brent was working hard to remodel this four-bedroom, three-and-a-half-bathroom home, and he hoped to have it on the market by early June. He'd already renovated the two upstairs bathrooms as well as painted and replaced the carpet in the three bedrooms up there. This week he'd been concentrating on the master bedroom and bath, and he'd asked Christine if she could get away to help him paint.

She strolled up the front walk, taking in the flowers she'd planted last weekend. A bright-red cardinal sitting on a birdbath took a drink and then fluttered away as Christine jogged up the porch steps. When she reached the screen door, Brent was already standing there with his arms folded over his wide chest. "There you are. I was just about to call you. I was afraid you got lost."

She shook her head while drinking in the sight of him. "I didn't get lost. My sister wanted to fill me in on what the girls have been up to at school. I'm so grateful Hunter's mother is helping Britney with the twins now so she can work at the store part-time when I need her." She grinned. "Or when you call me to come help you."

When Brent let her in, she reached up and touched his glorious dark curls. "I'm also glad you let your hair grow out. I couldn't stand it short."

"Well, it was part of the deal, so I had to comply." He took her hand. "Get over here." He pulled her to him and kissed her, making her toes curl in her sandals.

"How was your day?" he asked when he released her.

"Good. Busy. My new advertising campaign seems to be making a difference. I have more customers from out of town now. Maybe between us, we'll put Flowering Grove on the map, so to speak."

"Great." He pulled her into the house and closed the door behind them. "So I need your opinion on something, and it's really important."

"What is it?"

His hand found hers again, and then he steered her toward the first-floor bedroom. "It's the color on the master bath walls. I'm not sure I like it."

"I thought we decided on gray."

"Well, I made a change."

She halted and faced him. "Without consulting me?"

"You might approve when you see it." He looked as if he were up to something, but she couldn't imagine what.

"Okay," she said. "But I thought we decided on colors together."

"Just come see." When they entered the bedroom, he slowed his steps and released her hand.

She reached the closed bathroom door but then faced him again. His expression sobered, and concern trickled through her mind. "Are you okay?"

"Just open the door and tell me what you honestly think."

She tilted her head, studying him. "Brent, what's wrong?"

"Nothing." He gave a nervous laugh. "Please just take a look at what I did."

She turned the knob and pushed the door open with no idea what to expect. But when she stepped into the large bathroom, she cupped her hands to her mouth as she read the words scrawled across the far wall—in bright-magenta paint.

Christine, will you marry me?

Her eyes filled with tears, and when she turned to face Brent, she found him on bended knee holding an open ring box. She pressed both hands to her chest as the air whooshed from her lungs.

"Christine Emilia Sawyer," he said, his voice quavering and his expression hesitant, "will you please make me the happiest man in the world and marry me?"

"Yes! Yes! Yes!"

He popped up, lifted her into his arms, and spun her around as she squealed. When he set her feet back on the floor, he pulled her close and kissed her until she was breathless. As he released her, he pulled a ring from the box and slipped it on her finger.

"Brent!" she gasped, taking in the cluster of jewels shaped like a flower in a gold antique setting. "This is beautiful."

"It's a late-nineteenth-century Victorian diamond ring. I thought you'd like something old that's new to us as we start our life together." He took her left hand in his, and his eyes glistened. "And speaking of Victorian, I have another surprise."

"What?"

"The Victorian house across the street from your place just went up for sale, and I put an offer on it yesterday."

"You did?" Her words came out in a squeak.

He nodded. "Aunt Midge was all in. I don't know if I'll have the chance to buy it, but I would love for us to build our life there. And we could decorate it at Christmas like you've always wanted to."

"Oh my goodness! That would be another dream come true."

He rubbed his thumb over the back of her hand. "Chris, I never imagined that I could be as happy as you've made me. When we reconnected, I'd convinced myself I wasn't worthy of love and a happy life. I thought I'd failed too much, trusted the wrong people, had nothing to offer. But you showed me I am worthy, and I want those things with you and only you."

She sniffed as he touched her cheek.

"I've never loved anyone as much as I love you," he continued. "And I'm so grateful you gave me another chance after I left town like a jerk. Or as my sister would say, like a doofus." He grinned.

She laughed. "I love you too. But when I started falling for you, I was convinced you'd never be interested in me because I'm not like Britney. I've spent my life thinking I was lost in her shadow, but I'm not. I'm not Britney, and I never will be because I'm Christine."

"And Christine is who I want as my wife," he said, his voice a little husky. Then he kissed her again, and she soaked in his nearness.

When she pulled away, she pointed to the wall. "Now do you believe me when I tell you magenta is the perfect color for a bathroom?"

"If that's what makes you happy."

"*You* make me happy." She smiled up at him. "Tell me something. How did the nerdy twin get lucky enough to win the quarterback?"

His lips twitched and his eyes sparkled. "Actually, I heard the quarterback managed to capture the *stunning* twin's heart." He cupped her cheek as his eyes expressed tenderness. "*I'm* the lucky one."

As she enjoyed her fiancé's lips against hers, Christine gazed into the glorious future waiting for them.

At last.

Acknowledgments

As always, I'm thankful for my loving family, including my mother, Lola Goebelbecker; my husband, Joe; and my sons, Zac and Matt. I'm blessed to have such an awesome and amazing family that puts up with me when I'm stressed out on a book deadline.

To my husband, Joe, thank you, thank you, thank you for putting up with my random text messages asking you about refinishing furniture, remodeling bathrooms, painting walls (magenta!), and football terminology. You're a saint for putting up with my crazy! I love you more than words can express.

Thank you to my mom and my dear friend Maggie Halpin for proofreading the draft of this book and for encouraging me to believe in Christine and Brent. You're an inspiration!

To my dear friend DeeDee Vazquetelles—I can't thank you enough for your encouragement with this book. I'm grateful for your football knowledge and your willingness to attend games with me. Thank you for also volunteering to proofread. Your friendship is a blessing! I don't know what I'd do without your daily texts and endless emotional support. As we always say, I'm so grateful our kids brought us together. You're my ride or die!

A million thanks to Gracie and Dalton Craig for your patience with my many football questions, both in person and over text. I can't tell you how much I appreciate you! Y'all are the best neighbors!

Thank you also to my coworker Ben Krise, who answered my silly football questions. I'm so glad we work together.

Janet Jeter—I'm so grateful for your help with the twin research. You're so blessed to have not only a twin brother but another set of twins in your family! Thank you for sharing stories that have worked their way into my books—especially the anecdote about the infamous book birthday gift! I'm so grateful to have you as one of my work buddies.

I'm so grateful for my dear friend Sarah Hollingsworth, who took the time to explain what it's like to work as a paralegal. I cherish the fun and crazy memes you share with me. You are a blessing to me!

To Jessica Miller—thank you for always answering my crazy medical questions. I appreciate your time, and I'm so grateful for your friendship.

Thank you also to the Goodman family—Lesa, Danny, Caleb, Aaron, and Josh—for taking time out of your busy schedules to allow me to pick your brains with my football questions. I enjoyed our Olive Garden meal and hope you like this story as much as I do.

I'm so grateful to my wonderful church family at Morning Star Lutheran in Matthews, North Carolina, for your encouragement, prayers, love, and friendship. You all mean so much to my family and me.

Thank you to Zac Weikal and the fabulous members of my Bookworm Bunch! I'm so thankful for your friendships and excitement about my books. You all are amazing!

To my agent, Natasha Kern—I can't thank you enough for your guidance, advice, and friendship. You are a tremendous blessing in my life.

Acknowledgments

Thank you to my wonderful editor, Laura Wheeler, for your friendship and guidance. I appreciate how you've pushed me and inspired me to dig deeper to improve both my writing and this book. I'm so excited to work with you, and I look forward to our future projects together.

I'm grateful to my editor, Jean Bloom, who helped me polish and refine the story. Jean, you are a master at connecting the dots and filling in the gaps. I'm so thankful that we could work together on this book. You always make my stories shine! Thank you!

I'm grateful to every person at HarperCollins Christian Publishing who helped make this book a reality.

To my readers—thank you for choosing my novels. My books are a blessing in my life for many reasons, including the special friendships I've formed with my readers. Thank you for your email messages, Facebook notes, and letters.

Thank you most of all to God—for giving me the inspiration and the words to glorify You. I'm grateful and humbled You've chosen this path for me.

DISCUSSION QUESTIONS

1. Christine is convinced her business, home, beloved nieces, and the rest of her family are all she needs in her life. But then, at least to herself, she admits she wants a husband and family of her own. What do you think causes her to realize the truth?

2. When Brent arrives in Flowering Grove and strikes up a friendship with Christine, Britney warns her twin not to trust her former boyfriend. She's convinced Brent cheated on her during college, causing their breakup. Even though Brent seems like a nice guy, Christine is determined to honor her sister by not getting too close to him. What would you have done in Christine's shoes and why?

3. Brent returns to Flowering Grove to help his great-aunt after he loses both his business and his girlfriend. Have you ever experienced an overwhelming change in your life? If so, how did you adapt to it?

4. When Brent's aunt sells two paintings, she gives him the money and says he should use it to get back on his feet after losing his business. But instead, he gives it to Christine to help save her store. Why do you think he did

that even though he refused to believe they had a future together?

5. By the end of the story, what has Brent learned about himself? How does that influence his thoughts about a future with Christine?

6. Christine has always felt stuck in Britney's shadow. She's convinced she's the inferior twin while Britney is the perfect twin. Have you ever felt compared to a sibling or another relative? If so, how did you handle that?

7. Brent and his younger sister, Kylie, are close to their great-aunt Midge. Do you have a special relative with whom you're close? If so, who is that relative and how did he or she influence you and your life?

8. Christine fell in love with antiques when visiting antique malls with her grandmother. Have you ever visited an antique mall? What finds did you discover there?

9. Christine and Pam have been best friends since childhood. They're each other's support, especially during rough times. Do you have a special friendship like that? If so, what do you cherish the most about that relationship?

10. Determined to have his son live out his broken dreams, Brent's father constantly criticizes him and the decisions he's made. By the end of the story, though, he realizes he was wrong and apologizes. Do you think Brent should forgive his father and try to forge a better relationship with him? Why or why not?

From the Publisher

GREAT BOOKS
ARE EVEN BETTER WHEN THEY'RE SHARED!

Help other readers find this one:

- Post a review at your favorite online bookseller

- Post a picture on a social media account and share why you enjoyed it

- Send a note to a friend who would also love it—or better yet, give them a copy

Thanks for reading!

ABOUT THE AUTHOR

Dan Davis Photography

Amy Clipston is an award-winning best-selling author and has been writing for as long as she can remember. She's sold more than one million books, and her fiction writing "career" began in elementary school when she and a close friend wrote and shared silly stories. She has a degree in communications from Virginia Wesleyan University and is a member of the Authors Guild, American Christian Fiction Writers, and Romance Writers of America. Amy works full-time for the City of Charlotte, NC, and lives in North Carolina with her husband, two sons, mother, and five spoiled rotten cats.

◆ ◆ ◆

Visit her online at AmyClipston.com
Facebook: @AmyClipstonBooks
Twitter: @AmyClipston
Instagram: @amy_clipston
BookBub: @AmyClipston